ISBN 978-1-331-18095-1
PIBN 10154958

1 MONTH OF
FREE
READING

at
www.ForgottenBooks.com

By purchasing this book you are eligible for one month membership to ForgottenBooks.com, giving you unlimited access to our entire collection of over 700,000 titles via our web site and mobile apps.

To claim your free month visit:

www.forgottenbooks.com/free154958

Similar Books Are Available from
www.forgottenbooks.com

THE MAULEVERER MURDERS

BY

A. C. FOX-DAVIES

Author of

" The Dangerville Inheritance "

LC

NEW YORK: JOHN LANE COMPANY. MCMVII

LONDON: JOHN LANE, THE BODLEY HEAD

Copyright, 1907, by
JOHN LANE COMPANY

THE MAULEVERER MURDERS

CHAPTER I

TWO men were sitting in the Park, talking politics there, as they had done elsewhere ever since they had lunched together at White's. They had discussed every other possible complication which could be foreseen on the horizon of English diplomacy, for the elder of the two had been an Ambassador. He was one of the men who had seen and done things, and for that reason, if for no others, the one thing upon which he hated to talk was his work. He would have preferred to say nothing. But the younger was garrulous upon the point, with the persistency of the type which considers it a refinement of manners to confine the conversation to matters within reach of the listener's occupation. With a fellow-tradesman every man loves his "shop" as a topic of conversation, but with one in a different calling that is the one subject the workman abhors. The elder man relapsed into silence. Presently a scarlet outrider was seen, the traffic was stopped, a clear passage was made, and the two men stood uncovered as the Queen drove by.

The traffic was hardly set in motion again when the attention of the two was once again arrested. Near enough to profit by the clear avenue in which the Queen had passed through the thronging carriages, and yet far enough behind to give no suspicion of attempting to suggest a unity of party either real or assumed, followed a coach, perfectly appointed down to its smallest details.

The four piebald horses, which came dancing along on their toes, would in any case have been striking enough without the added attraction that they were admittedly the finest team which had been seen in London for some seasons past. The coach had several passengers in addition to the two menservants in their white and scarlet liveries; but, alone on the box-seat, sat a handsome woman, chiefly noticeable on account of her brilliant flaming hair and the excellence of her costume. She handled her horses amongst the crowd of vehicles with marvellous dexterity and consummate skill, under far from easy circumstances. The younger man raised his hat, and was acknowledged.

"Who's that, Alan? When one's out of England so much, one loses touch of the new beauties."

"Well, if you want to know, she's a mystery. Who she is or what she is nobody has really found out yet. I can tell you no more than you can already guess. She is a wealthy, beautiful woman, associating with and reputed to be one of the swell set amongst the demi-mondaines. But at the same time she is a little lady of very decided opinions, and one it pays nobody to take liberties with. Young Lord Salford—but then he always was an ass— presumed a bit too much a month or two ago; but she paid him out."

"What did he do?"

"Oh, he only wrote a letter without the formality of an introduction, in which he took a little too much for granted."

"How did she pay him out?"

"Just threatened to sue him for breach of promise—said she knew she hadn't a chance of a verdict, but thought his letter was such an interesting piece of evidence it would be a thousand pities to deprive the press of a legitimate opportunity of publishing it—said she knew they liked big names."

"What happened?"

"She gave him the alternative of a public apology in the advertisement columns of the *Morning Post.* He sent her an apology marked 'Private,' and a cheque for £500, and he had both of 'em back by return of post, with an intimation that usually it only took her forty-eight hours to make up her mind. The letter was distinctively characteristic of the lady."

"I suppose he apologized?"

"Yes; he enclosed her a letter addressed to the *Morning Post,* with the signed apology and the

cost of the advertisement, and asked her, if she considered the wording of the apology to be sufficient,
to please post it on.   She tore 'em both up, and he
heard no more of it, which also was characteristic.
But whisperings reached one or two of us, and
young Tommy Salford has been on thorns ever
since, lest his prospective old father-in-law, who is
something in the Dean or Bishop line, should get
to hear of it."

"She seems a curious young person.   What's her
name?"

"Vivienne Vane.   Didn't you notice the two
interlaced V's on the coach?   She's rather proud
of that monogram; she had such a lot of trouble
about it.   Tried all the stationers in London, and
said that all of them had a fixed idea that two V's
made a W.   Then she wrote to the P.R.A., told
him what she wanted, and said if he couldn't do
it she'd give it up; but that if he would, he could
have a cheque, or he could come to tea, or paint
her portrait, whichever he liked.   He sent her the
monogram, and 'might he come to tea,' but his
wife got to know, and said he would do no such
thing.   Now all the village is taking a hand in
the story, and trying to fix up a tea-party for him
so that he shall meet the fair Vivienne.   Since then
everybody has been getting to know just a little
more about his wife than they knew before.
Vivienne says that if the lady doesn't untie the
apron strings pretty quickly she will go and pose

to him as a model for the altogether, but I doubt if it really came to the point. She came in here yesterday driving a pair of donkeys, tandem, in a coster cart, with a man in livery behind. She did bring them along. I believe she could drive a team of runaway zebras. The only other woman who is a patch on her at the Jehu game is the Duchess of Merioneth. They are not unlike each other in appearance, and Miss Vivienne knows that, and rather trades on it. We've tried hard to run 'em both in to the same driving competition down at Ranelagh, next Saturday. They are both entered, but I expect the Duchess will fight shy if she hears Vivienne has been put down for the same event. It all depends whether she spots the fair Vivienne as the 'Miss Vane' who is entered. Luckily there are plenty more of the name about, and the secretary didn't smell a rat, so perhaps Her Grace won't either. Shall I introduce you?"

A whimsical smile spread over the Ambassador's face; then he burst into a short laugh.

"No. I'm going to Russia next; it's been settled to-day, and I don't think it would be much of a recommendation if I turned up at Petersburg with the odour of Miss Vane's skirts traceable. You see 'we' have to know things, and I have an idea I've heard Miss Vane's name before. I dare say you'll know later on. Those things always leak out. But I think I shall turn up at Ranelagh next Saturday."

Chapter II

"GOT anything on to-night, Ashley?"
"A suit of clothes, shirt, pants, etc."
"Oh, don't be more of an ass than usual; you know what I mean. I'm in a bit of a hole. I said I would take Vivienne Vane to the Gaiety, and on to supper at the Savoy, and, like a fool, I forgot all about it, and I have promised to meet the Danvers crowd in their box at the Opera, and go to supper with them at the Carlton. I can't do both, and it's serious business with me over the Danvers girl. She's a lady with a dot."

"Well then, hand the fair Vivienne over to me."

"Do you know her?"

"No, but I imagine she is not unlike the usual young person, who is agreeable to sup unattended with a mere man at the Savoy."

"That's just where you make a mistake, Tempest. I don't suppose she will object to meal with you instead of with me, for she is distinctly of the type which is always hankering after 'some new thing'; but she is very far from being like the

6

usual run. I don't flatter myself I am the only one; a man who gets that idea, when he hasn't done the usual parade to 'The voice that breathed o'er Eden,' must be a fool, and, what's more, a silly fool."

"They always say every woman has got her price, though there are some that want their weight in diamonds."

"I know the old saying, Tempest, as well as you do; but if there ever were an exception, that exception is Vivienne Vane. She seems to be wealthy beyond the dreams of avarice. She is, without exception, the most attractive woman that I have ever met in the whole of my life; she is certainly the most beautiful, and from beginning to end, the woman is an enigma. Of course it is the usual thing, and with her a mere commonplace, to say that she is a lady; but I am certain that somewhere or other, in some country or other, the woman has rank, and high rank, behind her. She may be a divorcée, or she may be a 'wrong side the blanket,' but the breeding is there unmistakably. If she were a woman of forty, with twenty years of experience and life behind her, one could understand her better, but at the outside she is only twenty-three or four, and she puzzles me. I can't even make up my mind what her nationality is: she speaks English without the slightest trace of an accent, but she's as fluent as they make 'em with French and Russian and German. I've tried her with Danish and Spanish and Greek, and she was more than my match in any of those languages; but then I don't know much of those particular lingos myself.   And, to crown it all, she has the most gorgeous, flaming, brilliant red hair I have ever seen.   It's worth going a mile to see."

"Sort of admirable Crichton, I suppose, with all the virtues, and the additional one of not being too virtuous."

"Tempest, you'd make a splendid judge, you're so damn good at summing up."

"Ah well: 'Faith is the substance of things hoped for,' and I suppose every barrister looks forward to the substance of the judicial flesh-pots."

"Well, if I stand the dinner will you take the lady out afterwards?"

"Certainly; I shall be delighted."

"Then meet us at Prince's at seven."

The two men separated shortly afterwards, to dress—Ashley Tempest to return to his chambers in New Square, Lincoln's Inn, and Herbert Mauleverer, his most intimate friend, to proceed to his rooms in Jermyn Street.   Tempest was the busiest junior at the bar.   He had never taken silk, for he thought it good policy not to, and being a brilliantly clever advocate, he was making a big income.

Mauleverer was a younger son, who admirably contrived to enjoy life, and do nothing on an allowance of £500 a year.   Absolutely without ambition of any description, his chief occupation seemed to be the promulgation of an intimate acquaintance with his many friends. A charming man as all his men friends admitted, he was nevertheless one with whom a woman could do anything.

In a few hours the two met at Prince's, and Tempest was introduced to Miss Vivienne Vane. He at once admitted to himself that in none of his remarks about the lady, had Herbert Mauleverer exaggerated in the slightest degree. Vivienne Vane was the most beautiful woman he had ever seen. But Mauleverer had given him no hint of her wit and power of repartee, and it would have been impossible, had he tried, to convey any sense of the *diablerie* which was an integral part of Miss Vane's curious and complex character. Tempest evidently attracted her, and she made not the slightest demur at his substitution as her escort to the Gaiety and supper; in fact, after the proposal had been mooted, she seemed to wish to facilitate such an arrangement.

It could not be a matter of surprise that a man and a woman of the world, each attractive to a host of others, and each brilliantly clever, should have quickly passed from the conversational status of acquaintances to a more familiar and intimate footing. In the pauses between the acts their conversation had lapsed to the confidential tone to which two people "in sympathy" so easily progress, and before they parted for the evening, when

Tempest put her into the dainty well-appointed brougham which was waiting to take her from the Savoy, each had come to regard the other as an old familiar friend.

Tempest shook his head at the hansom cabbies who severally offered themselves to him, and walked home, a sense of well-being pervading him. He had enjoyed his evening.

The remembrance of that remarkably well-chosen supper, and possibly of his companion, frequently occurred to him the next day.   In the evening he attended a large and solemn dinner party, and was surprised to find that comparisons rose constantly to his mind between that evening and the one before.   He was found somewhat distrait by the very bright and sprightly lady of a certain age, whom he took in to dinner.   She confided to her hostess afterwards that she had been very disappointed in the celebrated Mr. Tempest.

Tempest made his adieux as early as he could after dinner, and heard the hall door close behind him with a deep breath of relief.

"Ten-thirty! Feels like two!   I *must* have been there more than two hours and a half.   Gad! There's plenty of time."

A passing hansom stopped at his signal, and he jumped in.

"24, Russell Square!"

"Right, sir."

The horse jogged on at a good pace, and Tempest lighted a cigarette with an odd feeling of elation. He wasn't quite sure what impulse was driving him on, but whatever it was, he rather liked it. He got out when he arrived at the address he had given, and walked upstairs to a flat on the second floor.

"Was Miss Vane at home?"

She was, she had just come in; and Tempest followed the maid down the long passage with the curious feeling of elation growing stronger. Vivienne Vane was sitting in her small, exquisitely furnished drawing-room, a lighted cigarette between her fingers. She was in evening dress, some wonderful copper-coloured gown that toned with her brilliant hair. A long coat lay over a chair.

"Why, Mr. Tempest!" she said.

"I am so fortunate to find you," said Tempest. "Will you take compassion on a poor chap who has been bored to extinction?"

She smiled. "Are you the poor chap? Well, what shall I do?"

"Will you come again to the Savoy, and let us see if they can beat last night's supper?"

"My dear man, I've just come in. I've been dining out already."

"That doesn't matter; so have I. Come."

She hesitated, looked at him and smiled again.

"All right."

She held out her arms, and he slipped on the coat, and they went down the stairs.

"But what made you come?" she asked, when they were in a hansom.

"Didn't I tell you that I had been bored to extinction? I've been to a beastly dinner. I didn't want to go, to begin with; I always hate them. The food was badly cooked, and there was far too much of it, and I had an awful woman to take in, who wanted to talk shop to me, and asked me about my cases. And all the time I was thinking about the delightful little supper I enjoyed last night. The contrast was too poignant. I felt that nothing but getting you to come and have another supper could readjust matters."

"We are quite mad, you know. Here we have each of us just finished an enormous dinner, which we each found too much, and we start off to have supper. I'm afraid you are not very consistent."

"I am really. I'm the most consistent man I know. Here we are!"

Tempest was one of those men whom women feel they can trust to do things. He chose the table she would have chosen herself; he settled her in the best position and she leant back in her chair feeling quite sure that the supper would be quite right. There is nothing that is more characteristic of a man than the way he will take a woman out to dinner or supper.

The supper *was* just right, and when Tempest took out his watch and said, "Turning out time— we must be off," each had found the other a pleasanter companion even than the previous night. They came out slowly, and Tempest lit a cigarette.

"What a lovely night!" she said. "It is so warm; what a shame to be indoors!"

"Don't go in. Are you game for a motor ride?"

"To-night? At this time?"

"The very best time," said Tempest. "I'll leave you at Russell Square to change and put on something thick, and I will go on to the Garage where I keep my car, and call for you in half an hour. Have you ever motored in a fast car on a moonlight night like this?"

"Never." Her eyes were shining in the gaslight like a happy child's.

"Then you've something to live for," said Tempest.

Half an hour later he tucked her warmly up in the front seat of his car and moved gently off.

Slowly through the still crowded streets, till in wider Piccadilly he let the car go a little, and on the Hammersmith Road where nearly all the traffic had cleared off, the speed crept up and up. The girl spoke not a word, but Tempest knew in some innermost consciousness that she was enjoying every moment, and the car rushed on, till soon the street lamps ceased, and they were between hedges in the brilliant moonlight.

Tempest bent down "How do you like it? Isn't it better than going home?"

"Like it? It's heavenly! Why haven't I ever done this before? I feel like a child who is out for a spree. You wonderful magician! And I thought I was tired and ready to go home to bed!"

Tempest opened his lips to answer, but did not say anything, and drove on. His brows wrinkled into a frown beneath his close cap. He had hastily come to the conclusion, and the suddenness of it was rather startling though he knew that there was no going back. He weighed the pros and cons, but he knew beforehand that the pros had it. Presently he put the car on lower speed, and turned to the girl.

"This is rather jolly, this expedition of ours, isn't it? I should like to do it again. You are the best pal I have ever come across. Will you marry me?"

She started and looked up at his face, but it was watching the straight road in front of him, and she could not see his eyes.

"Are you joking?" she said. "It's not a very good joke, is it?"

"I shouldn't joke over a thing like this. I am more in earnest than I have ever been over anything."

"Do you want me to believe that you are seriously asking me to marry you?"

"Of course I do." Tempest looked into her face. "Will you?"

"But what do you wish to marry me for?"

"Do you want me to say that I have fallen in love with you? I will if you like, but it is a phrase I have always had a great objection to. I'm no youngster, and dozens of men I've known who've been in love, proud of it, boasting of it, have married the girls they loved," and Tempest added grimly, "and I've seen them five years afterwards, and the love—well, there didn't seem to be much left of it. Look here, yesterday afternoon, I hadn't seen you; and to-day I feel as if I had known you all my life, and I couldn't do without you. What does it matter if we only met yesterday? We've spent two evenings together; if I never see you again, I shall never forget these two evenings—and we've talked intimately. I know what sort of woman you are, and you're the one woman I wish to spend the rest of my life with. If you've half the perception I think you have, you know what manner of man I am."

She nodded in assent. "Yes, I believe I do. But—oh! do you know what reputation I've got?"

"Yes," he said steadily.

"You know I've lived with Herbert Mauleverer?"

"I guessed it."

"Then—how can you ask me to marry you? And are you playing the game squarely? Isn't he your greatest friend? And he introduced you to me."

"Will Herbert Mauleverer marry you? And

do you want to marry him? If so, I will say no more and stand aside."

She hesitated, and a deep flush reddened her cheek.

"No, to both questions," she said slowly.

"Then I do ask you to marry me."

The girl looked straight before her out into the quiet night, and there was silence between them, while the car slipped smoothly along.

They were almost at Chiswick, on the return journey, and Tempest slackened a little more; he meant to say all he wanted to say, before they got home.

"But I can't see what you are doing it for," she broke out passionately. "You are the only man who has ever asked Vivienne Vane to marry him!"

Tempest took one hand from the wheel and put it over hers.

"Can't you believe that a man needn't be all a brute?" he said gently. "You know I'm not humbugging you, darling. I never cared a rag for a woman in my life, thought I never should! Never had time This has quite taken me by surprise, you know," and he smiled. "But I know it's genuine. I'll give you as good a time as ever I can, and you'll find I'm not a bad sort of fellow to get on with as men go."

Vivienne sat quite still, her hands folded on her knees, her eyes fixed on his face.

"And your friends, your relations! What will they say if you marry me? Me! A woman with a past!" Her lips curved in a bitter smile.

"I don't care a damn what any one says. I don't know what your past has been, and I don't care. I only want to know what your future will be. You say you've lived with Mauleverer. Well, I can't pretend to like it, but I've got to accept it. My darling," his steady voice broke a little, "I know some devil has treated you scurvily, and brought you to this. But I'll make it up to you, sweetheart. You shall learn to forget it all, and you can trust me to keep you safe. No man shall look at you again, if you'll give me the right to see they don't. You haven't known me long, but you know that much about me, don't you, that I can look after my own, and more than all after the woman I love?"

She was still looking at him, but her beautiful eyes were full of tears, and her lips shaking tremulously.

"Oh, you man!" she said. "If I had met you years ago, how different things might have been. I never thought that any one could be so generous. You offer me your good name, your love, your consideration, all that you could give to a good woman. To me! Oh, I'm thankful to you, with all my heart I'm grateful—but I can't take it. Even if I loved you, I couldn't take it; I'm not low enough for that. You must not have any wife you could ever have to blush for. No, let me finish," for he had tried to interrupt her. "I can't ever tell you what your offer has been to me. It's given me back just a little of my self-respect. All my life I shall never forget that you would have taken me on trust, and that you thought me good enough to marry."

Tempest's face was very white. "Do you refuse to marry me?" he said. "And is it because, to quote your own words, 'I might have to blush for you'? Well, wipe that reason out. It is nothing. I'm the best judge of what I want. Is that the only reason, or is there any one else you care for?"

The woman hesitated. "That is the chief reason. But there is some one that I care for."

"And shall you marry him?"

"No."

"Why not? Hasn't he asked you?"

"Yes. But"—she looked down, and again the deep flush tinged her cheek—"he does not know that there is anything against me."

Tempest nodded silently; he understood. "I give up," he said, "for the present. But they say all things come to those who wait, and I shall wait. If I can't be your husband I can be your friend, and I will, if you'll let me. Remember, if you ever need me. It's good to have a solid buffer at your back, to know it's there, even if you don't want to use it."

Her eyes looked up at him. They were full of tears. Something within her was clamouring loudly, "Oh, take your chance. Take it, it will never come again." All the force of the man's character, the generosity of the love that could forgive everything, swept over her. If he had looked at her then, had seen the hesitation, the almost yielding in her face! But Tempest's keen eyes were on the road in front of him, his mouth was set very tight, and his strong square jaw looked hard and stern. They were nearly home, and neither spoke again till the car stopped in Russell Square.

Tempest helped her out, and kept her hand in his. The Square was deserted, the bright moonlight threw odd shadows everywhere; they might have been in a world of their own.

"So it's good-bye," he said. "Somehow it doesn't seem very easy to say. Well, tell me you've enjoyed your ride."

"Indeed I have! She hesitated, and then exclaimed impulsively. "Oh, I'm sorry! I'm sorry!"

"Don't! It's not your fault. Do you think you could kiss me once? I'll never ask you again, but because you're generous give it me now."

She leant towards him mutely, and he kissed her on the cheek.

"Good-bye. Remember, if ever you want me. Have you your latchkey? Let me open the door."

The heavy door shut behind him, and Vivienne

stood still inside. She heard him go down the steps and mount the car. There was a little click.

"Call him back! call him back!" the inner voice said. She turned, and with shaking fingers unlatched the door. "Ashley," she cried, "don't go." But it was too late, the car was beyond call, and as she watched, it went out of her sight. "Oh, you fool, you fool!" she said. It was not Ashley Tempest that she meant.

CHAPTER III

A FORTNIGHT later the Ambassador and his nephew met again.

"Can you dine me at your club to-night, Alan?" the elder man presently asked. I'm at a loose end."

"By all means."

Later on, in the same evening, the two men were sitting smoking in the hall of the New Club in Grafton Street. They had dined and had played a couple of games of billiards, and were filling up the interval before they parted, with whisky and cigarettes. Whilst they talked there came the quick rattle of a hansom on the asphalt, the cab was sharply pulled up at the door, and an elderly man of the spruce and ever young variety, came briskly up the steps of the club. As he passed through the hall into the cloakroom beyond, the elder man remarked to his nephew, who had nodded—

"Alan, who's your friend?"

"Colonel Mauleverer."

"Who's he?"

"Surely you know. He's the man whose two sons were murdered, the one two months ago, the

other a month ago.   Jove, I think it's a month
to-day—the porter would know."

"That's the worst of going abroad," said the
other; "something interesting is always happen-
ing, and one loses the thread of things.   Did they
find out who did the murders?"

"No, there isn't the slightest clue, except that
in each case a knotted rope in the form of a noose
was found round the neck.   The one son, Captain Mauleverer, George I think his name was,
was found shot in his quarters at Knightsbridge,
and Henry Mauleverer, one of his younger brothers, was found dead in the river, a mile or two
above Oxford."

The conversation turned to other things, and
just as they were discussing their departure, the
tape machine in the outer hall began to click.
Neither had enough energy to go to the instrument
as the paper strip rolled out, but in a moment or
two one of the club servants tore off the slip and
pinned it to the board.   The younger of the two
men strolled to the board and looked at it, and
stood transfixed with horror.

"Gad!" he ejaculated, "here's another."

His uncle jumped to his feet, and strode across
the hall, and read the ominous message.

"Eleven o'clock.   Mr. Herbert Mauleverer, son
of Colonel Mauleverer, C.B., and a brother of
Captain George Mauleverer, who was murdered
two months ago, and of Mr. Henry Mauleverer,

who was found drowned on the 30th ultimo, has been found lying in his chambers in Jermyn Street with his throat cut. The same peculiarity of the knotted cord round his neck is noticeable in his case, as in those of his two brothers."

"The old man can't know," said Alan.

The words had scarcely left his mouth when down the stairs from the smoking-room came the Colonel. In spite of his debonair air, the strength of character that the man possessed was clearly marked in his features. Twenty years on the North-West frontier of India, in various capacities, twenty years in which he had carried his life in his hand, and twenty years in which the lives of other men had been at his mercy and control, had all left their mark on the face bronzed and heavily lined, but showing in every line the enormous will power and self-control which lay behind the cynical smile that half betrayed the sensual side of his character. Seeing the two standing at the notice board he joined them with the remark—

"Anything come through except those rotten speeches in the House?"

Without venturing to reply each man edged slightly away, and the Colonel slowly spelled out the awful message about his son. Minute after minute he stood in front of the board, saying no word and making no movement, and in the tense horror of the situation the others watched the smile fade away, and watched the heavy underjaw slowly close as if with the grip of a bulldog. They saw the lines deepen on his face, and a ghastly grey colour slowly overspread it as the Colonel put out his hand to one of the others to support himself.

"Waiter, some brandy, quickly!"

It was brought, and the Colonel swallowed it undiluted, but said nothing, and stood there all the time, as if he were trying to realize what the message meant. The others muttered some half-audible attempts at sympathy. They might have been speaking to a stone image. At last, still without a word, the Colonel pulled himself to-gether, squared his shoulders, and with the familiar toss of his head which the men in his regiment had known so well, he slowly walked through the doors and down the steps. Immediately the tongues of the others were loosed.

"Whatever can be the meaning of it? It's the most ghastly thing I've ever heard of. Three sons, one after the other like that. I wonder what on this earth the Almighty is making the old boy pay for!"

Next morning the whole of London rang with the crime. Remarkable in itself with the mystery attaching to the single occurrence, it was rendered doubly and trebly remarkable in conjunction with the tragic deaths of his two brothers. Of course according to the press the police were in possession of several clues, and an immediate arrest was ex-pected. Equally of course the inquest was adjourned, after evidence of identification, without any clue having been made public, and at this third adjournment the verdict was, "Wilful murder against some person or persons unknown." The real truth was that the police were at their wits' end, and they could not even suggest any plausible explanation of the triple crime.

CHAPTER IV

THE Duchess of Merioneth lay back in her favourite low chair on the balcony opening from her boudoir, and looked out on the Park before her with half-seeing, half-dreaming eyes. She was alone, and that to a busy woman is sometimes a luxury. She sat with hands folded idly in her lap, and reflected with satisfaction that she had two clear hours before she need dress for dinner. The boudoir door opened, and steps came slowly through the room. The Duchess sat up, a frown on her face.

"Jack," she said, and the frown melted into a smile, "I'm so glad it's you, Jack; goodness knows who it might have been. You see, I was just enjoying having a few minutes to myself, so I didn't feel particularly glad to see any one."

"Shall I go?" But he stepped out on to the balcony, and put a hand on the other low chair, which stood near the Duchess.

"No, not now you're here. Sit down, and help me to be lazy comfortably."

Jack Mauleverer sat down, and then leant forward to study the Duchess's face gravely.

"What's the matter, Pauline? You look rather mopy. Are you tired, or what?"

"Not tired, only bored. I've been lunching with some stupid tiresome people. Why does one lunch or dine? I shall go and live on a desert island, and perform the operation by myself every day. Only Andrews would have to come too. Andrews is my cook, you know, Jack. It *might* be somewhat awkward, Andrews and I on a desert island all by ourselves. Scold me for talkink nonsense, Jack! Why didn't you come to tea?"

"I thought I might find you alone if I left it till later. This balcony on a summer's evening is the nicest place in London." He turned and looked at her, a twinkle of laughing admiration in his eyes. "And the handsomest woman in London is sometimes to be found here at this time."

"Thank you. I believe you have mentioned that before."

"Well, I know you expect it, you see. It is one of my stock remarks, when I see a balcony, and a woman, and two comfortable chairs, and a nice calm, peaceful evening like this, you know. Of course I don't say it when the *tout ensemble* is not all right."

The Duchess surveyed him reflectively. "You are rather good at saying that sort of thing. I wonder how many times you've been in love, Jack?"

"Lots," said Jack, comfortably.

"And I wonder how many women have been in love with you?"

"I believe, to the best of my recollection, that the exact number is seventeen. Of course I am only counting those who have told me so. The ones who have tried to conceal the fact I don't mention to you. But seventeen's a good number, Pauline."

"It's a lucky number to stop at, Jack."

"Remember, I am but young."

"How old are you—let me see, you are twenty-nine, ar'n't you? I always have to reckon up by my own age. You always used to be six years older than I was in the good old days at Tibberton. I used to be awfully frightened of you, I know, because you were so old. And how you used to torment me sometimes!"

"It was all for your good. Curious how the tables are turned, isn't it? I'm quite frightened of you sometimes now."

"Whatever for?" laughed the Duchess. "I didn't know I was so awe-inspiring."

"When I come and propose to you I'm as frightened as anything. Positively shivering in my shoes. Look at my hand, how it's trembling." He held out a brown fist for her inspection.

"It's as steady as a rock. But why should it be trembling now. You haven't come to——"

"Yes, I have," said Jack, meekly but persistently.

The Duchess leant back in her chair with a resigned sigh.

"Well, it is a waste of time, you know. And I thought we were having such a nice chat! I was beginning to feel quite cheered up."

"Then now you can begin cheering me up. That is only fair. Now I'm going to talk seriously. Will you marry me?"

"No, sir!" Her grey eyes were smiling wickedly.

Mauleverer's face was quite unmoved, and he drew his chair nearer hers, and squared his shoulders with an air of settling down to the fray in earnest.

"I believe *you've* said *that* before!" he remarked. "But somehow I have never felt exactly inclined to take it quite literally."

"That is not my fault, is it?" remonstrated the Duchess. "I have always understood that when a man asked a woman to marry him—well, *not* a dozen times, but only once—and she said she wouldn't, that there was no more to be said."

"You see, I've never asked a woman to marry me before, so I'm not well up in the correct procedure."

The Duchess shook her head. "I'm afraid that it is not all ignorance—you have no real wish to improve. I have pointed out to you before, that you have no business to propose to me again, and yet——"

"And yet I am doing it again. But what is a man to do, who only wants one thing in the world, and might have it to-morrow—to-day—this very moment—if it were not for the inconceivable pig-headed obstinacy of one woman who ought to know better than to put her will against mine. Upon my soul, it's enough to aggravate a man! It aggravates me, I can tell you, when I think of it."

"Ah!" said the Duchess, who felt her spirits rising to the occasion. "Aggravates *you*, indeed! And what about me? Now, just put yourself in my place. Here am I, quite happy and contented, and pleased with my lot, not wanting to marry any one, and a conceited, obstinate, tiresome man comes along, who can't imagine any one unwilling to fly for the handkerchief directly he throws it down, and makes my life a burden to me in this way."

"May I smoke?" Mauleverer asked, and lit a cigarette with care and deliberation, watching the Duchess's face with a smile of amusement in his eyes.

He was trying for something that he wanted more than he had ever wanted anything before, and he knew that it was a toss up whether he got it or not, but no anxiety showed in the handsome, careless face and steady fingers. He did not reply to the Duchess's last onslaught.

It is difficult to argue with a person who will not take up the glove you throw.

The Duchess looked at him, and suddenly laughed.

"You know, Jack, you only ask me again and again because I say 'No.' If I said 'Yes,' you would really be rather sorry; there'd be nothing to persist in!"

"Try me," said Jack, quietly.

She shook her head. Mauleverer leant forward, and put his hand over hers on the arm of her chair.

"Tell me *why* you won't, Pauline."

"Because I don't want to. I've got lots of friends, and heaps of money, and plenty of houses, and you to advise me for my good. What more can I desire?"

"Haven't I been patient? But there comes an end to patience. There's no other man, I'll swear—there's no other man you care a straw about." He stopped, and the Duchess hesitated.

"Well, no," she said. "There's no other man at all; I won't have one!"

"Then come to me, and I'll see there never is any one else. When once I have you, no other man shall have a chance to oust me. You like me, you're not bored with me, you can stand having me about you better than anyone else. Why, that's more than heaps of women think quite enough to marry on. If you can't give me love for love, I'll do without that."

The Duchess said nothing, but she let her hand lie quietly in his.

He waited, and then went on, "Tell me, am I such a brute in your eyes that you can never think of me? Have you been in dead earnest all these past weeks, when you've said no to me? Pauline, I've never believed you! I can't believe that I'm less than nothing to you! It's horribly conceited of me, but I can't! Look me in the eyes now, and tell me, have you no love for me, could you never have?"

The Duchess tried to look down, but his will was stronger than hers, and her beautiful eyes looked into his unwillingly.

"I do love you," she said; "but I can't marry you."

"Why?" Mauleverer's voice was steady still, but his hand held hers so tightly that she could have cried out, only some tension kept her still.

"Because, oh, because I'm afraid."

"Afraid of what? Not of me!"

"Partly. I daren't, Jack. Oh, if you knew what a time I had before!"

Jack did know some of it. There was hardly a man about town who did not know the reputation of the late Duke of Merioneth. And in spite of the brave face his wife had carried before the world, there had been times when the Mauleverers, her cousins, had been accorded peeps behind the scenes of the ducal domestic life which had hardly added to their respect for his Grace. Many a time since he had loved her had this thought turned Jack sick with horror and loathing, that the woman he worshipped had once been wife to that most notorious of *roués.*

"I know," he whispered softly. "But that's all over now, darling. You don't think I could ever——"

"No, oh no! But the horror sticks, Jack; and it has made me what I am. I feel so hard and bitter and old, so old! I feel years older than you. I can't let you do it. You don't know. I'm not fit to marry you."

"Why not—tell me. There *couldn't* be anything that matters, Pauline. The Duchess looked up quickly and tried to draw her hands away. "I can't tell you more; don't ask me. But I can never marry you."

Mauleverer stood up suddenly, and drew a long breath. He had thought the battle was won, and now it seemed that it had to be fought all over again. But he knew that it would go to him in the end, because she loved him. He leant over the back of the Duchess's chair, his arms over her shoulders.

"Pauline, my Pauline, it's no good! There is nothing now that can stand between you and me. Give it up, darling. What horrible things are there that could make any difference? Do you think if all the world stood between us that they could keep me from you now you've told me that you love me? Pauline, I didn't know you loved me, I never hoped for that, it's making me drunk with happiness. Aren't you happy too; doesn't it make your blood boil up a bit, when you think that you're mine and I'm yours, and all the world's before us? All the world, Pauline, no one else that matters or counts, but only just you and me. Do you know that you haven't said 'Yes' to me yet? It doesn't matter much, as you've said you love me, but I want it, I want everything. Say it, Pauline, say, 'Jack, I will marry you!'"

All her life long Pauline Merioneth remembered that moment, often in after years the sounds of London streets brought it back to her. She could sit once more in her long low chair, her eyes could see the Park before her, the trees green as they are in summer, her ears could hear the hum of the traffic of Park Lane beneath, the rattle of omnibus chains, the tinkle of hansom bells. And, whispering over her shoulder, the soft tender voice that held all she ever cared to listen to, the voice of the man she loved passionately to her dying day. For a moment she remained still, looking straight before her; then she leaned back her head on to his shoulder, as he bent over her chair, and gave him what he asked in unconditional surrender.

"Jack, I will marry you," she said.

But within a week Jack Mauleverer was found murdered in Lansdowne Passage, on his way from his club to the woman he loved.   Had Fate laughed in derision when they plighted their troth?

Chapter V

LONDON was again horrified, for the morning papers of July 31 contained the incredible announcement that Mr. Jack Mauleverer, the eldest son and heir of Colonel Mauleverer, had been found shot in Lansdowne Passage. At first this appeared to be quite inexplicable, and the mystery depended for its horror upon the fact of the occurrence forming the fourth in a sequence of tragic deaths in one family, and upon the coincidence of each having taken place after precisely the interval of a month. But when the further detail came out, it having been suppressed in the earliest accounts, that in this case, as in the three preceding ones, the neck was encircled by a noose of knotted rope, it was evident that the death of Jack Mauleverer was simply the fourth in the same series of crimes. Again the police expected to make an immediate arrest, but the matter had gripped the public notice to too great an extent for it to be put off with the usual sophistries with which an occurrence of this nature is usually treated by the press and police. There were wild rumours of a reappearance of Jack the Ripper, and the press

36

was full of interviews with insanity specialists, for it seemed beyond the bounds of possibility that any sane person, either from motives of revenge or any other reason, should deliberately plan and carry out a series of murders directed against four brothers, no single one of whom, as far as could be ascertained, had given any single person cause to bear them either ill-will or a lasting grudge. The authorities at Scotland Yard were simply bewildered by the rapid succession of murders, and by the absolute mystery which surrounded each one. They were always finding clues which never led to anything; they were continually evolving strange theories; but any practical advance towards an elucidation of the mysteries or an arrest of the criminals, seemed as far off after the fourth murder as it had been after the first. The whole series was, and seemed likely to remain, an absolutely unintelligible mystery.

It was the week after the murder of Mr. Jack Mauleverer that the Colonel was ushered into the rooms of Dennis Yardley, the most famous private detective in Europe, a man in whose hands had rested the reputations of Sovereigns, and whose marvellous brain had unravelled the mysteries of Courts. Never perhaps had that given period of time produced such a change in any man as had taken place in Colonel Mauleverer. The murder of his son, Captain Mauleverer, he had accepted after the manner of a man who must play the game and accept the buffets which Fate deals out. He took his second blow after the fashion in which a strong man plays the "stiff upper lip," but the third murder told heavily, and the fourth absolutely broke up even the iron will and strength of purpose of the man who had passed through twenty years on the Frontier with but little visible signs of its effect. It was with a hesitating step that he advanced into the room and it was with a faltering voice that he began to speak.

"I suppose you can guess what I have come about."

"Well, Colonel, I imagine there are very few people who are not acquainted with the awful experiences through which you have passed. I suppose you wish me to help you in finding some clue to the mystery?"

"That is partly so, but it is not my chief object in coming to see you. I had five sons; I don't pretend that they were mammy-reared; but I was on very good terms with all of my boys, and I am positive that if any one of them had got into serious trouble, he would have made no secret of it with me. And I am as certain of it as I am that I am sitting here, that no one of my sons has ever done any person such injury that such vengeance could have been anticipated. It is inconceivable to me that anything should have occurred which would implicate the four to this degree, and I am at my wits' end to think of any explanation which is plausible. But of one thing I am certain, that, whether the four murders have been committed by the same hand or not, there is one agency only at the back of it all, and the thing has been done so systematically that it seems to me the odds are heavy that my youngest and only remaining son is marked as the victim for the 30th of the present month. The thing cannot be coincidence, and it cannot be chance."

The old man pulled himself together, and some of his old character came back into his face, as, thumping the table with his fist, he said—

"My four elder boys are dead, and do what I will, and spend what I will, I can't bring them back. The claims of the living are greater than the claims of the dead. I have one boy left to me, and he has got to be protected, and I have come to you to ask you to do it. If you think the safest way to protect him is to try to unravel the four mysteries that are past, do it. If you think you can protect him more safely by taking other steps, take them; but I want you clearly to understand that money doesn't enter into the question, and that sufficient and adequate means must be adopted to put his safety beyond any question of doubt or risk. Now then, what do you think is the best way to set about it? Personally I have little faith in police protection."

The detective shrugged his shoulders, and answered—

"If you could persuade them to give you their best men and plenty of them, it would be all right. But money couldn't enter into the calculations of Scotland Yard, and they will not put six of their best men at the disposal of a private person for an unlimited period, possibly years in duration. For I tell you frankly, Colonel, that unless one can get to the very bottom of the whole business, you would not be justified in relaxing any precautions for the next fifteen or twenty years."

"Well, what do you suggest?"

"You're a member of the Yacht Squadron, aren't you, Colonel?"

"Yes, my yacht is lying at Ryde now."

"Well, if you put your son on your yacht, and take no single person on board that you haven't known for years, taking particular care to engage no new hands in any capacity, and give your skipper instructions that the first dark night after he leaves harbour, he is to alter the name of the yacht, then you will have reduced the risks to a minimum, and I can suggest no safer place. But at the same time, if you will leave your son at Eton, and let us watch him there, we may perhaps lay our hands on the explanation of the mystery, for I am as certain as you are, Colonel Mauleverer, that the life of your son will be attempted on the 30th of this month, and if that attempt is frustrated, that it will be tried again and again on the 30th of each succeeding month. To put it in brief it comes to this—are you willing to gamble with the life of your son? On the one hand, you may elucidate the mystery, and avenge your four dead sons, and as a natural consequence ensure the safety of your living son. On the other hand, you can 'play for safety' and secure a reasonable certainty of immunity for the boy; but, I warn you, at a most awful price, because neither he nor you will know one minute's ease of mind for, as I said, the next fifteen or twenty years. It's not a pleasant decision for you, but I am afraid it's one you will have to make."

The Colonel thought for a few minutes, and, like most other men of his character, his decision was made almost immediately.

"If it rest with me, I think after what you've said, that he must run the risk if I can depend upon you to take every precaution which human ingenuity can devise. But at the same time, if the boy himself is frightened, he will make but a poor subject, and so he shall decide for himself. I am going down to Eton this afternoon, and I will put it before him as far as I know it, and I will tell him you will see him—shall I say to-morrow?—and he can hear what you have to say, and then, if he is willing, I will put him into your hands."

On the following day the interview took place between the boy, Anthony Mauleverer, and Dennis Yardley. Though high-spirited, Anthony seemed to have in a marked degree his father's characteristics of a strong will, and the capacity for looking at things dispassionately. He was obviously much affected by the deaths of his brothers, and very evidently realized the gravity of the issue which his father had left for him to decide. He carefully considered everything that the detective told him, and though his decision was not made hurriedly, it was at the same time made without hesitation. He preferred to run the risk, rather than look forward to spending the best part of his life in a constant fever of dread and anxiety. The arrangements of Yardley were quickly made. A brief interview with the headmaster of Eton satisfied him that in the opinion of the school authorities such arrangements as the detective considered necessary were quite incompatible with school life. As Dr. Warre put it: "We have no wish, in fact we deeply regret doing or saying anything whatever that would add the smallest fraction of a degree to the worry and anxiety of Colonel Mauleverer, with whom we cannot but sympathize profoundly, but at the same time I have my duty to the College to consider, and its interests; and, if the boy's life is in anything like the danger that you suppose, or that your proposed arrangements would indicate, then he must be removed. I cannot have such a fearful responsibility thrust upon us here, nor do I see how the safeguards you suggest could be satisfactorily put in operation here."

Yardley returned to Town, and in the course of

a second interview with Colonel Mauleverer, the precautions to be taken were arranged. Briefly, it was decided that Anthony should go to his father's seat at Tibberton Mauleverer in Yorkshire, accompanied by four detective-assistants of Yardley, who, in relays two by two, were never for one single moment, day or night, to leave the side of their charge. On the following day, the 28th, they all left Town by the morning train, arriving between five and six, Colonel Mauleverer and Yardley travelling with them, the whole of the seven being armed.

Without a moment's hesitation the detective on his arrival went straight to the room prepared for Anthony and thoroughly examined it. It was on the first floor, but the height of the rooms at Tibberton Mauleverer was so great that the window was quite thirty feet from the ground. The door was at the end of a small corridor leading from the big gallery which encircled the hall, and on to which all the bedrooms opened. The two windows which were in the wall opposite the door looked over the garden front. The room was furnished in modern style; there was no second door, nor were there cupboards built into the wall, or recesses. The room had a handsome fireplace containing a dog grate, but, as was only to be expected from the age of the house, the chimney was big, and Yardley at once made a minute examination. With a gasp of horror, he put his arm up the chimney and found a slender knotted cord sufficient to bear the weight of a man hanging down inside, the end being about eighteen inches above the opening, so that it would not have been discovered without careful scrutiny. Ringing the bell, the footman came in response, and Yardley asked him to summon Colonel Mauleverer at once. The Colonel immediately appeared, and close upon his heels hurried the other detectives, who had accompanied the party from Town. Pointing out his discovery, the detective asked what access there was to the roof.

"Oh, there's a proper staircase from the attics on the next floor; but the entrance to the staircase is kept locked, and the key is in my room. We can soon see if the passage has been used."

Telling Anthony to go downstairs to the library, and sending two of his men with him, Yardley, accompanied by his two other assistants and Colonel Mauleverer, passed upstairs to the next floor, and carefully examined the doorway leading to the staircase to the roof. It was very evident that months must have passed since this way had been used; for the accumulation of dust and cobwebs, which could be seen through the keyhole on the other side, could not have been recently disturbed.

"Is it possible to get on to the roof in any other way?"

"Not as far as I am aware. But it might be just as well to ask Anthony. When the boys were all at home together, they often used to be fooling about on the roof."

The Colonel went downstairs, and fetched the key, and on his return, they all proceeded to the roof. It was a matter of a few minutes only to pick out the wide-mouthed chimney, which led to Anthony's room, and down which the rope was hanging. At the foot of the chimney was a neat little parcel carefully wrapped up to protect it from the weather, which, on examination, proved to contain a liberal supply of sandwiches and a flask of whisky. Even on the threshold of a tragedy the grim face of the Colonel relaxed into a smile—a ghastly one, but still a smile.

"Of all the damned infernal cheek——"

"Plenty of evidence of premeditation," acquiesced Yardley.

"What shall you do?" asked the Colonel. "Leave it?"

"Yes, we'll leave it; but I think we can manage a rather different ending from the one which has been planned. Can I send off some telegrams, sir?" he continued, as all filed downstairs again.

"Certainly," answered the Colonel; and he rang the library bell. "Where will you send them from?"

"Well, I'd rather send them from York, if you can drive one of my men in."

He sat down at the library table, and wrote the following wires:

"To Croxton Smith, Tooting, S.W. Can you lend me Holden and two of your bloodhounds? My man shall call to-night."

"To Jones and Co., electricians, Charing Cross Road, W.C. Please send down to-morrow certain to Tibberton Mauleverer Nr. York expert electrician assistants and materials capable of fitting complete installation burglar alarm in an hour."

"To Craven, c/o Duplicity, London. Go Scotland Yard and say imperative that I have two of their best men here at Tibberton Mauleverer midday to-morrow certain. Bring dogs as arranged."

The messages were written and handed to one of the assistants as the dog-cart came round. When he had gone, the Colonel turned to his son, and said—

"Anthony, how do you get on to the roof here?"

"Why, up the attic staircase, of course."

"No; that's the way I go. I mean the way you go," said the Colonel, with a smile.

Anthony laughed. "Well, it is *possible* another way, father, but I don't expect you'd care to try it. You know the little outhouse by the kitchen. It's quite easy to get on the roof of that, and then on to the kitchen roof. That joins on to the chapel, and from the chapel it's easy to get up on the other roof."

Yardley and the Colonel looked at each other and nodded.

"Guessed as much," the former muttered to himself.

The evening of the 28th passed away without any incident, and Anthony went to bed in his usual room, two of the assistants being with him. During the course of the next day the two men came down from Scotland Yard, together with the electricians, Craven, Yardley's understudy, and Holden, the latter having, in a leash, two of his master's world-famous bloodhounds.

Craven, together with Holden and the dogs, drove from York in order to avoid comment. Yardley instructed the men from Scotland Yard that they were to take it in turns to patrol the terrace outside the house.

The 29th of the month dragged wearily on. The suspense told heavily upon them all as the afternoon passed, and even Yardley and his assistants were glad when the night was over and the 30th dawned. That day was but a repetition of the former day, but with every anxiety intensified. In due course the gong sounded for dinner, and Anthony with his two guardians, the Colonel and Yardley, entered the dining-room which was large, occupying fully half of the frontage towards the gardens. The assistants took their places one by each door into the room, and the other three sat down to their meal. As they did so the detective looked at the Colonel, and asked—

"Do you always sit in the same places here?"

"Yes, I always sit at the foot of the table, and whichever of my sons was at home, for it was very rare for more than one of them to be here at a time, always sat at the head."

"Oh," Yardley grunted; "then, Anthony, suppose you sit opposite to me for to-night. I can't say I like things which are regular customs."

The dinner was over, and they were sitting lingering over the dessert. The servants had drawn the blinds, and lighted the gas, when all of a sudden every one heard a sharp report from a revolver, a scurry of feet on the gravel, and a second report, and a bullet had lodged in the back of the chair where Anthony should have sat. Jumping to his feet, Yardley called out—

"Craven, look after the boy, and call the other two. You two come with me"; and, rushing to the window, he leapt on the window-sill, crashed his shoulder through the glass, and dropped on a man. "I've got him; bring a light!" he yelled, as he gripped the figure by the throat and squeezed his fingers into the man's neck.

In a few moments lights were brought round to the front of the house. With a cry of horror the detective saw the dead face of one of the Scotland Yard men.

"Holden, bring the dogs," he called; and in a few minutes, straining at their collars, the dogs were brought round to the front of the house.

But the delay had been fatal. They were

quickly on the scent, and raced away in a straight line with the others panting behind them. But cleverly as their own plans had been laid, these they were trying to circumvent were cleverer   The dogs ran straight to the lake in front of the house, where, of course, they were brought up short. In a few minutes they had all reached the edge of the water, which was a long narrow piece.

"Can you wade across?" asked Holden.

"No, it's pretty deep in the middle."

"Nobody could have swum across in the time," interjected Yardley.

"Which is the quickest way round?"

"By the bridge; come with me;" and they all started off at a run to the right.

The distance was not inconsiderable, and it was a matter of ten minutes or a quarter of an hour before they were opposite the point at which the dogs had lost the scent. Backwards and forwards, backwards and forwards, each time taking a bigger sweep, Holden took his hounds along the edge of the lake, but without the slightest success. At last, in sheer desperation, he took them at a run all round the margin of the lake, and at the far end, in the opposite direction to the bridge, the hounds again found the scent, and tore off in the direction of the upper lake, only to be brought to a second standstill on the margin of the water. Profiting by his previous experience, he at once took the hounds round the margin of the lake, and had made the complete circuit, save for about twenty yards, when the hounds once more gave tongue as they raced 'back towards the house along the drive, making off short by the kitchen gardens. They jumped the park wall, a foot or two only in height from the inside, but a big drop into the road. Here they were again at fault. As Holden, when he had caught them up, took his hounds backwards and forwards along the roads, Yardley carefully examined the ground with the lantern, and there in the mud of the road could be plainly seen the mark of a bicycle tyre.

"Is there any train from your station here?"

"No, the last one went more than an hour ago."

He looked at his watch "It's more than an hour since that shot was fired. Can you telephone to the station?"

"Yes."

"Well, ask them what passengers went by the last train. What other stations are there within reach?"

"Satton, between here and York, and Linby on the other side of us."

"The train from Linby would pass through Tibberton, wouldn't it?"

"Yes, ten minutes afterwards."

"Well, they would guess we should go to the station here, so I don't think they would have chosen that one. You can't telephone to Satton?"

"No, I'm sorry to say we can't."

"Well, I'm afraid we can do no more here. Jones," he said, turning to one of his assistants, "you must drive to Satton at once, and make inquiries. Craven, you must go to York."

"He'd better go over on the motor," said the Colonel.

It was only a brief space of time before Craven, sitting in the motor-car, was taking his instructions.

"You must go to York and see the stationmaster. Find out anything you can about the passengers who got in at York. Tell the stationmaster it's a matter of life and death, that we pay any cost, and indemnify him for any expense; but the through train to London must not be stopped between York and the York Road ticket platform at King's Cross, that if there are any passengers to go by the train from Newark or Retford, we will pay for a special train to take them, and we'll pay for a special train to take any who are carried beyond their destination. But the train, which has now started from York, is not on any account to stop at any platform or any station. Wire to Scotland Yard, and tell them that the person we want to catch is in all human probability in that train. Tell them to send enough men to York Road to ransack the train from end to end, and to arrest everybody who is not well known, or cannot give an absolute account of themselves. Tell them one of their own men has been murdered, and that will put them on the *qui vive*."

Yardley and the Colonel turned back to the house.

"Well," said the Colonel, "what's the next move?" when they were seated in the library, where Anthony and his two guardians already were.

"We can't do anything more until we hear from London," was the answer. "You know, Colonel, one can't stand this sort of thing for ever; it's more than human nerves can stand, and we *must* find out who did it. We can't simply sit here and wait for events to happen. What have they done about that poor chap Peters?" '

"They've taken his body into the coach-house," said the Colonel. "Miles, my butler, tells me that he sent for Dr. Morrison at once. He's here now, and I have no doubt will come in before he goes."

As he made the remark the door opened and the Doctor entered.

"This is a terrible business, Colonel," he said.

"Yes, I'm afraid it is; and there's a good deal more behind it than one sees. I suppose that poor fellow was quite dead?"

"Yes, he was shot straight through the brain; he must have died instantaneously."

"I'm glad of that," remarked Yardley; "I shouldn't like to think I'd throttled a dying man."

The Doctor stayed with them talking for some time, before taking his leave, promising to give notice to the coroner, and to relieve the Colonel of all the formalities in connection with the inquest.

The Colonel rang the bell, and told the servant to send one of the stablemen to him, adding to the detective:

"I told them to loose the dogs, and I cannot for the life of me think why we never saw them. They are two huge mastiffs which we keep down at the stables, with by no means amiable tempers; in fact, in ordinary cases, it is none too safe for them to be about loose."—"Why didn't you loose the dogs as I told you?" he asked, as the stableman came into the room.

The man appeared half dazed, and it was with great difficulty that they could get an intelligible tale out of him.

"Please, sir, I didn't like to trouble you, sir, and I didn't find out, till after everybody had gone out, sir—you said to let them out about half-past eight, sir, and when I heard the shooting and the noise, I went into the yard, and they'd both been poisoned, sir. Turk was dead, sir, and Greek was foaming at the mouth; it must have been poison, sir, for I've seen dogs poisoned before. Greek wasn't dead when you sent for me just now, and we're doing all we can."

"Thanks! that will do. You'd better send for a vet, if there's any one who can go."

The man left the room, and the Colonel turned to Yardley, his face harder and grimmer than before.

"Gad! the preparations were complete."

The detective rose from his chair and walked backwards and forwards up and down the room.

"It's simply ghastly. In all my experience I never came across anything planned so devilishly, or in such cold blood as this has been."

"Well, I suppose we are safe for to-night, as our man has got away."

"How on earth do you know there's only one in it, Colonel? It seems almost incredible to me that it has all been the work of one person. If you could only give me some clue, even the wildest guess, why it is being done, we might make plans; but we are absolutely in the dark."

The Colonel carefully thought; one could see the far-away look in his eyes as he passed his own life in review.

"Well, I can honestly say that I know of no single person with whom I am at enmity. Why, man, I've lived all my life in India. It isn't twelve months since I gave up my regiment, and came home. I don't suppose any of the Afridis whom my men have sent to glory are coming back to trouble us."

"Anthony, are you ready to go to bed?" asked Yardley.

The boy said nothing, but stood up, and turned to shake hands with his father. Plucky though he was, there was no doubt that he was unhinged now that he was face to face with his own risk. He had sat like a log all the evening, and it was very evident that now he realized the fact that his life hung practically on the throw of the dice that Fate was holding.

"Don't give in, old boy," said the Colonel. "I think you know we're doing all we can to keep you safe."

"I know that, sir," said the boy, as he turned to leave the room with his two guardians.

Yardley sprang up. "Now nobody outside ourselves is to know it, but I'm going to change places with that boy to-night!" Turning to his assistants, he added, "Shift the boy's things to my room and stay there with him, and take care that none of the servants know that the room has been changed."

When they had left the room the detective told the Colonel—

"I've had that electrician at work in Anthony's room all day, and he's rigged up an alarm, so that a bell will ring directly that rope is moved, and we've weighted the rope to keep it steady. Of course, it's too far down for any one to notice this, even by daylight. I've got the bell muffled so that only a faint 'burr' would be heard, or of course it would give the alarm everywhere. That will tell us when our friend is coming down the chimney, and then, please God, we shall have him. I'm going to take the other two men to spend the night with me in that room. The other Scotland Yard man is patrolling about outside, though his nerves must be pretty good, after the fate of his companion. I think," said Yardley, as he turned everything over in his mind, "that we'll have Holden and his animals in the hall."

About eleven o'clock they all proceeded upstairs. The light in Anthony's usual room was turned down to the tiniest jet, and one of the assistants took his station immediately underneath it. Yardley took the bell of the alarm in his one hand, and holding his revolver in the other, sat on the side of the bed, within a few feet of the fireplace. Minute after minute the four men sat in the dark, every nerve on the strain. Accustomed as he was to deal with a crisis, the situation was more than the Colonel even could stand, and the perspiration rolled down his face, as he afterwards admitted, whilst minute after minute slipped by. An eternity seemed to have passed, when all of a sudden the bell gave a faint burr, and every one with difficulty suppressed an exclamation. But then the muffling of the bell slipped, and a loud harsh peal rang through the room.

"Damn it," said Yardley; "of course that's given it away."

Turning to one of his assistants he told him to stay where he was, and to shoot without warning if any one came into the room. Darting through the door, he yelled to Holden to loose the dogs, and to go to the kitchen door. He heard the bolts drop as Holden opened the front door, before he got to the end of the gallery. Running down the back staircase and through the servants' hall, he got to the kitchen door as Holden came round the house.

"I don't think he can have got down yet, so we will just wait for him."

Minute after minute passed, but nothing happened; so leaving Holden he went round to the side of the chapel, to a point from which he had a view of the only means of access from the roof of the house to the chapel roof. At that moment, just disappearing in the darkness, he saw a figure running at top speed, and at the same moment his eye caught sight of the rain-water pipe, by which descent had evidently been made. Calling to Holden he set off in quick pursuit; but the other had a long start. In a moment the hounds raced past him hot on the trail, and were lost to sight in the darkness. As he ran he heard, in quick succession, five or six reports from a revolver. He saw the flashes far away to his right, in an opposite direction to that in which he was going. Following the flashes, he stumbled over the bodies of the two dogs. He had lost all track of the fugitive, and could only go on groping blindly. Coming to a halt, he swore violently, and with every term to which he could lay his tongue, at the fiendish luck by which twice in the same evening he had failed to make his capture. It was utterly hopeless to attempt pursuit in the dark, the park wall was several miles in length, scaleable from the inside at almost any point, and there was nothing in the way of fences to prevent any direction having been chosen. On the other side of it, for the greater part of the distance, some road or other ran alongside the park wall.

By the time he had got back to the house he found that Craven had returned, and he eagerly questioned him.

"What did you find out?"

"Well, there were only fifteen people who travelled by that train from York. There was Lord Malvern and five friends, who had been staying with him for shooting, and they had two men-servants. There were three clergymen who turned up at the station in the Archbishop's carriage. There were four people whom the stationmaster said he knew as living in York, and whose names and addresses he wrote down for me, and there was a fat old farmer and his wife, who came by one of the local trains, and most certainly could not have given us the chase we had."

They had been walking as they talked, and by now were back in the library where the Colonel and the two assistants were waiting for them. In a few brief sentences Yardley told Craven what had happened since he left.

"I am not surprised there was no one left on the train that would answer our description. Have you got a Bradshaw, Colonel?"

As it was handed to him, he turned over the leaves and then glanced at the clock.

"I think any one on a bicycle could just have done it. The mail goes through in an hour from now. You'll have to go to York again, Craven, and the same instructions that I gave you before hold good again. Wire Scotland Yard that there has been a second attempt and that I want the mail train searched. If you start at once you may perhaps catch the train yourself, in which case you had better travel on it."

"I don't think he will," put in the Colonel. "The motor only manages about fifteen miles an hour, and it's about seventeen or eighteen to York."

Without another word Craven picked up his overcoat, thrusting his arms into it as he went to the door where the motor was still waiting.

"Back to York," he said to the chauffeur, as he jumped in beside him; and the machine whizzed away down the drive.

Yardley still lolled in the big chair by the library fire. The man had visibly aged during the night, and the depression consequent upon two palpable defeats occurring so closely together had left a very perceptible alteration.

"Colonel," he said, "I don't believe the man exists on earth who would make three attempts in one night, and I think we can go to bed." And with that he drained a tumbler of whisky.

The Colonel's spirits were visibly better, it was

the old lust of shikari coming back to him, for the hunting of men is the finest sport in the world. Yardley was right, and the remainder of the night passed without event. He was early afoot on the following morning, and spent hours in examining the scenes of the previous night's adventures. All the others had breakfasted before he turned up. As soon as he made his appearance the Colonel asked him what he had found out.

"Well," he said, "I've discovered several things. In the first place, come here;" and he led them to the window. "You see those two lines." He pointed out two scratches in the window-sill; they were by no means deep, but at the same time they were readily perceptible to the touch, and looked as if they had been cut with a penknife in the soft sandstone.

"Well, what are those?"

"Follow the direction of them."

The Colonel's eye rapidly took the bearings indicated, and saw they pointed directly to the chair in the back of which the bullet had lodged the previous evening.

"That's how the pistol was aimed," said the detective; "the blinds were drawn of course and it puzzled me how the aim could be so exact." He sat down to the table and proceeded with his breakfast, saying, as he did so: "I went down to the lake. You remember the dogs followed the scent to the edge and then lost it. The explanation of that is simple. We lost time going round to the right, over the bridge. Now, no one could have swum across it in the time nor could anybody have waded the length of the lake, for you can't run waist deep in water; but whoever it was we were after last night turned sharp to the left as soon as he was in the water, and ran along on the edge, in an inch or two of water, to the end of the lake. The footprints under the water can be plainly seen still, though I don't suppose they'll last many hours longer; they are a good deal defaced already. As we found out last night, the tracks led from the big lake straight to the upper lake, and we lost the scent again at the edge of the water there. If you remember, Holden there at once took his dogs straight round the edge of the lake, starting to the right. In that case he made a mistake, because if he had repeated what he did on the first occasion, and taken them backwards and forwards, we should have saved a lot of time. The murderer turned sharp to the left again, but there he only went a dozen yards in the water before he doubled back to the house on the scent the dogs picked up afterwards. You see, at each place we lost considerable time. Then I went round by the chapel. Did you ever get down the other side, Anthony?" said Yardley, turning to him.

"No, I didn't know you could."

"Well, I don't think you could get up that way, but it is as simple as pie to come down by that water-pipe. Whoever was concerned in last night's business knows this house well. Then I went down to the road where the bicycle marks were. Thank goodness your roads here take impressions. If, as I feel pretty certain, the criminal got on a bicycle there, one can piece the story together a bit farther. The bicycle marks were not continuous, but I could find no sign of any track towards York after you get out of the cross roads and on the main road. On the contrary, a treble track was very plain in places where the road was soft in the opposite direction. Now, I feel pretty certain the three tracks were made by the same bicycle, because the tyre was new, and had left the ridge marks from the corrugations in the india-rubber perfectly distinct. Those marks are the same as in the track in the side road by the wall at the point where the dogs took us to."

"But what on earth do you make of three tracks?"

"Well, the fact of there being three gives one the explanation, if it is really a fact that we are looking for a man on a bicycle. Whoever it was came from the opposite direction to York, that is, came from Thirsk, and came here on a bicycle, and after his first attempt he just rode round the park wall—there's your second track. Now, he would think that, having made one unsuccessful attempt, we should jump to the conclusion that he would be making tracks and that no second attempt would be made that night, and so we should not be on the watch, so he made his second attempt, and, luckily for us, we were on the watch. Then after we chased him the second time he made the third track, and I don't believe he went to York at all but went the opposite way, and we must look for him in the north."

"Oh, but he could go that way and turn off by Hobson's Farm," put in Anthony. "It's a trifle the longer way, but it's much better for bicycling. We generally go that way," he added.

As they were speaking, Craven entered the room. Yardley turned sharp round.

"Well?" he asked.

"I missed the train, I'm sorry to say; but I don't fancy it will make much difference. Two of the porters recognized a man in knickerbockers and bicycling clothes very muddy, who put his machine in the cloakroom and booked to London. There were two commercial travellers, several York people, some of them ladies who were known, and some people booked through from other places who had come in by various other trains during the evening and who had been subsequently seen about the platform who obviously could not have been here. He had hardly finished his report when a telegram from Scotland Yard was handed to Dennis Yardley.

"Names addresses everybody both trains secured and verified nobody likely first train second train commercial travellers identified by luggage and have discarded passengers with tickets from beyond York eight passengers coming from York gave names and addresses since corroborated as passengers by York stationmaster Archbishop's butler and Brown a lady's maid both identified and well known York and King's Cross and Jimmy Webb have arrested last-named nobody in bicycling clothes or knickerbockers."

Looking up, Yardley remarked, "That looks as if we've got the man;" and he passed the telegram across to the Colonel with a visible sigh of relief. The latter asked—

"Who is Jimmy Webb?"

"He is a man with about as notable a criminal career as I have ever heard of. He has always been suspected of the murder of Lord Delavel. I don't know if you remember it, about eight or nine years ago; but the police could never bring it home to him. His particular line is blackmail. A black-mailing letter was found in Lord Delavel's blotting-pad afterwards, threatening to murder him if he didn't pay some huge sum, I think £10,000, and the old man wouldn't, and one night when the butler went into the library to make up the fire before going to bed, they found Lord Delavel with his head battered in, and his note-case on the floor empty. He had cashed a cheque for £100 that morning and the notes given him at the bank came back from the Continent, and were traced to a firm of turf accountants at Flushing. The firm proved that each had come into their hands from a separate bookmaker after the Epsom Meeting. It was obvious that twenty bookmakers could not have been parties to a single crime, and they could none of them tell where they got them from. The police knew Jimmy had been at Epsom, but none of the bookmakers could identify him, so the thing fell through; but we firmly believe he was responsible. He has just been released on a ticket of leave, after seven years for blackmailing Lady Fauncetown, and I feel pretty sure that during the next few days, if Jimmy had not been caught, you would have had a letter offering to spare Anthony's life 'on terms' which would have been fairly stiff. Thinking it over in the light of this knowledge, I dare say you will find that's the explanation."

"But they tried to *kill* Anthony. Where's the use of blackmailing me if the boy's dead? And how about my other boys?"

"Do you think the attempts last night could only have been intimidation?"

"You don't seriously think that any human being in cold blood would murder four of my sons simply to frighten me so that he could blackmail me about the fifth. The thing isn't human."

"My dear Colonel, you may take it from me that Webb—we always nickname him Smiler—would stick at *no* crime to gain his ends, and I would believe anything about him."

"Well, then, you think it's all a plan to extort money from me?"

"No, I don't think; it doesn't pay me to think until I am sure. But, knowing the man, I put what I have said as a plausible explanation, which accounts for everything we know at present and which may be true. It seems to me the most probable story."

The Colonel went to his bureau and hunted for some minutes, finally tossing a letter he withdrew from it across to the detective.

"That's the only blackmailing letter I ever received."

"Well, there is not the slightest doubt Smiler wrote this. I know his writing, and the style of his letters."

The letter was a curt note, signed James Bohun, threatening a criminal prosecution unless £5000 were paid to an appointed messenger.

"Did you pay?"

"Not a cent; a blackmailer's accusations would have to be true before I took any notice of 'em. I never heard any more of this."

"No; but, you see, it is dated just before the date of the death of Captain Mauleverer. I dare say the man knew you were well enough off, and meant to have whatever money you could be plundered of, by hook or crook. Mind, I don't say for certain that we have got to the bottom of the business, but the presence of that man in that particular train is a long step towards a solution. You see a crime is committed, and the criminal in all probability escapes in a certain train. Now everybody on that train can be accounted for except this one man, who is a known criminal of bad type. Everything at present therefore points to his connection in some way with the crime, and we must wait and see what the explanation is."

CHAPTER VI

DURING the next few days Yardley suggested that they should all return to Town. "You see the attempts have been so determined that it doesn't seem to make much difference where you are, and they very evidently have means of knowing your movements. Added to which, it is no good hiding Anthony if we are to catch the criminal, that is, if we have not already got him, which I think we have."

The Colonel agreed, and the next day saw him settled at his Town house with Anthony, and his four protectors in attendance, whilst Yardley was deep in consultation with the authorities at Scotland Yard. When the prisoner was first brought before the magistrate, formal evidence of arrest only was given, and, a remand for a week was obtained. On that occasion the police merely outlined the details of the crime, indicating the probability of the prisoner's connection with it, and obtained another remand pending inquiries.

On the following occasion much the same procedure was adopted in spite of the repeated protests of innocence on the part of the prisoner. The

magistrate indicated that the police must be prepared to go more fully into the question on the
next occasion, but granted the remand asked for.
Webb was again brought up on the twenty-second
of the month, but the police had got no further
evidence of any importance. They confessed their
inability actually to connect the prisoner with the
crime, but pointed out the probability that whoever
committed it boarded the train at York. Various
railway officials gave evidence that a man in cycling
clothes arrived at the station just before the departure of the train, his clothes exceedingly muddy,
and that this person took a ticket to London, and
was seen to enter the train. Evidence was given
that the train made no stop at any station between
York and King's Cross, and that to ensure this
Colonel Mauleverer had paid for a special train
to follow it, picking up passengers who would otherwise have travelled in it, and had indemnified several people who had thereby been carried beyond
their destination. Evidence was also given that
a force of thirty police constables had boarded the
train at York Road, and that no passenger could
have escaped their notice. That every passenger
on the train had been closely questioned and detained pending verification of the names and addresses given, but no passenger in cycling clothes
or knickerbockers was found on the train. The
prisoner answered the general description given at
York, and he had been several times convicted of

various offences. Evidence was also given to prove the finding at the side of the railway by a plate-layer of a suit of bicycling clothes some twenty-five or thirty miles south of York. The prisoner em-phatically protested his innocence, and produced a ticket from Newcastle to London, and asserted that he had travelled through from Newcastle by that train. The ticket, however, was not punched as it should have been at York, which the magistrate considered a. most suspicious circumstance. The prisoner explained this by asserting that he was in the lavatory at the time. Yardley requested to be allowed to examine the ticket, which he did, care-fully making a note of its number. The prisoner was asked if he had anything to say, or if he wished to call any witnesses to prove his presence else-where. He admitted that he was unable to do so.

"Then," said the magistrate, "I'm afraid I must commit you to take your trial."

An audible sigh of relief escaped from the police inspector, but Yardley's face showed plainly that things had not gone as he would have liked.

"What's the matter?" said the Colonel, when they got outside the court.

"I'm afraid that's not our man, Colonel. Every-body who's ever been through York knows the tickets are examined on the train, and if the ticket had been obtained as a precaution or as a blind, he would have taken jolly good care not to have been in the lavatory at the time, or else to have come out when he felt the train slowing down. It isn't as if the crime were unpremeditated. Everything, as far as we can see, has been thought out to the tiniest detail, and every preparation made, and I don't think such an obvious precaution as that would have been missed. I don't know what to think," said the detective; "but now I am as certain in my own mind as I can be, that we are no nearer an explanation than when the crime was committed. The police are as keen as mustard to avenge their own man, and I think we can leave them to hunt up the antecedents of Mr. Jimmy Webb, and do all that is requisite to get the conviction, if he is really the criminal. I'm just going to telegraph to Newcastle to find out when that ticket was issued, but I think we shall have to start looking for somebody else. You don't often get a gang working at the same crime, particularly when it includes premeditated murder, unless it's a case of burglary on a big scale, and there's been no burglary in this case." He turned sharply to the Colonel: "How are your estates settled, Colonel?"

"They were re-settled by my father on my marriage, on myself and my sons in tail male, and my two brothers, who are now both dead."

"Who's the remainder man?"

"My boy Anthony, except that I fancy there's the usual final remainder, 'to his heirs whatsoever.' But I really forget."

"Well, suppose you and Anthony both died intestate, who would come in?"

"I'm sure I don't know. Anthony and I are now the two last of the family. As I had five sons I never thought about it."

"Well, it would be worth while making inquiries, Colonel. Who are your solicitors?"

In the course of the day the reply came from Newcastle that the ticket had been issued a few minutes only before the departure of the train. After reading the wire, Yardley passed it to the Colonel, with the remark—

"That's another point in his favour, because he couldn't have come down by an earlier train in the day, and he or a confederate travelled on that very train from Newcastle. If it were a confederate creating an *alibi* for him, that ticket would certainly have been punched."

The next few days passed quite uneventfully, but the awful strain and anxiety were telling upon them all, even on Yardley, in spite of his many previous experiences of strange positions.

As the day of the 30th slowly passed, the man's face grew positively haggard. Curiously enough, the victim of this strange machination was the least affected. Anthony, once the horror of that awful night at Tibberton had gone, was nearly himself again. For the nerves of youth have an elasticity that is denied to those of greater years who have known and seen and done things. Knowledge and experience have their uses and advantages, but those who claim to profit by those advantages must always pay the penalties which knowledge exacts.

As they took their places for dinner that evening, Anthony was the only one who attempted to talk. The grey-haired old butler moved round the table, filling the glasses. Contrary to his wont, Yardley asked for a whisky and soda. As his glass was filled, and he took it in his hand to drink—anxiety brings thirst—he paused for a moment as he replied to a question of the Colonel's. Then he raised his glass to his mouth, but in a moment he spat out what he had taken, and at the same time knocked Anthony's glass flying out of his hand, which he was barely in time to do.

"I knew there'd be another attempt. That's devilish, absolutely devilish!" he shouted.

"Good God, what's the matter?" And the Colonel sprang from his chair.

"I mean this, that my drink was half strychnine. If it's the whisky that's wrong, then Anthony was safe; but if it's the soda—well, then, they've risked poisoning the whole lot of us to make certain. Damn my soul, but these people do things wholesale. It's sheer butchery!"

"Miles," said the Colonel, "shut the door, and let's have this out at once. No! You two men stay here," he added, as the two men-servants attempted to leave the room. "Miles, pour out some whisky neat, and give it to Mr. Yardley."

He sniffed at it; then tasted it. "I think that's all right. Let's try the soda-water;" and the butler drew a tumblerful from the gasogene. "Oh, here it is; there's no doubt about this," he said, after the first sniff at the glass. "Has any one tampered with this gasogene, Miles?"

"No, sir; I charged it myself this afternoon."

"Could you have made a mistake by any chance?"

"I don't think so, sir. I've no other powders that I could have used instead."

"Have you got any of the powders left, Miles?"

"Yes, sir. I've got a full box; they came in fresh this afternoon."

"Came in fresh this afternoon! How did they come? Did you order them?"

"No, sir; it was rather curious, though I never gave it a thought at the time. A messenger boy brought a parcel and a note from Hunt's—that's the chemist's, sir," he added, turning to the detective. "They said in the note that they'd been having a lot of complaints about their gasogene powders, and they were afraid that some mistake must have been made. So would I please send back at once all the powders I had, and they would credit me with them; and they sent me another box, which they said I should find quite satisfactory."

"Did you notice any difference in the powders?"

"No, sir; the stuff looked just like the ordinary

white powders, the same as we always use. Shall I fetch the note, sir?"

"No, wait a moment," said Yardley. "You stay here for a bit," as he went to the telephone in the hall and rang up Messrs. Hunt.

In breathless silence they heard him ask, "Are you there? .   Are you Hunt's, the chemists? . . . Did you send any messenger to Colonel Mauleverer this afternoon for any purpose at all? . . . Did you send up to change some gasogene powders? You are quite certain that nobody in the place sent them up? Please ask very particularly . . . Have you been sending out any messages to anybody saying that there was some mistake in the powders you have been supplying? . . . Have you sold any gasogene powders to-day? . . . Did you keep the note? . . . What an awful pity!"

A minute or two passed in silence, as the detective listened to the reply he was receiving; then with a savage oath he crashed the receiver down.

"Done in again," they heard him remark.

Once more they heard him lift the receiver to summon head office.

"Put me on the central office of the District Messenger people. I don't know which is the head office of all these numbers of theirs."

A few minutes, and again the conversation began.

"Are you the head office of the District Messengers? . . . I'm Yardley the detective, and it's a matter of life and death, and it depends on you whether we can put our hands on the criminal in a case of murder. I want you to ring up every one of your depôts, and find the boy who took a note to Hunt's, the chemists, in Piccadilly this morning about eleven o'clock, with instructions to wait for a parcel, and who took a parcel away from them. I want that boy here as quickly as possible at Colonel Mauleverer's, 20, Berkeley Square. And then I want the boy who brought a parcel to this address this afternoon."

"Miles, will you fetch that note, and bring in the box of powders at once, please?" said the detective, sitting down, and adding, "We must eat, and I think we shall be safe now with the rest of the meal."

When Miles returned, the detective glanced sharply at the windows. They were both heavily shuttered, as he noticed with pleasure.

"Miles," he asked, "you said nothing to any of the other servants downstairs?"

"No, sir.

"Well," and he turned to include the two footmen in his remarks, "if you three men can keep your mouths shut and will do exactly—mind, absolutely exactly—as I tell you, we can prevent any further attempt on Mr. Anthony's life to-night. Tell the women downstairs that Mr. Anthony has been poisoned. You see," he said to the Colonel, "when the first attempt failed at Tibberton, a second was made. It is probably the same here. But the murderer must find out whether his first attempt has failed or not before he makes the second. If the first has been successful the second will not be necessary, and the murderer must find that out. He knows perfectly well that if anybody is taken suddenly ill here, we shall send for one, or probably two doctors, we shall send for the police if we suspect foul play, and there will be a general hubbub and commotion in the house. So I am positive this house is being watched at the present moment; it will be watched until we all go to bed on the chance of the poison being swallowed in the bedtime whiskies, etc. But if nothing happens they will know the first attempt has failed, and there will be another attempt made. We must let them think they have succeeded."

For the next half hour the detective stayed at the telephone ringing up, in quick succession, the police and five or six doctors. After a short interval, and close upon each other's heels, came a well-known Scotland Yard inspector of police, a dozen policemen, who posted themselves all round the house, and some of the best known medical men chosen by the detective in each case because their appearance conformed to the orthodox and popularly accepted type of the medical profession. Lights appeared in most of the windows of the house, and a crowd quickly gathered, attracted no doubt by the presence of the police. It then needed nothing more than the word "murder" to be plainly spoken in conversation in a loud voice by Yardley, a little matter that was arranged to happen at the moment when the door was opened to admit one of the medical men.

In the course of an hour or more the medical men left in a body. Several reporters were already on the threshold; but the doctors all point blank refused to answer any questions. One reporter, more pertinacious than the rest, pushed forward.

"I'm sorry to trouble you, gentlemen, but I don't want to waste my time if nothing's happened. I know this is Colonel Mauleverer's. Is it another murder?"

"It's a matter of murder, certainly, if that's what you want to know," answered one of the doctors; but the reporter could get no further details and the doctors each drove away. The police remained.

Yardley was right; no further attempt on the life of Anthony was made that night, but the next morning a small parcel arrived by post for the Colonel, who, on opening it, found it to contain a knotted cord fastened in the form of a noose.

Yardley had waited anxiously all through the night for news of the District Messengers for whom he had sent. But the boys must have been engaged on other messages or off duty or something, because it was not until breakfast was nearly over that the first arrived and was shown in to the detective.

"I suppose they have told you why you are wanted? I want you to think carefully and tell me exactly who sent you to Messrs. Hunt, the chemists, in Piccadilly, with a note, yesterday morning about eleven o'clock."

"Please, sir, I was rung up to go to the Café Monico, and one of the waiters gave me the note, told me to wait for an answer, and bring it back."

"Should you know that waiter again?"

"I think so, sir."

"Well, wait a minute, and you shall take me to him."

Jumping into a cab, Yardley and the messenger boy were quickly driven to the Monico, and passing through the swinging glass doors the boy at once pointed out a short, stout, bald-headed waiter as the one from whom he had received the note. Sitting down at a table, the detective nodded the waiter, and inquiring if he were busy or if it were possible for him to spare a few minutes, he asked him if he could explain anything about the note which he had sent by the boy the previous morning.

The man at once recollected the occurrence, and said a lady, very quietly dressed, had come in and sat down at one of his tables, and asked him to send for a District Messenger, and she had then said, after looking at her watch, that she was afraid she couldn't wait, that she gave him the note and said there would be an answer which he was to take charge of, and that she would call again soon after luncheon. She had called again, and had received the parcel. Yardley asked the waiter if he could describe her more particularly; but he said that he had taken no particular notice, thought he might, perhaps, recognize her again if he saw her, but she was not one of his regular customers, and he was not sure.

"But was there any name on the parcel, or did she leave any name?"

"No, none at all."

Yardley took out a blank card and wrote a name and address upon it.

"If she comes in again and if you can find out her name or anything about her, it will pay you to let me know, and if you will telephone at once and can manage to keep her here till I come, I don't mind finding a £20 note. But, mind you, you are not to talk about this. I suppose you are always to be found here?"

"Yes, sir."

And, giving the man half a crown for his trouble, Yardley went back and again rang up the central office of the District Messengers.

"Will you find out at once, please, which of your boys brought a parcel and a note to this address—Colonel Mauleverer's, 20, Berkeley Square—yesterday afternoon between three and four. I asked before for him to be sent. I expect he must be at one of the offices pretty close at hand."

In a few minutes a boy arrived from one of the Piccadilly offices; but all Yardley could learn from him was that he had been called up by the clerk in charge of the office, and sent off with a parcel. Yardley went back with him to the office and closely questioned the clerk in charge. Apparently he had forgotten the whole incident, and though he thought a lady had brought the parcel to be despatched, he did not pretend to be certain upon the point. Turning up the ticket he found that the name and address given was "E. Jones, 53, Henrietta Street, Covent Garden." The detective made a note of the address, and at once cabbed to Henrietta Street, only to find that there was no such number in the street.

When the detective returned to Berkeley Square he found that one of the regular agents from Scotland Yard had just called to interview Colonel Mauleverer, and he immediately joined them in the library.

"As you know, Colonel," Inspector Parkyns was saying as Yardley entered the room, "you authorized us to make a thorough search in the Jermyn Street rooms of the late Mr. Herbert Mauleverer. I believe we made you aware that a photograph was found in his letter-case. We have been carefully going through all the correspondence in his rooms. As you know, I expect, your son seems to have made a practice of keeping, or shall I say he has omitted to destroy, any letter he received. Of course the finding of a photograph of a lady amounts to nothing, but, as you assured me, you had not the faintest idea who the original of this portrait was, I thought it was just as well to ascertain the identity, as it might lead to our becoming acquainted with friends of his whom he had kept from your knowledge. If it's a painful subject to you, Colonel, I must apologize, but I am afraid it cannot very well be helped. I have been to Messrs. Ellis and Walery of Upper Baker Street, and they have referred to their books. The photo was evidently taken under an assumed name, for they have it simply as Miss Smith of Chicago. She had told them she was a member of the chorus in the Belle of New York Company, and the photograph was taken without charge, as of course is the case with most other professional photographs. The prints were to be sent to 469, Oxford Street. Of course I at once made inquiries, and found that the Oxford Street address was merely that of a tobacconist's shop to which letters were addressed at a fee of a penny each. Inquiries with the Belle of New York Company show that they had never had anybody named Smith in the chorus, nor, as far as they were aware, anybody who used that name, and on being shown the photograph every one at once denied that any such person had ever belonged to the company. So it was very evident that whoever it was who was photographed, wished to hide her identity."

The Colonel picked up the photograph and looked at it intently.

"She's an uncommonly beautiful woman," he said. "Somehow or other the face seems very familiar to me; but I can't think who it is."

"The same thing struck me," said Yardley.

Parkyns continued: "The face has been haunting me, and I've spent rather more time over it than perhaps I ought to have done, because we had no evidence to suggest that the original of this photograph was in any way connected with the murder of your son. Yesterday, however, one of the detectives at the Yard recognized the photo, and it turns out that the original is rather a well-known woman about town. She goes by the name of Vivienne Vane."

Yardley gave a long whistle. "That woman! I ought to have recognized her." He turned to the Colonel, and added, "You know she's the woman who trades on her likeness to the Duchess of Merioneth. As the Duchess is your cousin, I expect that is the likeness you thought you recognized, Colonel."

"Of course that is what I was thinking of."

"She's rather a character," Parkyns resumed, "and there's always been a mystery about her. She will disappear for months, and then suddenly turn up for a brief spell, and there's no escapade too wild

for her to be mixed up with, and there's no extravagance she won't commit. We've tried at
different times to find out the source from which
she gets her money, but we've absolutely failed.
She always has money to any amount, but she never
pays by cheque, or in any way in which money can
be traced. The curious point is that no matter
who may be her protector for the moment, we are
practically certain that she never accepts money
from him. There have been all sorts of wild
guesses to account for her existence; but it seems
most probable, in fact, we all of us are certain, that
she must be the mistress of some enormously
wealthy foreigner, probably a Russian, and comes
over here for a holiday sometimes."

"Yes; but what has she got to do with my son?"

"Well, with regard to your son, we run up
against a kind of blank wall. As far as you know
there was no motive whatever for anybody to
murder him. We can find no point of contact
between any known part of his career and any one
likely to have committed any such crime. In a
case of murder you must have motive sufficient to
explain a murder by a person not previously
criminal, or else you must have *dramatis personæ*
(if I may use such an expression) of such a type
and class that murder becomes less of an improbability. Bearing that in mind, we can connect this
woman Vivienne Vane with your son. He carries
her photograph and corresponds with her. I don't

as yet suggest she committed the murder, but that
is a side of his life, sir, of which you had no knowledge, and it seems to be the only unknown side in
which we can hope to add to what we already
know. With a woman of her type, one never
knows where such an acquaintance may lead, or
what other acquaintances may be made in consequence of it."

It would have been difficult to read from the
Colonel's face what construction he placed upon
the detective's information.

"Have you shown this photograph to Jones, his
housekeeper?"

"Not since it's been identified. I certainly asked
him, at the time I first came across it, if he knew
who the lady was, and he said he had no idea,
and to the best of his belief he had never seen
her."

"Would Jones have any reason for not telling
the truth?" asked Yardley.

"He might have, under the circumstances."

"How so, sir?" said Parkyns.

"Jones was butler at Tibberton until my father
died and the establishment was put down; as a
matter of fact, that was why my boy took rooms
with him. He was a very good type of servant,
very loyal to the family, and I think if he thought
he was preventing public scandal he would deny
any knowledge. Of course he might have had no
knowledge. It all depends on whether the woman

ever went to my son's rooms.   She may never have
done so."

The Colonel turned to Parkyns, and said, "Jones
would naturally be suspicious of replying to any
questions from you; but I think perhaps if Mr.
Yardley and I went round to see him, and explained
that it was all with the object of discovering who
murdered my son, we might perhaps get more out
of him.   I think we will go round now," he added.

The two men wended their way across Piccadilly, and were soon at the house in Jermyn Street.
Jones himself opened the door, and burst out with
a gasp, as he recognized his visitors—

"Oh, sir, I do hope it isn't true about Mr.
Anthony!"

"Mr. Anthony's all right, thank you, Jones.
We can't get at the bottom of it; but there's no
doubt that an attempt was made to murder him
last night."

"Oh, sir, it's been a terrible business!   I'm sure
my heart bleeds for you.   To think of those fine
young gentlemen, that I've known ever since they
were children, and one of them here in my house!"

"Ah, well, what's done is done, and we can't
alter it," said the Colonel.   "What we've got to
do now is to find out who did it.   And that's why
I've brought this gentleman round to see you,
Jones."

Jones slowly led the way upstairs to the rooms
that Herbert Mauleverer had formerly occupied.

"They're just as he left them, sir. I've not had the heart to try and let them again."

"Jones," said the Colonel, as he sat down, "just bear this in mind. It doesn't follow that because you tell us a thing, that we shall repeat it, and you can speak quite frankly now. Have you ever heard of Miss Vivienne Vane?"

"Yes, sir, I have."

"Did she ever come here to these rooms to see Mr. Herbert?"

"She was here the afternoon he was murdered, sir."

Yardley jumped in his chair, and glanced quickly at the Colonel, who said—

"Why didn't you tell us that before, Jones? It's rather important."

"Well, sir, I didn't think it was my business to know anything about that sort of thing. Young gentlemen will be young gentlemen, and you know how these dirty papers make a great story out of nothing."

"Tell us all you know, Jones."

"I don't know much, sir. Miss Vane had only been here once before, about six months ago, and the day Mr. Herbert was murdered she came here about four-thirty, with Mr. Herbert, and Mr. Herbert told me to bring up tea. The second time I went up with some buttered toast; I couldn't get it all on the tray at the one journey. When I got to the door I heard them speaking very loud. I heard Mr. Herbert say, 'I cannot help it, Vivienne; it's simply a damned shame, and it's my duty to tell him.' And she said, 'I tell you you shan't. I'll kill you first.' Then I coughed to let them know I was there, and went in with the toast."

"But, good Lord, Jones, you ought to have told us this. It may be the explanation of the whole thing."

"I think not, sir; because I heard them go downstairs, and Mr. Herbert let her out. That would be about five-thirty. The curious thing is, that about an hour afterwards I heard the front door slam, and I could have sworn Mr. Herbert had gone out himself, as I told the police, and as I said at the inquest. But when I went up to clear the things away, and put Mr. Herbert's clothes out for dinner, there was Mr. Herbert sitting in his chair with his throat cut."

"Were you in the house all the time?" said Yardley. "And you are certain you heard no one go upstairs?"

"No one, sir. Well, I was certainly in the house all the time, and I wouldn't have thought it was possible for any one to have come in without me hearing them."

"I wonder if the woman came back?" said the detective. It was evident that he was turning his new-found information backwards and forwards in his mind, and, like as with so many other people, his fingers were moving in purposeless action as his brain worked. Thoughtlessly he was busy turning over the pages of a book that was lying on a side table, and as he did so a scrap of paper flew out and fell to the floor. It was the last part of a letter, and read—

" . business it is of yours. Why should you tell Jack? I have never led you to believe that you were any more to me than many others, and you have no control over what I do. My life is my own, I will do with it what I like, and I warn you that I will not stand your interference."

Yardley read the slip of paper aloud, adding the remark—

"I expect that this is the explanation."

The Colonel read it, and evidently read it again.

"I can't say I see daylight. It couldn't have been my son Jack, because, as every one knows, he got engaged, and he was the last man to have had a clandestine affair going on at the same time. It wasn't like him."

"I think I see the next steps we shall have to take. Even if Miss Vane herself was not the criminal, the probabilities nevertheless are that she knows something about it."

The address of Miss Vane was of course easily obtainable, and returning to Berkeley Square to pick up Inspector Parkyns, Yardley told him as much of the interview which had just passed as he thought necessary, and hailing a cab, the two proceeded to the flat in Russell Square, which belonged to Miss Vane. The only occupant was an elderly woman, between fifty-five and sixty, who either would not, or could not give them any information about her mistress. The story that she told them to the effect that Miss Vane had not been near her flat for more than a month, and that she had no idea as to her present whereabouts, might possibly have been the exact truth. On the other hand, it might be an absolute fabrication, and Yardley inclined to the latter conclusion. By skilful cross-questioning, they elicited from the old woman that the last occasion she had seen Miss Vane, was when the latter had left her flat on the 31st.

"That looks as if she came over from somewhere specially to have this matter out with Herbert Mauleverer," was the inward comment of Yardley, as they turned away.

The police in every capital in Europe were at once put on the *qui vive* in order to ascertain the whereabouts of Miss Vane. But week after week slowly slipped by, without the slightest clue coming to hand—in fact, it was a few days only before the date fixed for the trial of Webb—when London was startled by one of the amazing stories which from time to time grip the attention of every person who reads a newspaper.

CHAPTER VII

THE National Vigilance Association had for some weeks been organizing a monster campaign against the White Slave Traffic, and other forms of immorality in London. Addresses at Exeter Hall were advertised to be given nightly during the week of the Campaign which it was intended should reach its climax on the Friday night, for which evening the advertised attractions were addresses by the Bishop of Leominster and Mr. Home. To make the meeting on that evening a thorough success, the whole of the arrangements had been given much publicity by means of both circulars and press notices, and it was announced that the chair on the Friday evening was to be taken by Lady Henry Tudor, who was to entertain the Bishop of Leominster during the stay he purposed making in Town for the meeting which he had promised to address. The publicity and the importance the campaign had acquired showed forth plainly as the consequence of the guiding hand of the experienced journalist of sensationalism, Mr. Home. The arrangements of the Bishop were known, it being public property that diocesan engagements prevented his arrival earlier than by the six-thirty train at Paddington, from which station he was to drive direct to Exeter Hall. The Bishop arrived as had been arranged, and a wildly enthusiastic meeting took place. The *Times* and the remainder of the morning Press reported the unctuous and sonorous periods of the Bishop with due emphasis and importance.

But the *Daily Tale*, which brought out a second edition, had a magnificent journalistic scoop to its credit the following morning. Using "scare" headings, in which it surpassed itself, it announced the Abduction of the Bishop of Leominster and Mr. Home, with a wealth of glowing and picturesque detail—such as only the *Daily Tale* can produce—detail which in this case unfortunately was largely imaginative.

Now, in England we are not accustomed to the abduction of our Bishops, and though the Press Association had notified the whole of its subscribers of the news of the abduction, the Press generally declined to take the item seriously. They were sick of the supplied paragraphs concerning the Campaign with which they had been deluged. As an old-young sub-editor on the *Standard* remarked: "It's sure to be all a fake, just a put-up job of old Home's, and I'm hanged if we make fools of ourselves advertising him." Such was the attitude with which Fleet Street generally received the news. The steady-going Press prefers its news to be accurate so far as the exigencies of journalism will permit. Melcarite Street, on the other hand, looks out upon the world differently. Exact accuracy in that quarter ranks rather less highly. News when obtainable, good news at any price, sensation at every opportunity. As the *Daily Tale* sub-editor put it: "It may be a fake, probably is, but it's damned good copy, and one of their best reporters was immediately sent to Lady Henry Tudor's to collect additional particulars. The sum total of his discoveries did not amount to much. Lady Henry, and some other guests who had been present at Exeter Hall, had returned in one of her carriages, leaving the Bishop and Mr. Home, the former of whom had been detained in conversation by some one for a few moments, to follow in the second carriage. The separation of the party had been pure chance, to which Lady Henry Tudor never gave a thought. She was well aware that her men-servants could deal adequately with any emergency, and not contemplating even an emergency of the mildest character, she drove home. But no ecclesiastic followed her. At twelve-thirty she telephoned to Exeter Hall, and learnt from the police on duty that the Bishop and Mr. Home had driven away immediately after the meeting—it was thought to Lady Henry's. At one o'clock the second carriage returned empty, and the footman on being questioned, stated that he was standing at the door, and thought he saw the Bishop coming through the hall, and called up the carriage, which he thought drew up opposite the doorway. That just as he moved forward to open the door he was hustled away, and saw another footman holding the carriage door, and then recognized that it was not Lady Henry's carriage, so presumed he had made a mistake and that it was some other Bishop, so went back to the doorway to wait for the Bishop of Leominster. That the carriage waited until after the doors were closed and he had been informed by the police that the Bishop had left some time previously.

Lady Henry Tudor at once recognized that a serious mistake had occurred, and telephoned to Mr. Home's house, only to learn that his family were still anxiously awaiting his return.

The story of the footman left little doubt that the Bishop and Mr. Home had been abducted. The *Daily Tale* reporter collected his facts, elaborated them with a due regard to the picturesque, and the *Daily Tale* brought out its second edition.

London was highly and hugely amused and chuckled amazingly. The *Daily Tale* on that morning had a record sale.

London read the account through a second time, and then picked up its *Morning Post* for the second course in its daily journalistic meal. In the guinea announcement column that paper gravely informed its readers that—

"Owing to an unforeseen change in his plans, the Bishop of Leominster, during his present short stay in London, is the guest of Miss Vivienne Vane, who is well known for her great interest in Rescue work. Mr. Home accompanied the Bishop, and a numerous and select party were assembled, last night, at Miss Vivienne Vane's to meet them."

London read the announcement, and gasped!

The Bishop of Leominster might be ignorant of Miss Vivienne Vane's notorious reputation, even Mr. Home might possibly be ignorant; but London knew—London of the Clubs was better informed, and it just lay back in its comfortable club chairs, and rocked its sides with amusement. The *Morning Post* on that day had also a record sale; but the Editor, who for weeks afterwards was most unmercifully chaffed, promptly wired for the immediate return of Mr. Murcat, then absent on a brief holiday. Clubland had barely comfortably digested the news, and was still chuckling with amused delight at the long vista of complications which might ensue, when the first edition of the *Star* was published. Now the *Star* is far from being squeamish, and it's not a paper for which much demand exists in the good class clubs, which get their sporting news, "latests" and "results" off the tape without the necessity of awaiting the publication of the successive editions of the evening Press. But the *Star* had a gorgeous innings on that particular Saturday. To use the word "abduct" in his case would be too strong; but a typical *Star* man had been "persuaded" to be present on that evening at a supper party at Miss Vane's.

She had rightly calculated on the strength of a man's ruling passion, and having secured the presence of a pressman, she left the rest to chance, wherein she was wise. The *Star* man quickly saw that his own presence there had been the result of trickery, but his journalistic sense became too strong when the copy for "The finest story in the world" was gradually evolved before his eyes. That the law was being infringed he never doubted, but being himself in no way responsible, and the thing being a fact, and consequently "news," and being moreover amazingly good "copy," he sat down there and then, and wrote a detailed and accurate account of everything that had taken place in Miss Vane's house from the moment of the arrival of the Bishop and Mr. Home.

But even the *Star* has its limits, and much of the report was suppressed, the bare truth, even, in most of the paragraphs, was "toned down" before publication, but the final result in published print ran to four columns, and was a finished and detailed account of the wildest saturnalia that has ever been described in the Press. As the report concluded, "The Lord Bishop and Mr. Home remained throughout the entertainment, which was of a character running to limits and extremes that were

probably undreamt of by either of the abducted."
Even bowdlerized and abbreviated, the report remained both picturesque and substantially true.
London shouted itself hoarse as it laughed and as
it pictured to itself two favourite sanctimonious
humbug participators in such a carnival. The *Star*
on that day had likewise a record sale, and when in
sheer desperation the machines ceased printing at
night time, copies of the paper were selling at a
premium.

Yardley carefully read the account.

"H'm! I think Miss Vivienne Vane must certainly have returned to Town" was his inward comment, as he put down the newspaper.

On the Monday morning the sensation deepened.
The whole of the press contained a brief announcement of the arrest of Miss Vane charged with the
murder of Herbert Mauleverer.

CHAPTER VIII

IN the meantime the date fixed for the trial of Jimmy Webb had steadily approached. Little fresh evidence had been obtained, and on the day of the trial when counsel for the Crown closed its evidence for the prosecution the case against Webb stood upon the following "basis." That whoever attempted to murder Anthony Mauleverer had escaped from Tibberton on a bicycle That there was just sufficient time for a person to have ridden from Tibberton and caught the train at York. The station-master and several porters had sworn to the arrival of a slight, clean-shaven man in bicycling clothes, who had deposited a bicycle in the cloakroom, removing from the bicycle a small valise, and had been seen to enter the train to London from York. That the train had not been stopped until the York Road (King's Cross) station, when it had been boarded by thirty police from Scotland Yard. That no person in bicycling clothes was then on the train. That everybody on the train except Webb had been identified as well known or else had supplied the police with details which had been since authenticated. And that Webb was a notorious criminal who had served several terms of imprisonment for blackmail and forgery, and was a known associate of the most desperate characters. It was proved that the bicycling clothes had been found upon the line the following morning by one of the permanent way staff, and the clothes had been identified by the station-master and several of the porters at York. It was also proved that Webb was alone in a first-class carriage, and had had ample opportunity of changing his clothes, and that he was unable to prove where he was during the time the attempts were being made. Webb had been asked at the commencement of the trial whether he wished to be defended, and the judge had offered to supply him with the services of counsel. Webb had insolently replied that he didn't want to have his pitch queered by any of the thundering young duffers who defended prisoners for nothing, and had elected to defend his own defence. There could be no denying that he did it in a masterly way. Dealing first with the evidence which had been proved against him, he admitted that the clothes fitted him. They consisted of knickerbockers, and a loose jacket of grey cloth, a grey cloth cap, and a white woolen sweater. A belt had also been found, but no stockings, though, on the other hand, the prisoner was wearing stockings at the time of his arrest. Webb pointed out that a sweater would fit anybody, and would cover other clothes, also that the knickerbockers and jacket were ready-made clothes of a stock size, that would probably fit scores of people. Asking for the belt to be passed to him, he pointed out that it was made of webbing, and that it could not be altered by an adjustable clasp, as is the usual method with belts. He pointed out that it was fastened with a leather strap and buckle, that it was a comparatively new belt, and that, very plainly only one particular hole in the strap had ever been used. Buckling the belt in that hole he asked for it to be measured, and an audible exclamation echoed through the court when the measurement was announced as twenty-three and a half inches. Putting the tape round his own waist he asked for some one to verify his own measurement as thirty-six inches. Turning to the jury he added—

"Now, gentlemen, you can strap yourselves in a bit, and it is quite possible that with a strong belt like this, I might, if there was any reason for it, pull myself into twenty-three and a half inches, but I put it to any one of you, if you wanted to do what they say I did at Tibberton, would you have pulled your guts in till you couldn't breathe, and could you have bicycled eighteeen miles in an hour and a quarter strapped up like that? It isn't as if there was any reason why I should pull the belt tight." Webb continued, "I suppose these dirty police thought I should do something to them, and I've never had a chance of closely looking at these clothes yet. Can I look at that cap?'"

The cap was passed to the prisoner in the dock, who examined it closely. It was of the ordinary shape, but very large and overhanging. Like many other caps which one buys ready-made, it had the appearance of having had a great deal more stuff put into it than there was any necessity for. Holding it out, Webb said—

"Now, look here, each side of it is ram jam full of pin-holes. What the hell do I want to pin my cap on my head for? Whoever has been wearing this cap has been using a hat-pin. Do I look as if I'd got anything on my head to pin a hat or a cap to? And then, how about the boots? The police at York road got hold of my luggage. You heard them say what they found in it—a pack of marked cards. Well! what do they matter? You don't try to shoot a chap with a pack of cards. They found a night-shirt, a vest, and some drawers, and a lot of papers. But they didn't find any boots. They make a lot of fuss because I was wearing stockings. Well, they found two other pairs of stockings in my bag, and I always wear them. And why? Well, I'll tell you. When you are doing time at Portland you have to wear them, and good thick ones, too, and when I came out the last time my legs were always so cold if I wore socks, that I made up my mind to go on wearing stockings, and I have done ever since. Now, you heard the railway people say how carefully they searched the line. Did they find any boots? Not a blessed one. Now, the police examined the boots I was wearing in the train. Here they are," and he put one leg on the side of the dock and showed that he was wearing a neat pair of patent leather boots, "and they looked at my boots. I didn't know why at the time. But a few minutes ago you heard me ask the copper who examined me in the train if my boots looked wet or muddy or dusty, as if I'd been walking in a blessed lake for half a mile, and you heard him say my boots were quite clean and quite dry. Now that bicycle has got rat-trap pedals, and if I'd ridden from Tibberton to York that would have marked the soles of my boots. Now, the soles are fairly new, and there isn't a sign, and there isn't a scratch on the patent leather. So whoever rode from Tibberton to York didn't ride in this pair of boots. Well, then, where's the other pair? I tell you what it is. That's a woman's belt, and a woman's cap, and she knew that if she threw the boots away they would be found, and she would be spotted as a woman, so she stuck to them; but she never thought about the belt or the cap being noticed. Whoever it was that rode up to York station in bicycling clothes was a woman who had her own reasons for changing her clothes on the train, and I wasn't that woman. But, after all they've said, they haven't proved that that bicycling woman was the one who tried to murder the young beggar. No woman could have shinned down a rainwater pipe or run away from a pair of bloodhounds, and there are precious few who will use a revolver or bicycle twenty miles in an hour and a quarter, and I don't believe any woman's got the pluck to do all they want to make out was done that night at Tibberton. They find some blessed bicycle marks at Tibberton, as if there's only one bicycle in the world, and somebody turns up at York with a bicycle, so they think it's that person who did the shooting. And then, because they can't find anybody in knickerbockers at King's Cross, and because they find me on the train, they want to make out I am a murderer. I've never been to Tibberton in my life. How was I to know the way over the chapel roof? Whoever did the job must have known the house and the places about jolly well, must have been born and lived there. But because these dunderheaded duffers of police can't find anybody else, and because they've got their eye on me, they pitch on me. As I told the magistrate, I booked at Newcastle just before the train started, and I got in there, and came right through, and because I didn't get my bally ticket punched at York they want to make out I wasn't on the train. As I told the magistrate, I was in the lavatory when they came round about the tickets. The police told you all about my marked pack of cards, as if they had anything to do with a shooting job. Well, there were three others in the carriage with me from Newcastle to York, and we were playing poker, and, of course,

I cleaned them out. They said they were commercial travellers, but one of 'em had an uncommon fine pair of shoulders, and he was wearing a pair of regulation boots, and when I thought I'd cleaned 'em of every cent, he trots out a £50 note, and I asked him if he'd been robbing the canteen. And he wanted to fight me first, only he thought better of it, and tried to win back what he'd lost before. Well, and then I won his £50 as well. And the police know I had that £50 note, and that's what I've been spending in those advertisements the police made such game of. Said they were all a blind."

"What advertisements were those?" asked the judge.

A copy of the *Daily Tale* was handed up and the following advertisement pointed out to the judge:

"Will any one of the three gentlemen, one of whom was swindled out of a £50 note at cards in the train between Newcastle and York, please communicate with XYZ, c/o The *Daily Tale*."

"Rather a curious advertisement," commented the judge.

The prisoner continued: "Now, that's why I didn't tell the magistrate. I didn't want to be prosecuted for card sharping, so I just said nothing till I saw how things were going so badly for me, and I saw that another dose of penal servitude was better than being 'scragged.' But none of the blighters have answered, else I could prove easily enough where I was when they were potting at young Mr. Anthony Mauleverer. And that's all I've got to say, and I put it to you whether I could have worn that belt or whether I was likely to have put a cap on with pins. Now, look here, gentlemen, I haven't got a lawyer, but just you remember those two points, and you play me fair, even if I am no particular shakes on other points."

The reply for the Prosecution was brief. Counsel ridiculed the idea of the *alibi* to be established by witnesses who would not respond to such an alluring advertisement as had appeared in the *Daily Tale*. As counsel truly said, it had appeared therein everyday for a fortnight, and in the advertisement columns of a good many other papers, and the grotesque terms in which it had been couched had caused it to be reprinted as a curiosity in practically every organ of the Press. If the prisoner's story were true it was inconceivable that the loser of the £50 had not responded. The ticket from Newcastle, it was suggested, was procured by an accomplice who got out at York, handing over the ticket to the prisoner for the purposing of proving an *alibi*, or else was a duplicate ticket purchased and brought to York. The cap would certainly appear to have been usually worn by a woman, but that was no proof it was not worn by the prisoner on the night in question.

"I put it before your consideration, gentlemen," said counsel, "that the cap, the belt, and the missing shoes are all pieces in a clever puzzle which was thought out beforehand by the prisoner, who is a consummate adept at criminality, and arranged by the prisoner that he might use the facts for the very purpose for which he has used them, namely, to divert suspicion from himself. The prisoner professes not to have closely examined the cap or belt until he did so in your presence to-day. He asked permission from the prison authorities for facilities to that end, and was definitely refused some time ago. Perhaps it is just as well, as, had this not been the case, we should have had no guarantee that the pinholes in the cap existed at the time the article was found on the line. You have seen and heard the prisoner, and know the style of man he is. Now, I say it requires a trained and practised intellect and a brain of no mean calibre, and it requires trained powers of observation and deduction to have done what the prisoner professes to have done, that is, to have immediately noticed those two salient points and without a moment's hesitation to have drawn the deduction which I admit is an unimpeachable one, and I say unhesitatingly that such observation and such deduction were beyond the brain power of the prisoner. I frankly admit the clothes, since they have been found, have remained in the custody of the police—trained both to observation and to deduction—for several weeks. Trained detectives who have examined the clothes failed to observe the details the prisoner noticed in a moment or two. Then, again, why did the prisoner ask to see the clothes almost immediately after the charge against him, and the evidence to support it, had been elaborated during the various hearings before the magistrate. The answer to that question is simple. The prisoner having arranged matters beforehand knew what to look for and knew what conclusions to draw. But there remains the belt to be accounted for. Obviously the prisoner could not have worn it. I agree with what he says—it is plainly one which has been worn by a lady. I also agree with what the prisoner says, that no woman could have committed the crime. The prisoner simply wore his braces when bicycling and wore the same pair of braces when he had changed his clothes. The belt from beginning to end is simply a 'blind' introduced by the prisoner. The prisoner has remarked that there is more than one bicycle in the world. Quite so. But there are not so many that had on that particular day raw-new tyres which leave a rather curious impression where it is visible, *e.g,.* in soft mud. When all is said and done, gentlemen, you come down to this hard bed-rock fact, that whoever attempted the life of Anthony Mauleverer escaped on a bicycle, and boarded the train at York.

Everybody else on the train except the prisoner can be satisfactorily accounted for, and the story enunciated by the prisoner is too wildly improbable to be accepted without corrobation, which corrobation the prisoner cannot produce.

Counsel was about to conclude his speech when a folded note was handed to him. A breathless silence reigned in court, as he carefully read it and mastered its contents. Beckoning Yardley to speak to him, a hurried consultation took place. Turning to the jury to continue his remarks, he added—

"During the last few moments, Mr. Dennis Yardley, the well-known private detective, who has been engaged in the interests of Colonel Mauleverer in the apparently hopeless endeavour to elicit some solution of the mystery attaching to the deaths of Colonel Mauleverer's four eldest sons, has provided me with some startling evidence. It appears that the £50 note of which the prisoner has spoken, is one of two notes each for that amount which are now missing, but should have been found amongst the effects of Captain George Mauleverer, another son of Colonel Mauleverer, who was found murdered in his quarters at Knightsbridge Barracks, a little more than four months ago."

"Then that's why the bl—— cur wouldn't answer the advertisement. Blast him!" shouted the prisoner.

Turning towards the dock, a perceptible sneer

slowly passed over the face of counsel as he looked the prisoner up and down, and replied—

"Perhaps so; but I think the more obvious probability is the one the jury will be most inclined to accept."

The judge, however, at once intervened. Sternly reprimanding the prisoner for the language he had made use of, he turned to counsel for the prosecution and reminded him that his action was not allowable, and quite out of place at that stage of the trial.

"I cannot permit the life of a prisoner to be jeopardized in this manner by the introduction of a wholly unsubstantiated assertion when the opportunity to rebut on behalf of the prisoner had passed.

"You know perfectly well," continued the judge, "that by merely making that statement you have created an immense prejudice against the prisoner —you have done the mischief, and it will be quite impossible to remove the prejudice arising from your statement, even if, as is most probable, I have to instruct the jury wholly to disregard the fact."

"I'm sorry, my lord; but, as you saw, the information only that moment came into my hands."

"In that case you ought to have informed me before making it public. However, as you have said it, you had better prove the point, if you can. Of course the prisoner must have the opportunity of replying. You had better put Mr. Yardley in the box."

Yardley having been sworn, the judge at once asked—

"Why was not this point brought forward before?"

"Proof has only been put in my hands, my lord, since I came into court this morning. If you will permit me to explain, you will see this is not through any fault of mine. It appears that Captain Mauleverer was treasurer of the mess of his regiment, and when the regimental accounts came to be settled after his death, it came out that he was exactly £100 short in the money which should have been in his possession. Of course it is strictly against regulations, but some officers do mix up their private money and the mess money, and no officer would have blamed Captain Mauleverer for not having the requisite amount of hard cash in the regimental cash-box at any particular moment, if he had an ample margin banked to his private account. Whether any slur rested upon Captain Mauleverer, therefore, depended entirely upon the amount of money in Captain Mauleverer's possession over and above that in the regimental cash-box. It was only possible to ascertain the fact by application to his relatives until his will is proved if he ever made one. The matter was talked over at mess, and as Captain Mauleverer was one of the most popular men in the Army, and every one being averse to running the slightest risk of adding to Colonel Mauleverer's misery by approaching him on the subject, it was decided that nothing whatever should be said, and that the sum should be made up by the other officers, as they put it, 'for the honour of the regiment, for the good name of Captain Mauleverer, and to save Colonel Mauleverer pain in case the Captain had managed to get his accounts muddled. Seeing the importance that has really proved to attach to the matter, it is much to be regretted that it was only three days ago that Captain Brabazon returned to the regiment after a prolonged absence on sick leave. He had left the barracks the same day the murder of Captain Mauleverer was committed. On his return to the regiment he was asked for his contribution to the missing hundred pounds, and then for the first time heard of the matter. He inquired how much was in the cash-box, and learnt that only three pounds odd was found in it. 'But he changed me two fifty-pound notes out of the regimental cash the very morning I went away.' Captain Brabazon's answer put an entirely different complexion on the affair, for it left no doubt that robbery had been committed, inasmuch as the two banknotes which Captain Brabazon saw placed in the box a few hours before Captain Mauleverer's death were missing when his accounts were taken over. Fifty-pound notes are not difficult to trace. Captain Brabazon could at once tell us that he had received them from Mr. Richard Dunn, a well-known bookmaker, at a certain race meeting. Mr. Dunn remembered being paid them by Mr. John Corlett, the proprietor of the *Sporting Times.* Mr. Corlett's bankers were able to supply the numbers. It then became necessary to trace the note that the prisoner admits was in his possession. His account was, to a certain extent, corroborated, because he did pay for the advertisement with that money. He sent it with a note to the *Daily Tale*, asking them to keep enough to put it in their paper every day for a fortnight and to spend the rest in advertising in other papers. The *Daily Tale* have supplied me with the number of the note which was sent them. I have had their reply during the last few minutes and the note was certainly one of the two which Captain Mauleverer changed for Captain Brabazon."

Yardley passed the memorandum he had received from the cashier of the *Daily Tale*, up to the judge.

"Do you propose to summon the necessary witnesses to prove this?"

"That depends upon whether your lordship is willing to adjourn."

The judge asked the prisoner what he had to say.

"I dare say this last bit is all true enough," said Webb. "I told you how I got the note, and these gentlemen will bear me out that I told them I had asked the man I got it from whether he'd been robbing the canteen. But I'm not being tried for the murder of the Captain, and the bank-note has got nothing to do with young Mr. Maul-everer."

The judge adjourned the case for the luncheon interval, and intimated on the reassembling of the Court that, after consideration, he did not see his way to adjourn the case, and that he should instruct the jury entirely to disregard everything in connection with the incident of the banknote. He added—

"Before the prosecution was aware of the existence of the banknote—though, of course, the police knew of it—the prisoner had himself referred to it, and given a very plausible explanation of how it had come into his possession. Unfortunately they had only his word, but the whole circumstances of the disclosure were, in his opinion, very much in favour of the prisoner's innocence on that point." Turning to the prosecuting counsel, he said: "If you attach importance to the matter of the banknote, which, as the prisoner says, has nothing to do with the crime with which he stands charged, you can charge him with the murder of Captain Mauleverer. If the jury in the present case find him guilty, it will not be difficult for the Crown to put their hands on him when they want him; but if the verdict is 'not guilty,' it is a very simple matter to rearrest him." The judge then proceeded with the summing-up, and the jury retired to consider their verdict. After a lapse of five hours, they sent a note to the judge saying they could not agree, and there seemed no possibility of their ever doing so. The jury was therefore discharged, and Webb consequently remained in custody.

CHAPTER IX

YARDLEY, immediately the Court rose, went to Knightsbridge Barracks and interviewed several of the officers. He asked particularly who would have access to Captain Mauleverer's quarters. Captain Brabazon remarked—

"Only ourselves and the Captain's servants. Of course, there is nothing to physically prevent any of the men coming in; but they never do. So unless the murderer took the money, or one of them knew the Captain was dead and went to plunder his rooms, none of the men are likely to have been loafing round. So that the thief was either the murderer, or a stranger, or Mauleverer's servant, or one of us."

Yardley asked if he could see the Captain's servant, but was told he had bought himself out of the army about a couple of months afterwards. His name was John Smith, and they could none of them suggest any special method by which Yardley could ascertain his present whereabouts.

"His buying himself out rather looks as if he had lifted some cash," put in one of the other officers—Major de Crespigny—who was present.

"Yes," replied Yardley; "but if his servant did

the robbery I should rather doubt his doing the murder. He could have done the robbery easily enough without murdering. He probably found Captain Mauleverer dead, and helped himself before he gave the alarm."

"Yes, it *was* Smith," answered Major de Crespigny, "who gave the alarm."

"The curious point is," said Yardley, "that Captain Mauleverer's cheque-book was lying on the table when we made the first examination of his quarters—presumably it was there when he died. A man may leave his cheque-book about if he's very careless, but he doesn't leave it open. There was a cheque partly written. The counterfoil was filled up 'Charity 10s. 6d.'—the cheque was dated, but in place of the name of the payee was simply 'The' at the beginning of the line. It was evident Captain Mauleverer had been interrupted whilst writing the cheque, because, if he had simply changed his mind about sending it or had been interrupted on an earlier occasion and never completed it, the cheque-book would not have been found lying open. So I think he met his death before he finished writing it, and was interrupted to meet it *whilst* he was writing. I suppose *you* can't suggest anything. It wasn't a regimental subscription, or anything of that kind?"

"Why, don't we all know everything?" put in Major de Crespigny, adding: "That never came out at the inquest."

"No, it was carefully withheld, because it seemed the only possible clue, and it was such a very slender one we preferred not to publish it."

"I wonder if it was the same woman who came to me—a Sister of Charity. She brought round one of those collecting books. I talked to her for some time, an elderly, not bad-looking woman, about forty to forty-five, very lady-like, seemed to know an awful lot, and pitched a most piteous yarn about the kids she was collecting for, and wheedled a guinea out of me. I knew Mauleverer was rather soft-hearted, and I asked her if she had asked him for anything. She said she had known him personally in better days, or something of that kind, and didn't care to ask him. So I never thought of connecting her with him; besides, I am not sure it was the same day. But I gave her a cheque. I'll go and get my cheque-book and see."

He went to his quarters and came back almost immediately. The counterfoil was dated the 29th.

"Ah, well, it's not the right date," said Yardley. "The man was murdered on the 30th."

"But it just happens that it is," said Major de Crespigny. "When I was quite a cub, when I had just started having a banking account, I once sent my man to cash a cheque. I had made a mistake in dating it, and put the date a day forward. Now I was waiting for that money. I forget why, but I remember I was most awfully annoyed when the man brought the cheque back and said they wouldn't pay it, because it was after bank hours. Since that little episode I have always made a point of dating cheques one day behind to be on the safe side. So that one of my cheques, dated the 29th, would mean that it was drawn on the 30th."

"Then it was the right day after all?"

"Yes."

"I wonder if that's the clue we want?"

"But then she said she wasn't going to see Mauleverer."

"Oh, it doesn't matter what she *said*. Did she go? Who was the cheque payable to?"

"I've only got 'Children's Home' on the counter-foil. I don't suppose that was how I made it out."

"No, but we can get at the actual cheque at your bank."

The next morning, by arrangement, Major de Crespigny took Dennis Yardley to his bank——Coutts'—and they together interviewed one of the officials. But Yardley had drawn a blank again; the cheque had never been presented.

"What do you make of that?" said the Major, as they walked away together along the Strand.

"Just this—that she killed him, and called on you to demonstrate her assumed identity as a Sister of Charity. The whole thing was a blind."

"But that was in the morning about twelve o'clock. Mauleverer must have been dead in his quarters for hours, for his body wasn't found till ten o'clock at night."

Yardley whipped round at the remark. "That's what I was confident of, only that ass of a doctor said he was only just dead."

"His servant certainly ought to have found him before then."

"He did find the body and lifted the cash, and then waited in the hope that somebody else would make the discovery, knowing that suspicion would fall on him if he were the first to find the body and if the money were missed."

Yardley walked away after parting with the Major, turning everything over in his mind. Twist it how he would he came back to the same conclusion. That there was some connection between each of the four murders, and also between them and the attempt on Anthony's life. Vivienne Vane was in custody for, and probably guilty of, the murder of Herbert Mauleverer.

Everything pointed to a woman having murdered Captain Mauleverer; many things indicated a woman as the person who had attempted Anthony's life; and yet, how could a woman have been their antagonist at Tibberton? And then, again, in each case there was the knotted cord. What did that mean? Yardley had ransacked the records of Scotland Yard, and the memories of all its officers; none of them knew of any secret society of which it was an emblem. None of them remembered any similar case from which an analogy could be drawn. So it came back to the fact that it had some special connection with the four sons of Colonel Mauleverer, and yet no four men standing in the relationship of brothers had fewer friends in common, or led more utterly distinct lives than the four Mauleverers. To any one knowing their lives intimately, it seemed almost inconceivable that all four should have established contact with an agency which should embrace them all within its punitive action. And how on earth could the boy Anthony have earned sufficient enmity in any quarter to have carried his life in his hand as he was doing? There seemed to be but one bond between them, and that was their relationship. The thought jumped to Yardley's mind that the revenge was not directed against the sons, but against the father, who would suffer equally as each of his sons was murdered, and, as it took five murders to dispose of his sons, would be punished five times. Yardley argued the point out with the Colonel, who either would not admit or could not remember any incident in his life that could even suggest a necessity for any revenge.

"My dear man," he had snapped out at Yardley, "I've not been a plaster saint. I've lived an ordinary man's life, no better and no worse, spending my substance, or rather such parts of it as the trustees thought fit to let me get my hands on, with harlots and riotous living. You can't find any explanation there. I never bilked a woman, I never served a friend a dirty turn, and, as I told you several times, the rest of my life was spent in India. I've hung a few Afridis, and I've shot a good many more, but it was no Afridi that we chased that night at Tibberton. But," ended the Colonel, testily, "it's not my life that I'm paying you to rake up. Let the dead past bury its dead. Your work"—and he rapped on the table and looked straight at the detective—"is to find out who killed my boys, and to take care of Anthony. It's late in life for me to start a father confessor, and, frankly, I don't see the necessity for it."

There was a piece of evidence, however, of which Yardley had learnt at Scotland Yard, which had seemed to him might possibly afford a clue which had been overlooked. On the floor of Captain Mauleverer's room a plain hemstitched handkerchief had been picked up. It bore no name or embroidery, but in one corner were a few stitches in coloured thread, evidently a laundry mark. The police had circulated a photograph of the mark, and had made inquiries in every single laundry in London and the suburbs without the slightest result; and it being impossible, in their opinion, to identify the owner, little if any further attention had been paid to it. Yardley had obtained possession of this handkerchief, and had immediately been struck by the curious scent which was perceptible. Though pleasant enough as a perfume, it was distinctly noticeable as unusual. His first step in the matter was a visit to the establishment of Messrs. Atkinson in Bond Street. Asking to see the manager, he was ushered into the latter's sanctum, and, producing the handkerchief, he asked the manager if he could identify the scent. The reply was a decided negative, and the manager added—

"You can take it from me that that scent is not on the market. It is either an accident, or else it is some scent made from an exclusive formula for some particular person. There are a good many of these exclusive formulas; for instance, we ourselves supply twenty or thirty to special people to whom they belong. I'd advise you to try one or two other firms like ourselves; but if you have no success, then I can only suggest that you should interview the head chemist at Gosnell's down in Newgate Street, and any other firms like them whom you can come across. They are wholesale people, of course, and will not be able to tell you who it is that is using it; but if it has been made in their laboratories, then they can tell you the firm they supply it to, and it will be an easy matter for you to trace it."

Yardley did as the manager had suggested to him, and ran his quarry to earth at the very first attempt. The chief chemist at Messrs. Gosnell's immediately recognized the perfume.

"Yes," he said, "we made this. We had an inquiry from a firm of milliners in Bond Street, asking if we could supply a perfume which should be exclusive to them, and asking if we would guarantee, providing a sufficient order were placed with us, not to disclose it to any one else, or to supply it to any other purchaser. We submitted three different scents, two others and this one, stating, with regard to this one, that we had one customer for it in Russia, and asking if this was an objection. This was the scent that was selected, the condition being made that, though we were to be at liberty to continue to supply it if required to our single customer in Russia, it was not to be sold to any one else. As we have been paid very well, it follows, as a natural consequence, that we have not supplied it except through these two channels. Who the two people are to whom it eventually gets of course we do not know, though we believe our Russian customer is Prince Kentchikoff."

Yardley then went to the milliner with whose address he had been supplied, and met with a point-blank refusal to give him the information he sought.

"Well," he said, "I personally cannot compel you to give me this information, but I can subpœna you as a witness, and I can put you on your oath in a court of law. If you then decline to say who it is you sell the perfume to, you will be committed to Holloway for contempt of court. If you give us wrong information, and it proves to be wrong when it is tested, by an examination of your books, and other inquiries which we shall make, I will promise you on my own account that you shall be prosecuted for perjury. But if you will tell me what I wish to know, then I will promise you that the matter shall not be mentioned, and no use shall be made of the information, unless it proves to be vital to the case."

At last he obtained the information—the perfume was supplied to the Duchess of Merioneth. With inward disgust Yardley left the shop. It was about as likely that the Duchess had committed the murder as that he had himself. The Duchess was the cousin of the Mauleverers, and had spent her childhood with that family, and half a hundred reasons might be suggested to account for one of her handkerchiefs being found in Captain Mauleverer's quarters. But Yardley could not bring himself to believe that the Duchess, spending that huge amount in dress, which the society papers were constantly advertising, would be content to use a plain hemstitched handkerchief of a kind that could be bought in any shop for sixpence halfpenny.

CHAPTER X

ONE point which puzzled the detective enormously, was his utter inability to persuade himself whether the murders were all the work of a single person, or whether a gang had taken them in hand. If one person only was at work, then the events which took place at Tibberton seemed utterly beyond the capacity of a woman, whereas he felt convinced that Vivienne Vane was guilty at any rate of the murder of Herbert Mauleverer. Webb, under his ticket-of-leave, had reported himself to the police at such times and places that it was absolutely impossible that he could have been concerned in his own person with anything beyond the murder of Captain Mauleverer and the attempt on Anthony. But then, the detective was by no means disinclined to believe the story Webb himself told. But if a gang were concerned, it seemed inconceivable to human intelligence that there could be any motive which would induce a number of people to commit such a cold-blooded series of murders except in anticipation of large financial plunder, circumstances difficult to arrange and control by a third party, unless the explanation could be found in some political society. Up to the present point, Yardley could find no trace of anything political except in relation to the murder of the eldest son, and with him the only suggestion lay in the fact that he was an *attaché* to the British Embassy in St. Petersburg. This fact had of course been almost the first upon which Yardley had pitched when he began to make his inquiries, but it had been quickly abandoned. The British Ambassador, when questioned, had made it very clear that Mr. Mauleverer cared nothing whatever about his work, took no interest in it, and never lost the smallest chance of being absent on leave. As he was an unpaid *attaché,* and as his work at the Embassy was a mere *façon de parler,* it seemed ridiculous to suppose he would ever have been mixed up with any Russian political society. Yet there was another circumstance which might conceivably have some relation to such a supposition. Vivienne Vane undoubtedly had some connection or other with Herbert Mauleverer; the "Jack" referred to in the note, might—in spite of the Colonel's opinion—be really the eldest brother She had evidently unlimited money at her disposal, the origin of which remained a mystery; and it seemed probable that in some way or other she was connected with the death of Herbert Mauleverer. Therefore, if the series of murders were the work of a gang, she must have some association also with the murder of Jack Mauleverer. But an income of the proportions of the one which she palpably possessed could not exist unknown to others besides herself. There was but one country in Europe where such an income could accumulate, and could be enjoyed unembarrassed by the attentions of the press. That country was Russia; yet the Russian police had absolutely, and almost vehemently, denied the very smallest knowledge of Miss Vivienne Vane. They even stated that they had never known any occasion when she had been in Russia. It was plain, therefore, that their statement was either true, or that their knowledge was being hidden purposely, because such a personage as Miss Vane could not exist in Russia without the knowledge of the police. The curious point was that Miss Vane spoke Russian, and letters in that language had been seized in her flat. True, they were only love-letters of a type none too refined, but they were plain evidence of Russian connections. Like a flash it dawned on Yardley that Miss Vane was a paid spy in the service of the Russian Government. In a moment scores of the details fitted into their places. The bravado of her *liaison*, brief indeed, but a nine days' topic, with Lord Daventry, the Under-Secretary of State for Foreign Affairs, who had been "broken" in consequence—her knowledge of Russian—her mysterious comings and goings—her great wealth—the periods of her life which were unaccounted for, and last, but not least, the unequivocal point-blank denial of knowledge on the part of the Russian police. If she were a Russian spy everything was explained. Spies are not to be depended upon, as no Government knows better than the Ministers of the Czar. If she were drawing salary from the Russian Government, the odds were that she was also drawing it from some secret society, for it is difficult to find in the Russian Secret Service any single person who is trusted. Their work of espionage is controlled and dictated, and their reports are received and read, but no one knows better than the Russian Minister of the Interior that the information so supplied is only acted upon in those cases in which the Government judges that it does not happen to be to the interest of the spy to play them false. If Miss Vane were in the employment of the Russian Government, anything was possible. The first point to ascertain was whether she was or not, and the next little item of information which was wanted was the knowledge of whether the murders had any relation to this Russian connection, and, if so, whether they were due to the instigation of the Russian Government, or whether they had been planned by some force in opposition thereto.

And yet Yardley was puzzled! Jack Mauleverer, Captain Mauleverer, and Herbert were old enough to have involved themselves in mischief, but it seemed doubtful that this could be said of Henry at Oxford, and it seemed absolutely impossible for Anthony. Yardley quickly decided that the only way to get any definite knowledge from Russia was by playing the game of bluff, and that night saw him on his way to the Russian capital.

Even with the introduction which the British Ambassador supplied him with, he found it was by no means easy to obtain an interview with the Russian Minister of the Interior. He was, however, in the end successful, though at the opening of the interview the minister warned him that it must be brief. Yardley, who had planned that interview and rehearsed it beforehand, at once opened the ball, asking M. de Plehve what was the true explanation of the murders of the Mauleverer brothers. M. de Plehve jumped in his chair, and asked for an explanation of the remark.

"I don't pretend I am ignorant of the murders. As chief of what is probably the finest police force in the world, it pays me to keep *au courant* with crime in other nations. Russia, *mon ami,* is cosmopolitan. Crime and criminals have no nationality, and the English murderer of to-day may be the Russian cardsharper of to-morrow. I *have* to know! Besides that, as a student of crime, the mystery attaching to these purposeless murders has interested me from—what shall I say?—the professional point of view. I have made such inquiries as were possible. I needn't tell any one in your position how closely the police of different countries work in common, and I expect I know as

much about it as your police know, but I assure
you I know no more."

"Excellency, that's rather strange, isn't it? One
of your secret agents is arrested for the murder of
one of the brothers. I cannot but think that you
can supply the explanation."

The minister sat silently in his chair and
drummed gently with his finger-nails on the table, as
a curious animal expression, half leer, half cunning,
overspread his coarse features.

"Ah, *mon ami,* you mean the beautiful Miss
Vane; but that is just where you make a mistake.
Miss Vane was *not* in our service."

The minister paused, and Yardley showed plainly
his amazement.

"But—but——" he began.

"My friend," quietly interrupted de Plehve, "I
moved heaven and earth to get her for one of our
agents, but she refused every offer point-blank."

If Yardley had been amazed before, he was considerably startled by the frank disclosure of the
minister.

"Of course I am not talking for publication, but
Russia has no wish and no need to screen the
criminals of other nations, and I am quite willing
to tell you that, though we have never been able to
obtain absolute proof, we have always had the
strong suspicion that the interests of Miss Vane
lay in this country, and that she was a revolutionary
agent. There is an utter mystery about her ante-

cedents, which has puzzled the police of Europe, and there is a still greater mystery as to her income. But we flatter ourselves that we are nearer the solution than our English *confrères*. As of course you know, Miss Vane pays for everything in gold. If it is £2000 for a motor-car, or £2 for a bottle of scent, it is just the same, the payment is made in gold. Now, I dare say you've heard of Prince Kentchikoff. He always insists on the whole of his rents being paid in gold, and, like our English friend, he uses no banking account, but pays everything in gold. We know him to be the head of one of our many revolutionary bodies, and that particular body depends upon his enormous revenues for its existence. We have always supposed that a large proportion of his income passes into the hands of Miss Vane; but what has always puzzled us is to find out how it passes, and, if it passes in specie, how the money is changed. Now, there is another point. Of course, Mr. Yardley, your reputation is international! If I thought for a moment that I was giving you news, I should not allude to this matter, but I have no doubt you already know as much of the following facts as I intend to tell you. His late Majesty the Czar Alexander had a daughter by Mademoiselle Sarcelle, the well-known French actress. For the last five or six years, in spite of all our efforts, we have absolutely lost sight of that girl. She was a most beautiful girl, as I dare say you've heard, and the latest photographs of her—I never actually saw her myself—bear a marked resemblance to Miss Vane. We cannot find the slightest trace of Miss Vane during the time when the lady I have referred to was living in Paris under our observation. The latter disappeared a few months only before the first news we can get of Miss Vane, and we firmly believe that the two are identical. Consequently there is every reason why Russia should leave no stone unturned to prove Miss Vane innocent. We cannot have Miss Vane executed as a murderess, and we know your English newspapers too well to count upon her obtaining pardon if she is proved guilty. Now you have the reason why I have taken so much interest in the case and why I have spoken so frankly. I have carefully studied every atom of evidence I can get into my hands, and speaking now merely from the point of view of a police officer, I do not myself believe Miss Vane committed that murder with her own hands, although she may have been in some way connected with it. Of course if the identity I have hinted at is not really a fact, which I admit we cannot prove, although we have very strong suspicions, the Russian Government has not the slightest interest or concern in the matter; but, as I say, we think it is a fact, and for that reason I am specially authorized by his Majesty to assist you. With the official English police we cannot deal as I can with you, but I am speaking advisedly when I say that, if Miss Vane proves to have been only an accomplice and not the actual criminal, she will be sentenced to a term of imprisonment to satisfy the publicity of your English justice, and then will be quietly liberated and placed under such control as my august sovereign, His Majesty the Emperor Nicholas, thinks fit—so that if in any way the Russian Government can quietly help you to arrive at the true solution I am commanded to give you every assistance. It will pay us to find out the truth. Now, I have a theory of my own—of course it is only a theory, but it is based on knowledge which possibly is not in your possession. Now, you have four sons murdered, and an attempt at the murder of the fifth son. The knotted cord in each case probably really signifies what it is intended to indicate, namely that one and the same agency (whether this be a single person or a gang is immaterial) is concerned in all the murders. The most prominent, in fact the only common bond between the five sons is their relationship—the one thing they derive in common from a common source."

"That is what I have insisted all along till I came here. I have told Colonel Mauleverer, over and over again, that I was certain the explanation was to be found in his own life."

"Ah," said M. de Plehve, "I think you are wrong. The sons had a mother as well as a father."

The point had never dawned on Yardley. Mrs.

Mauleverer had died a few weeks after the birth of Anthony, the youngest child; the Colonel never alluded to her, and she might never have existed, so small a part did her memory seem to play in the lives of Colonel Mauleverer and his sons. Yardley·might well be excused for not having taken her into consideration.

"I see you don't know who she was," continued the minister. "Mrs. Mauleverer you will find described in the 'Landed Gentry' as the only child and heir of Admiral Hay, C.B., and Admiral Hay's mother is here given" (M. de Plehve took down a copy of Burke's monumental work as he spoke) "as Sonia, elder daughter and coheir of Sir William Codrington, K.C.B., Consul General for H.B.M. at the City of Kischineff."

With his fingers on the book, the Czar's watchdog turned to Yardley, and said—

"My friend, if you desire to succeed in your profession, I strongly advise you to study genealogy. It's a most interesting science, but most of those who study it waste time on their own pedigrees, and spend money like water in a vain endeavour to prove that some particular but quite unimportant John Smith or William Robinson was the son of Thomas Smith or Joseph Robinson. You and I, my friend, who haven't got any pedigrees, ought to know better. Genealogy, as I have said, is a most fascinating study, but the part that interests me most is the unwritten side of genealogy. Most people whose pedigrees are worth putting into print have two genealogies, the one *à la* Mrs. Grundy, which gets into works like this one, and the other, which, being true, has a great deal more importance, but which somehow never gets any publicity. Those are the pedigrees which I advise you to study. I am quite an expert authority on them myself. They really repay close attention. The present is a case in point. No doubt you have heard of the province of Moritania, on the southern border of Poland. It is very small, which probably accounts for the fact that its annexation by Russia and its previous history find no prominence in any European history book. Of course we don't put that kind of thing in a Russian school book," was the cynical remark of M. de Plehve. "Moritania was originally a Sovereign principality. It was always by alliance or *force majeure* under the protection of some powerful State, usually Poland, but it always retained its nominal independent Sovereignty. Its chief characteristic was that its population was almost entirely Roman Catholic, a characteristic it still retains, in spite of our continuous efforts during the last century and a half to increase the Jewish and Russian elements. The last *de facto* Prince—Prince Ivan Soyonoff—was always a violent enemy of Russia, and naturally, in the final conflict, threw in his lot with Poland, and in consequence we were compelled to depose him. He was a most intimate friend of Sir

William Codrington, and fell at the battle of
Ladoff. Now, Sir William, when he was a resident Consul, was childless. He resigned and returned to England, and a few years afterwards
the Russian Government ascertained that he was
everywhere accompanied by two daughters. The
exact age of the girls could never be ascertained,
but the elder of the two, certainly from her age,
must have been born some years before Sir William
returned to England from Kischineff. The
younger child was apparently just of that age at
which she might have been born immediately after
the return of Sir William, or immediately before
he left Moritania, but everybody judged her to be
rather older, and like her sister, undoubtedly born
in Moritania. Sir William did certainly have one
daughter born at that time. The two daughters
of Prince Ivan were said to have perished after
the battle of Ladoff, but we subsequently ascertained
that they were simply handed over to Sir William
on condition they took his name and were known
as his offspring. Six months later a child of Sir
William died, but whether it was his own child who
died, or the younger daughter of Prince Ivan, we
have never found out, though most things point
to its being his own blood daughter. The elder
child unquestionably was the daughter of Prince
Ivan. She it was who married Admiral Hay's
father, Sir Thomas Hay, and was the grandmother
of Mrs. Mauleverer. The younger child married

Lord Townsend, and became the ancestress of that family. The true facts we know are common talk in the Province, and they know there the truth about the younger child—a point on which his Majesty has no certain knowledge. The daughter of the Emperor Alexander we have good reason to know is thoroughly democratic in her sympathies. She had collected a considerable following, and is undoubtedly the figurehead of the revolutionary ferment with which we have to deal at the moment. I by no means assert that no marriage ceremony took place between his late Majesty and Mademoiselle Sarcelle. As a matter of fact, I believe they were married some time before his late Majesty's marriage with the Empress Dowager. But, like your English Royal Marriage Act, the House Law of the Romanoffs utterly vitiates the legality of any such ceremony, and it troubles us little, except that, unfortunately, the Roman Catholic Faith has a most inconvenient disregard for these Family House Laws, and a most curious belief in the consummation of marriage as the determining factor, and the bulk of the Moritanian population being Catholic, accordingly prefer to regard this lady I have alluded to as the true and only heir to the late Emperor. They believe in Divine right and disregard the Salic law. Then of course the Socialist forces in Russia, the chief article of whose creed is that they are against the Government, and who firmly believe that any violent change would be of a certainty for the better, are only too ready to adopt this lady as their candidate for the throne, whilst her known democratic sympathies render her one whom the Russian Government cannot afford to lose sight of.

"It is a curious circumstance that, from a military point of view, Moritania is an ideal 'jumping off place' or cradle for the revolution which we are told is coming. So that if Moritania goes wholeheartedly with the Pretenders their chance of success is by no means negligible. There is only one contrary factor and it is this, that I think the average Moritanian is truer to his principles of loyalty and personal fidelity than to his religion, and for that reason the descendants of Prince Ivan, who are known to exist somewhere in England, amount to an absolute bar to any claimant asserting a right as the true heir of the Emperor Alexander. Moritania is practically essential to any real *de facto* revolutionary movement. Consequently Moritania is the basis of the movement I have referred to; but you can't rebel in a hostile territory, and so long as the heirs of Prince Ivan exist, they, without any efforts on their part, are assured of the sympathy of Moritania, which will continue. As a matter of fact, I very much doubt if the Mauleverers really know the position in which they stand, but this pestilent book"—and M. de Plehve put his hand on a volume of the Almanach de Gotha— "in spite of all our efforts, will continue the as-

sertion that the descendants of the elder branch of
the family are now domiciled in England; and the
traditions connected with the disposal of the two
children of Prince Ivan are carefully treasured in
Moritania. Of course it is our business to know
these things, but from the fact that the Mauleverers quarter the arms of Hay and Codrington
in preference to using the sovereign achievement of
Moritania, it would seem to argue that they really
are unaware of their descent. But whether that is
the fact or not, their mere existence is a very powerful factor in opposition to the revolutionary movement, and his Majesty's Government of late has
found it quite in consonance with its policy to rather
encourage this pathetic historical loyalty to the
descendants of Prince Ivan. We look upon it
much as in England you look upon your White
Rose League, a harmless and chimerical ideal. It
suits us a great deal better than the more actual
forces we have to combat."

"Then," said Yardley, "you put it that the
Mauleverers are being murdered to further the
claim, or rather to remove the obstacles from the
path of the present revolutionary movement?"

"My dear young friend," replied the minister,
"you put it too strongly. Sitting in this chair, one's
brain starts to work, and knowing the evidence concerning these murders, one tries to evolve a reason
why they should have been committed, and, being
in possession of information of which you were not

aware, one comes to a conclusion; at any rate, one evolves a motive, and, mark you, my friend, no murder was ever committed without a motive. In this country we are not given to splitting hairs over legal technicalities. If it is for the good of the State that a man should be executed or transported, well, he is"—cynically commented the Minister—"and we don't trouble much whether his crime be murder or manslaughter. Your wonderful English law is different, and you have decided that without motive, or rather without intention, there can be no murder. Now, I have suggested a motive to you, which fully explains everything you know, and to be aware of the motive of a crime is a long step forwards to finding the criminal. But do not forget that all I have told you amounts to no more than a theory, and that theory"—said M. de Plehve, speaking slowly and emphatically—"entirely depends upon two things. There is first the identity of Miss Vane with the lady I have alluded to, which is the point upon which his Majesty's Government would give a good deal for certain knowledge. There is also the point as to whether Miss Vane really did commit the murder for which she is now under arrest. On the evidence I have seen I doubt it! I am afraid I must wish you good morning, Mr. Yardley." And the Minister, half rising from his chair, bowed the detective out of the room.

Yardley gained the street in a perfect haze of

bewilderment. Accustomed as he was to startling assertions and unexpected developments, even he could not, at a few moments' notice, readjust his ideas to an entirely new conception of the whole case. As the French say, "It gave furiously to think!" Wildly improbable to the last degree as the whole story seemed, the moment he had left the presence of M. de Plehve he could not but admit that it was the only logical explanation which up to that moment had been suggested. In spite of the fact that the Russian Minister had warned Yardley that he only enunciated a theory, he had nevertheless spoken as one who knew, and Yardley never for a moment doubted that there was all-sufficient reason behind that knowledge. The all-important fact to be ascertained was true and definite knowledge as to whether Miss Vane was, or was not, the daughter of Mademoiselle Sarcelle. On his return from Petersburg he spent some days in Paris, in a vain endeavour to track this daughter of the Emperor and the actress. As de Plehve had stated, she disappeared at a certain date, and from that moment there did not appear to be one solitary trace of her existence.

Proceeding to England, he quickly sought an interview with Colonel Mauleverer, and asked him point-blank if he was aware of his wife's descent. The Colonel gazed in amazement as the detective unfolded his story.

"Admiral Hay," he said, "died of cholera in the

West Indies when my wife was between two and three years old, and her mother died during the following twelve months. The Admiral had made my father my wife's guardian, and she was brought up at home. She certainly knew nothing about it, because she was openly proud of her Codrington descent. There was a curious little book she had which none of us could read, which was left to her with instructions that it should be carefully treasured, in her grandmother's will. Her grandmother died a few years after her parents. The Colonel opened a drawer in his bureau and took out a small parchment manuscript book which he threw across the table to Yardley. The latter knew enough Russian to be able to decipher from the book an exact confirmation .of the story he had heard from M. de Plehve; there was no doubt the latter had spoken with knowledge. Yardley had been supplied with introductions from M. de Plehve to the Russian Ambassador in London, who was asked to bring Yardley into contact with such of the accredited agents of the secret service as had been concerned about the inquiries about Miss Vane, and about the daughter of Mlle. Sarcelle, and he lost no time in presenting his credentials. He could never quite make up his mind whether in the many happenings which occupied him during the ensuing period he was being helped or hindered by his Russian associates. He always felt that somehow or other his professional capabilities were being made use of by others, for their purposes and not his own. Obviously it was to the interest of the Russian Government that he should be successful in his search; but he encountered many checks, and he went into court on the morning of the trial of Vivienne Vane having gained no solitary atom of provable information as to her antecedents prior to the day, some three or four years previously, when she had taken London by storm as its most beautiful and fascinating and its most extravagant member of the demi-monde. The police had, meanwhile, been working steadily on their more ordinary lines of inquiry, and not wholly without result. But Yardley had been busy with an ultimate object in view widely differing from that which animated the police. They were interested only in the detection and punishment of the actual criminal who had been guilty in the past: Yardley's concern was with the future, and with the safeguarding of Anthony by the elucidation of the mystery of the crimes.

CHAPTER XI

THE Old Bailey, as was only to be expected, was packed to suffocation. In an absolutely unemotional, impartial, almost uninterested voice the Crown Counsel carefully built up the evidence fact upon fact into a damning indictment against Miss Vane. He described her intimacy with Herbert Mauleverer, who was in possession of her signed photograph, the first clue in the chain of evidence that had been collected; he produced the fragment of the letter (which the prisoner admitted she had written) which indicated a serious issue of some kind between the deceased and the prisoner —the point at issue being very apparently one which it seemed to him the jury might be allowed to presume, and which in his opinion was one quite unnecessary to put into words. Counsel also stated that he should call Jones, the landlord and valet of Mr. Herbert Mauleverer, and prove by his evidence that Miss Vane called at Mr. Herbert's rooms on the afternoon of the murder. Jones, the landlord of Herbert Mauleverer, counsel believed, would be asked to give evidence that Miss Vane left the rooms of Herbert Mauleverer at five-thirty. Counsel had no wish to discredit the evidence of Jones, who, there was no doubt, was devoted not only to the Mauleverer family, in whose service he had been for many years, but also especially to Mr. Herbert Mauleverer. Colonel Mauleverer gave him the highest character any servant could desire, and though the explanation very likely might be that Miss Vane had returned after Jones had heard her let out by Herbert Mauleverer at five-thirty, there could be no doubt whatever that she was present in Mr. Mauleverer's rooms at a later hour. He proposed to call medical evidence to show that death could only have taken place a matter of half an hour or so before the body was found. An intense air of expectancy pervaded the hushed court as counsel explained an item of evidence the sensation of which had not been discounted by publication in the press. Counsel stated that the body was found seated at the writing-table, and hidden in the fur rug that was underneath the chair had been discovered a lady's watch. This, which was one of the usual kind worn hanging from a brooch, was of plain gold, having on the back the initial "V" in diamonds. If the initial itself were not sufficient evidence, any doubt as to the ownership of the watch would be at once set at rest because he proposed to call as a witness the jeweller by whom the watch was sold to Miss Vivienne Vane.

"The watch," said counsel, "would be handed

to the jury for examination, and they would notice that very evidently it had been trodden upon: the glass was broken, the case was dented and flattened, in fact the whole watch was so damaged that it must have stopped at the moment at which the accident happened to it. The hands of the watch were flattened against the dial, but they showed the time at which the watch had fallen and been trodden upon. The time indicated was five minutes to seven.

"To sum the whole case up," concluded counsel, "here was Miss Vane's watch stopped at 6.55. The body was found at 7.15, and before 7.30 a doctor had been present who would be called to prove that death had taken place within half an hour. Miss Vane was known to have had a violent quarrel with Mr. Herbert Mauleverer. No other solution of the mystery had been put forward on her behalf, and the conclusion of her guilt was irresistible.

"It was difficult to suggest a motive for the murder, but Mr. Dennis Yardley, the well-known private detective, would be called, and would give evidence which would disclose the probability that Miss Vivienne Vane was one and the same person as a certain Vera Sarcelle. If that identity were a fact," remarked counsel, "then the motive was less obscure, for the Court would then be dealing with a crime which had a political basis and origin, amply sufficient to supply the motive, for it was to the palpable interest, an interest both personal and political, of Miss Vera Sarcelle, that the whole of the five Mauleverer brothers should be removed. Miss Vivienne Vane stood indicted for the single murder of Herbert Mauleverer, but counsel presumed it was to such an extent common knowledge that he need not enlarge upon the point that four out of Colonel Mauleverer's five sons had each already met a violent death within as many months, and no less than three attempts had already been made on the life of Anthony Mauleverer, the only remaining son. The circumstances of each death left little doubt the four murders emanated from one controlling agency, and, although not the slightest connection could be traced between Miss Vane and any of the crimes he had referred to save the one for which she was now indicted, there could be no doubt that Mademoiselle Vera Sarcelle stood to reap benefit from each of the four deaths, and, moreover, from each equally. That lady represented and was the figurehead of a vast movement concerned with interests far greater than those of a mere personal character, and a movement which could at any moment provide any required number of desperate agents. As far as the question of the motive he had outlined existed, it depended upon the identity of Vivienne Vane and Vera Sarcelle, but neither that motive nor that identity, if both were disproved, and neither of which counsel could assert as definitely established, could remove the very precise and particular evidence which connected Miss Vivienne Vane with the murder of Herbert Mauleverer, for which offence she was now on her trial."

The first witness called was Inspector Parkyns of Scotland Yard. He described the summons to Mr. Herbert Mauleverer's rooms, and the subsequent finding on different occasions of the photograph and the watch, as had been already detailed. Mr. Ashley Tempest, counsel for the defence, allowed the witness to pass without any severe cross-examination; the questions, which were few in number, being merely asked in the effort to elicit more precise exactitude.

Dr. Henry Atherton was then called and sworn. He described how he arrived at seven-thirty and examined the body of Herbert Mauleverer. A knotted cord was closely thrown round the neck, but death was due to the fact that the throat was cut, and that blood was, at the time he saw the body, still slowly oozing from the wound, and he estimated that death had taken place about half an hour previously. The wound in the throat had been made from left to right, and was much deeper on the right-hand side than on the left, so witness had no doubt whatever that the wound had been inflicted by some one standing behind whilst Mr. Mauleverer was leaning over his writing-table. The blotting-pad on the table over which the body was leaning was soaked with blood, which

had evidently poured from the wound in pro-
fusion.

Mr. Tempest rose to cross-examine. "You say
the wound was inflicted from behind. What leads
you to that belief?"

"The fact that the cut is plainly from left to
right. It is a mere scratch on the left side of the
throat; it is a deep wound on the right where the
knife had been forcibly dragged through the
throat."

"I put it to you that Mr. Mauleverer committed suicide."

"No, I think not, because if he were right-handed
the wound would certainly be also from left to
right, but would be deepest on the left side. A
man cannot exercise much strength when his arm
is bent to the extent it would be when he had
extended the wound to the right side of his
throat."

"But the razor was his own, and was found just
below his hand exactly where it would have fallen
from it."

"It is practicably impossible he could have made
that wound himself; besides, he wouldn't hang
that rope round his neck."

"Pardon me, that is hardly a point upon which
you are justified in giving expert evidence."

The next witness, one of the assistants of Messrs.
Ellis and Walery's establishment, proved having
taken the photograph produced, of a lady, whom

he now identified as Miss Vane, but who was photographed in the name of Miss Smith.

Cross-examined, the witness stated he had no shadow of doubt it was a photograph of Miss Vane.

"When was it taken?"

"Eighteen months ago."

"I gather it was taken professionally, the copyright belonging to your firm?"

"That is so."

"Then you have published copies of it which are purchasable at different shops?"

"Yes."

"Anybody could buy them?"

"Certainly."

"How many have been sold?"

"The illustrated papers have very largely killed the sale of prints of copyright photographs—we look now to copyright fees for the right of reproduction—but this particular photograph has been exceptionally popular, and we have sold several thousand copies."

"Then the possession of this lady's photograph by no means proves personal acquaintance?"

"Certainly not."

"There is a question which I caused you to be informed I should ask you. Have you ever photographed any one giving the name of Mademoiselle Sarcelle?"

"Yes. Once about two years ago."

"Have you brought the copies of that negative as I requested?"

"Yes."

The copies were handed to the jury and counsel.

"I don't quite see what you are driving at, Mr. Tempest," interjected the judge.

"If your Lordship will pardon me, it will all be apparent in a moment."

"Now then," added the counsel, turning back to the witness, "will you carefully examine the photograph, and then will you look at the prisoner?" Counsel paused whilst the witness did so, and then asked, "Now, do you think the two photographs are photographs of the same woman?"

"I decline to say."

Counsel pressed the point, but could get nothing more out of the photographer than the fact that the two faces seemed remarkably alike, and the witness was then allowed to leave the witness-box.

The next witness called was Mr. J. H. Durrin, expert in handwriting, and counsel for the prosecution asked him—

"You have been given a fragment of a letter which was found in Mr. Herbert Mauleverer's rooms, and which you have heard read to the jury. I understand you have examined it. You have also had under examination the signed copy of a photograph of Miss Vane, with a certain written inscription. Will you kindly tell me whether in your opinion the two were written by the same person?"

The witness unhesitatingly asserted them to be, in his opinion, in the same handwriting, and proceeded to point out the similarity of the letters "e" in each, and also the curious form of the small letter "v."

Counsel then produced a letter which he asked witness to examine.

"What is that letter?"

"It is a letter which has been supplied to us by the Russian Embassy, and is in the handwriting of Mademoiselle Sarcelle."

"Do you find the same peculiarities in that?"

"The letters 'e' and 'v' are certainly shaped in the same manner."

"Is the handwriting the same?"

"That is difficult to say. In the previous letter I have alluded to, the writing is very evidently done with a stylograph, and is upright. So is the writing on the photograph. This writing slants, and looks as if it had been written with a J-pen."

The examination of the witness being concluded, Mr. Tempest rose to cross-examine.

"For how many years have you been engaged as a handwriting expert?"

"Nearly thirty."

"Have you any idea in how many cases you have given evidence?"

"I really can't remember. I have never counted them."

"How many times have you been proved to be wrong, Mr. Durrin?"

"I decline to admit that I have ever been wrong. I merely point out the similarities in different specimens of handwriting, and express my opinion."

"You don't pretend, then, to make a definite assertion of fact in any case—not even the Fleck case, for example?"

"No; though I am often so certain that I have no doubt whatever in my own mind."

"Now, Mr. Durrin, there are as good fish in the sea as ever came out, so I presume that it is quite possible for another expert to exist as clever as yourself. Would you care for the life of any one you were interested in to depend on expert evidence in handwriting?"

"Of course it is only opinion, and you can't hang a man on opinion."

"Ah!" said the counsel; "then yours is nothing but opinion, and you merely profess to have pointed out that the handwriting in the letter and on the photograph are both written with a stylograph, and that peculiar 'e's' and 'v's' occur in both?"

The witness assented.

"Will you take your oath they were written by the same person?"

"No, I cannot," said the witness; "I am merely giving my opinion."

"It's not unusual for people to use Greek 'e's,' is it?"

"Oh, dear, no."

"Or to use stylographs?"

"Certainly not."

"Have you ever seen any one make a 'v' like that before?"

"No; I have never met with that peculiar shape."

"Now, if I can bring you cheques in which precisely similar 'v's' occur, dated before the date of this murder, written by no less than three people, you would be surprised?"

"I certainly should."

"Well, I propose to do it later. But I put it to you, Mr. Durrin, that if the thing were unique in your experience, and I can find examples readily enough elsewhere, it rather discredits the value of your opinion and the extent of your experience."

The witness merely shrugged his shoulders, and, as Mr. Tempest intimated that he had no further questions to ask, left the witness-box.

The next witness called gave his name as Ernest Wilson, one of the assistants at the Goldsmiths' Alliance in Regent Street. On being shown the watch, he was asked if he recognized it.

"Yes," he said; "I sold it myself."

"To whom did you sell it?"

"To Miss Vane."

"Can you give me the date?"

The witness did so, and his cross-examination then commenced.

"Was this watch made to order?"

"No; it was sold from stock."

"May I presume, then, it is an ordinary stock pattern?"

"Yes."

"Which might be purchased in any good jeweller's shop?"

"I know no reason to the contrary. They are sold with these initials in diamonds ready made. We always keep three or four of each initial in stock, and I expect other big firms do the same."

"Now, you admit it is a stock pattern, and that this pattern is sold through the trade in the ordinary way. How on earth dare you attempt to identify this particular watch as the one you sold to Miss Vane? All you know is that she bought a watch with the initial 'V' upon it."

"I can identify it very easily. Every solitary article in the shop is marked and numbered, and directly any article is sold, a note of the number is taken, and it is marked off in the stock-book. I have referred to the number in this watch, and I find that this particular one was sold to Miss Vane."

"It seems to me almost incredible that every article should be entered like this. Do you mean to say that the practice is invariable?"

"Yes; it is necessary for the purpose of burglary insurance. We have no other way of proving burglary except by the stock-book, and the assessors for Lloyds, where our stock is underwritten, are very particular about the manner in which the stock-book is kept."

"But you have kept no record that this particular watch was sold to Miss Vane," said counsel, after examining the stock-book which was handed to him.

"No; but the entry in the stock-book shows that it was sold by me at that particular date, and it happens to be the only watch of that pattern that I have ever sold. I had heard a great deal about Miss Vane, and I was naturally curious when she mentioned her name, and I have a very clear recollection of the circumstances."

"But it comes back to this, that your evidence is merely a matter of your recollection?"

"Not quite. I have examined the stock-book carefully. A good many watches of this pattern have been sold, but only two with the initial 'V.' "

"Might not this be the other one?"

"No; the other one was purchased by Sir William Vincent—I suppose for some member of his family —he has an account with us, and the number appears in the day-book. Consequently the other one must have been the one I sold to Miss Vane."

"You see the watch has been trodden on. Is it possible for the hands to have moved after that had happened?"

"I think not; the whole works are crushed in, and it is quite impossible for the hands to have moved. They are quite flattened on the dial."

"You conclude, then, that the watch was trodden on at six-fifty-five?"

"Yes, I am certain."

"But could not the hands have been moved, by catching in anything, for example, after the watch had stopped?"

"I think not in this case."

The next witness, Jones, in his examination described how Miss Vane had come in with Mr. Herbert Mauleverer; how he had taken up tea, and how on the second occasion when he took up the hot buttered toast, he had heard them quarrelling violently. He then described how he had heard Mr. Herbert come downstairs with Miss Vane and let her out, and then, how he had thought he heard Mr. Mauleverer go out about six-thirty, but had discovered his body on going upstairs to his sitting-room. In answer to a question, Jones admitted that he had seen Miss Vane in Mr. Herbert's rooms on a previous occasion.

Mr. Tempest then took the witness in hand.

"Why do you now give all these minute details about Miss Vane being at your house, when you were absolutely silent at the inquest?"

The witness did not answer; but the question was pressed.

"I thought it better not to."

"But why?"

"For Mr. Herbert's sake."

"No other reason?"

"I had to think of the reputation of my house."

"Oh! One for him and two for yourself. But as you carefully said nothing about all this at first, you wouldn't be surprised if nobody believed it now?"

"It's quite true."

"Do you appreciate the fact that the *suppressio veri*, and the *suggestio falsi*, are really ordinary lies?"

"I don't understand, sir."

"Ah, well, perhaps it doesn't matter. When did you first tell this story?"

"I told it to Colonel Mauleverer and Mr. Yardley when they came to see me."

"Did you see Mr. Herbert Mauleverer and Miss Vane when they came in?"

"No, I only heard them."

"Then there might have been three people who came in together? You didn't see them?"

"No, sir, I didn't; but I didn't hear any one else, and nobody else was in the room when I took up tea." .

"Might not the other person have been in the bedroom when you went up?"

"I only saw two people in the room, and I only heard two people come in."

"Did they ring for tea?"

"No, I took it up, as I always did when Mr. Herbert was in. He had called out that he wanted tea, as he went up the stairs."

"Did they drink it?"

"One cup was used."

"Was whisky and soda in the room?"

"Yes."

"Were there glasses there?"

"Yes."

"How many were used?"

"Two."

"Well, then, somebody had both tea and whisky."

"Yes, sir, I suppose so."

"Isn't it much more likely that the two men had whisky, and the lady tea?"

"Yes, if there were two men."

"You wouldn't say whisky and tea were a usual mixture?"

"No, sir."

"Did you see Mr. Mauleverer let Miss Vane out?"

"No."

"What makes you think that was what happened?"

"Miss Vane had a very rustly silk petticoat on. It almost drowned what they said"—an audible titter went round the court—"and I heard her petticoat rustling when they came down."

"That rustling might have prevented you hearing a third person go in."

"It might, sir."

"Then you thought you heard Mr. Herbert go out. Why did you think it was he?"

"He sometimes did about that time, and it seemed to me more of a man's tread, though it was not a heavy tread. But then, Mr. Herbert was a light walker."

"Did you hear the silk petticoat rustling?"

"No, sir."

"The tread couldn't have drowned it?"

"No, sir."

"Then you feel pretty certain it was not Miss Vane who came down the stairs just before you went up?"

"I don't think it could have been her, sir."

"Mr. Yardley suggests, I think, that Miss Vane returned."

"Then she must have taken off her petticoat, sir, if she did."

"What time was it when you heard Mr. Herbert and Miss Vane come in?"

"Between four and half-past."

"What time was it when you heard them go out?"

"About five-thirty, sir. But it was before five-thirty, because I went out to post a letter, and the five-thirty slip was still in the pillar-box, and the pillar-box at the corner is where they always begin collecting."

"What time did you hear the second person go out?"

"I don't know, sir, but it was before seven, and it was after half-past six."

"Is the door at your house kept locked?"

"Not during the daytime, sir."

"Then any one knowing your house, could have walked straight up to Mr. Herbert Mauleverer's rooms?"

"They *could* have done, only I think I should have heard them, sir."

"Well, but you say you heard two people come in, and Mr. Herbert is dead in his rooms, and yet you heard two people go out. Is there any balcony on your house that any one could get in that way?"

"No, sir."

"Could they get in by the trap door in the roof?"

"No, sir; that's bolted on the inside, and it was bolted when I went up afterwards to look."

"Who found the watch on the floor?"

"Inspector Parkyns, sir."

"Did you notice if Miss Vane had it on when you took in the tea?"

"I don't think I noticed."

The next witness was Mr. Dennis Yardley, who, in answer to the questions of the prosecuting counsel, told amid the hushed silence of the court, how, in investigating the cause of Mr. Jack Mauleverer, he had visited Russia, how it had been there suggested to him that Vivienne Vane was only an *alias* for Vera Sarcelle, how everything that he had been able to ascertain fitted into this supposition, and how it was probably correct. He was proceeding to relate what he had been told of the latter person, when Mr. Tempest at once objected to the evidence, his objection being upheld by the judge. Rapidly explaining that this evidence had taken him wholly by surprise, Mr. Tempest asked that the cross-examination of this witness might be postponed. The prosecution therefore called the next witness, who gave his name as Paul Sirotkin, and described himself as a member of the police in Russia. Being asked if he knew Miss Sarcelle, he stated that until a year or two ago, when they had lost sight of her, she was very well known to the Russian police as a persistent conspirator; that though they had been unable to ascertain her whereabouts, many things pointed to her presence in England, and that there was no doubt she had been actively engaged in revolutionary propaganda at a date long after she had disappeared from the observation of the Russian police. The witness said that he had seen Vera Sarcelle on several occasions, and he firmly believed Miss Vane was the same person.

This closed the case for the prosecution, and Mr. Tempest after his opening remarks called his first witness for the defence, who gave his name as Andrew Milner, a bank clerk in the Law Courts branch of Lloyd's Bank.

"I asked you," said counsel, "carefully to exam-

ine any cheques that you could lay your hands upon
that were more than six months old in which you
could find 'e's' and 'v's' made in the same fashion
as those to which Mr. Durrin called attention."
Counsel added in explanation, that it was fortunate
the letter "v" was one selected because, as it occurred in the words "five, seven, eleven and twelve,"
it would often need to be written upon a
cheque.

The witness produced eighteen or twenty
cheques, in all of which the curious "v's" and
"e's" could be found, these being cheques made
out by different people.

Counsel then called Miss Vivienne Vane, who,
leaving the dock, took her place in the witness-
box.

"Did you go to Mr. Herbert Mauleverer's rooms
in Jermyn Street on the day he was murdered?"

"Yes, I did."

"Did you have tea there?"

"Yes."

"And whisky afterwards?"

"No, I never drink whisky."

"What time did you leave?"

"I left before half-past five."

"On your oath now, did you return to Mr. Mauleverer's rooms afterwards?"

"No, I did not; I never saw him again."

"Was that your watch which has been produced?"

"I had a watch like that, which I have lost. I am not sure when I lost it, because I did not miss it until after I heard this one had been found."

"Were you on good terms with Mr. Mauleverer?"

"I was on very intimate terms; but we had had a disagreement, in fact, a violent quarrel, which was why I went to his rooms with him that afternoon, but we made it up before I left, and he agreed to do as I wished."

"Are you Miss Vera Sarcelle?"

"No, I am not; I never heard the name until it cropped up in this case, nor have I the ghost of an idea what they are driving at."

Mr. Tempest then handed over the witness to be cross-examined, and the first question she was asked was—

"What was the subject of the quarrel between Mr. Mauleverer and yourself?"

"I decline to say."

Threats and persuasions seemed equally useless in any attempt to extract an answer, and at last counsel gave up the attempt, and asked—

"Where did you go when you left Mr. Mauleverer's rooms?"

"I decline to say."

Again counsel urged the question, and the judge, speaking in a kindly tone, added his persuasion.

"I don't wish to prejudge the case, Miss Vane,

but I don't think you realize the importance of this question. If you can give a satisfactory account of where you went and how you spent the next hour or two, there can be no doubt of your innocence, whereas your refusal to say in itself creates suspicion."

"I am very sorry, my lord; but I have no alternative. I really cannot say where I was."

With a supercilious smile, as if he little need trouble any further, counsel asked—

"Do you know Russian?"

"Yes."

"Have you ever been in Russia?"

"Yes, I have stayed there several times."

"Have you ever been in Moritania?"

"That was where I stayed."

"And you persist that you know nothing of Vera Sarcelle?"

"I have never heard the name before, and I don't know who the lady is."

"Have you ever heard of Prince Kentchikoff?"

"Yes, I have seen his name in newspapers; but that is all."

"Where does your income come from, Miss Vane?"

"I inherited it."

"Who was your father?"

"My father has been dead for fifteen years, and has nothing whatever to do with this case. You don't suppose his name was Vane?"

"No; that is the very point," replied counsel. "I want to know what his name was."

"I think it unnecessary to answer, and I think it ungentlemanly of you to ask."

The judge looked up, and said: "I don't think that is a question which ought to be pressed unless you have some special reason."

"Well, my lord, if Miss Vane will say who her father was, we might be able to prove that she is not Vera Sarcelle; whereas we think she is, and her refusals give colour to the belief."

Miss Vane's beautiful face flashed round to the speaker.

"Do I look of common origin with parents whom it does not matter if I bring disgrace upon? Do you think I am proud of being here? I *am* here, but I don't intend to pander to your curiosity. It *cannot* matter who my father was."

"Which is your bank?"

"I haven't got one."

"But how do you get your money, then? You appear to spend a large income."

"It is paid to me in gold, and I keep and spend it in that form."

"Where do you exchange it into English money?"

"What do you mean? It is paid to me in sovereigns. Those are English money, surely."

Counsel laughed, and passed on to his next question.

"Who was the 'only man' you ever cared about whom you mention in your letter to Mr. Mauleverer?"

"I decline to say."

"Was it about him you quarrelled?"

"Well, yes, in a way, it was."

"What did Mr. Mauleverer threaten to tell this person?"

"I don't think it necessary to answer."

"I suppose it was an account of your career?"

The witness made no answer.

The question was repeated.

"Oh, well, that will do as well as anything else. Have it as you like."

The judge at once interfered. "You may, if you care to run the risk of the suspicion the refusal creates, refuse to answer a question, but you must not answer in the manner in which you replied to the last question."

· Yardley and Paul Sirotkin were then recalled for cross-examination, and Tempest eventually pinned, each in turn, down to the final admission that there was no particle of evidence of any sort which would prove the identity of Vivienne Vane and Vera Sarcelle, and that the supposed identity was mere surmise.

In an eloquent speech for the defence, Tempest did all that human wit could suggest in favour of his client. Taking each witness in turn he attempted to break down the evidence given, and show its unreliability where it was contrary to the interest of his client, emphasizing it where it told in her favour. He ridiculed as utterly preposterous any attempt to identify his client with Miss Sarcelle. He pointed out that the latter had not been proved to have had the smallest connection with any of the murders, and said it was absolutely purposeless to attempt to trace the identity which he denied.

"If," said counsel, "it were any use my going into the witness-box myself, I or others with the same knowledge would do so, and swear to having known many relatives of Miss Vane intimately, and to knowing her history in detail from the time she left the nursery. But under Miss Vane's instructions, I may not say who she is, and I can only offer you my own unsubstantiated assertion that she is not Mademoiselle Sarcelle, of whom also I know a little." He admitted the watch was probably the property of Miss Vane, but she could give no account of how it came to be found in the rooms of Mr. Mauleverer. "Gentlemen," he added, turning to the jury, "do you think if my client knew that watch had been torn off in a struggle (and if it had then been trodden on she would certainly have known), do you think she would have had no ready explanation? God in heaven! do you think, gentlemen, I couldn't have invented some plausible tale that would have fitted facts she *knew,* and disproved the conclusion you are asked to draw?"

A murmur of angry dissent ran through the court.

Turning to the gallery with a sneer, Tempest added—

"I am fighting for my client's life. I *know* she is innocent; fighting to save an innocent woman's life—what would have been a lie more or less compared with that? We know she left Mr. Mauleverer's rooms at half-past five—an hour before the murder was committed—and did not return, yet we daren't invent a story for the simple reason that at any moment the true explanation may turn up. If we knew the truth we could fight it, but we do not know the explanation of the watch being found. My client doesn't even know whether she wore it when she went to Jermyn Street or not, and I am hampered by that ignorance. All she knows is that, when she learnt such a watch had been found, she looked for her own, and missed it. I say that watch, which was not found for several days after the murder, was stolen from Miss Vane and purposely placed there."

Counsel at once admitted the truth of the allegation that the fragment of the letter, which had been produced, and the signature on the photograph, had both been written by Miss Vane.

"My client has no wish to deny either."

With a bantering commentary on the evidence

of Mr. Durrin and its lack of value, counsel passed to the evidence of Jones, which Mr. Tempest remarked that he accepted in every word.

"Transparent truth rings in every word of it, together with no little observation."

He admitted once more that Miss Vane did go to Mr. Mauleverer's rooms and did quarrel with him. But the quarrel passed, and Miss Vane had tea, but she had no whisky, and a man does not usually drink whisky out of two glasses at the same time.

Turning to the jury, and in slow impressive tones, he added—

"If you can find who drank from that other glass, then you know who murdered Herbert Mauleverer, and Miss Vane was not that person."

He then carefully repeated the evidence of Jones which showed that the rustling silk petticoat which Miss Vane took in with her at four-thirty went out (the witness need not have seen to have been certain what he heard) at five-thirty—of that there was no doubt. "Now, gentlemen, ladies don't usually change their rustling silk petticoats in a gentleman's rooms over afternoon tea, and as the petticoat went out at five-thirty, presumably Miss Vane was inside it. But in order to prove Miss Vane to have been guilty, it isn't enough to prove she came in at four-thirty; for we know she went out at five-thirty. The other side have got to change her petticoat, and get her into the rooms again, and give her a different step—a man's tread. And they *can't* get her in there again, because we know she wasn't there. And Jones knows she wasn't there, and yet, because this watch is found, which may have been there for weeks, or not put there till afterwards, you, gentlemen of the jury, are to be asked to jump to the conclusion that she went back without her petticoat, for Jones must have heard that, and committed that murder for no reason whatsoever, without the slightest motive. Gentlemen, the idea is preposterous. Now, the rug was under the writing-table, and under the chair in which he was sitting. Mr. Mauleverer was found leaning over the writing-table, and this was saturated with blood; there was blood on the carpet. There is the rug before you, gentlemen—there isn't a trace of blood on it—yet the watch is found in the rug. Miss Vane never went near the writing-table, which stands in a little alcove, and that is one reason why she is so certain that there is some explanation of the watch being found there."

Hour after hour her counsel pleaded and fought for the life of his client. No point was too small for examination, too trivial to be disproved; no stone was left unturned. Applause rang through the court when he sat down, for his defence had been masterly, and the judge let the applause pass unchecked. A faint and pitiful smile passed over the prisoner's face as she nodded to Tempest in recognition of his efforts.

Again the evidence was carefully gone over by counsel for the Crown. Disdaining to employ any approach at emotion or eloquence, he simply reviewed the evidence, and concluded—

"The defence may say what they like, gentlemen; they may, as they have sought to, weave the evidence into a tangled web of confusion, from which it is difficult to derive a conclusion logical to the whole; but they cannot—I say they cannot—get over the consequence of these two facts, that Miss Vane's watch is stopped at the hour at which the murder must have been committed, namely at six-fifty-five, which *primâ facie* would point to her presence there at that moment, and that Miss Vane declines to give us the slightest hint where she passed that evening after five-thirty. I say that, even now, if Miss Vane will say where she was she can leave this court a free and an innocent woman. She will not, and I leave you to draw your own conclusion. Of that conclusion and its consequence the prisoner had warning from his Lordship."

The Court adjourned for the day, and the next morning the judge commenced his summing up. This was passionless and impartial; but it was pitiless in the impersonal manner in which the jury were directed to the evidence under which the innocence of the prisoner had little chance of recognition. The conclusion seemed, after the summing up, almost inevitable; but it was evident that the speech of Mr. Tempest had exercised great effect, for it was two hours before the jury returned to the court. The hum of conversation slowly subsided. The prisoner leant slightly forward, not a trace of anxiety in her face, not a hint of any personal feeling, unless it were a slightly interested amusement. But it was otherwise with her counsel. His face had gone a ghastly grey, and the perspiration stood in beads over his forehead, as he sat at the table, nervously closing and opening his hands on the pencil with which he had been making notes. The suspense of the past two hours had left their mark on him, and any one would have supposed, from looking at his face, that he it was rather than the prisoner whose life hung in the balance.

The jury filed into their places, and, in answer to the inquiry of the clerk of the court, the foreman rose and gave the verdict "Guilty."

A quick-drawn sob from the public, a shriek from a woman in the gallery, and a shuffling of feet as all eyes turned on the prisoner.

The wardress, who was in the dock with her, motioned her to stand up, and the setting sun, reflected through the dusty window of the court, seemed to settle in a perfect blaze upon her figure. Beautiful when judged by the strictest standard, with a glorious wealth of bright copper-coloured hair, a brilliant complexion, and a faultless figure, she would have been remarkable in any assembly. Here, where she was the central figure of the drama which was being played out, her beauty seemed enhanced, and was rendered all the more remarkable by the utter impassiveness of her face.

The judge stretched out his hand along the table to reach the black cap as Mr. Tempest rose to his feet.

"My Lord——" he said.

But the judge at once interrupted him. "I can only hear you in mitigation of sentence, Mr. Tempest."

"My Lord, it is my duty to state——"

"Mr. Tempest, I cannot hear you."

"I only wish to say"—and as the judge again attempted to silence him, he continued in a voice that weighed down all opposition—"this trial is absolutely invalid!"

"Will you kindly explain yourself? This is most unusual."

"I cannot help it, my Lord; I have my duty to do, and I should have thought the number of years I have had the honour of practising before your Lordship would have obtained for me a hearing even in circumstances which I know to be unusual. It is the bitterest experience of my life that my abilities have fallen so far short that, knowing, as I do, that, beyond doubt or question, my client is innocent, I have been unable to prevent the verdict of guilty being brought in against her."

"Mr. Tempest," said the judge, "I am willing to extend to you as much indulgence as to any man practising before me. But you know, as well as I do, that your remarks are most improper. You say this trial is invalid. Will you kindly explain that remark at once, sir?"

"My Lord, my client pleads privilege of peerage. She is a peeress of the realm, and demands to be tried by her peers."

"Really, I must ask for some explanation of such an extraordinary statement."

"Strange as the statement may be, it is the literal truth. I quite realize that this plea should have been entered before the trial; but having been arrested in the name of Miss Vivienne Vane, I felt, as her advocate, and I think if your Lordship can divest yourself of the traditions of the bench, you will agree with me, as a man, that I had no alternative but to endeavour to prove her entire innocence in that capacity. Knowing as I did, and as I shall presently explain to you, that she was absolutely innocent, and had not the slightest connection with this case, I saw no reason why I should impose upon her the penalty of having to acknowledge in her proper person her identity with Miss Vane. But in the face of the verdict which the jury have just brought in, I have no alternative, as I can only prove her innocence by disclosing the fact that she is the Duchess of Merioneth. Of course, although this trial is invalid, her person has been arrested by the Crown, and even in her identity as the Duchess of Merioneth, she still stands charged with the murder of Mr. Herbert Mauleverer. I understand it will be the duty of your Lordship to hand her over in custody to the Gentleman Usher of the Black Rod to take her trial before the House of Lords, and for that reason, though I am aware it is quite irregular, I think, if your Lordship will permit me, it will simplify matters if I at once produce such evidence as will satisfy your Lordship of the entire impossibility that her Grace could have been concerned in the murder."

"It certainly is most irregular, but perhaps it will be better if you do."

In rapid succession Mr. Tempest produced the publishers of the *Times* and the *Morning Post* of the day following the murder to prove the publication of the issues of their papers for that day, copies of which were produced. In each was an account of the dinner party her Grace had given on the previous evening to meet their Royal Highnesses the Prince and Princess of Wales. He then called Henry Ellis, the butler of her Grace, who gave evidence, that, being uncertain of some of the arrangements for that dinner party, he had been anxiously awaiting the return of the Duchess, who he understood, had been staying in the country. That he had expected her by an earlier train and had become very anxious and distinctly remembered that at half-past five she had not arrived. That she arrived almost immediately afterwards in a cab and told him her luggage was being sent direct from

Euston, and had then listened to the arrangements he had to suggest in connection with the dinner, and that he saw her at momentary intervals until she went upstairs to dress after seven o'clock. That it was quite impossible for her to have been elsewhere at any time between her arrival shortly after five-thirty and midnight on that evening.

The prisoner had removed the wig she had been wearing, showing a neat little head with her natural dark hair closely arranged. The last witness unhesitatingly identified her as his mistress, the Duchess of Merioneth.

At the request of the judge, Colonel Mauleverer, her cousin, also identified the prisoner as the Duchess.

Turning to counsel the judge said, "Of course, Mr. Tempest, the Crown if they are so disposed can again place her Grace on her trial in the House of Lords, but in the face of the evidence you have just produced, I think you may take it from me that this will not be done, and on your undertaking that the prisoner will not attempt to leave the jurisdiction of his Majesty's Court for the present, I do not think it will be necessary that she should remain in custody. I don't know whether the prosecution wish to raise any objection to that course?" the judge added.

On hearing to the contrary the Duchess bowed slightly to the judge and left the dock. The expression on her face had hardly changed. It was the same unseeing, unthinking indifference which had characterized her attitude during the whole of the trial.

"I wonder if it was worth it?" she said, as she shook hands with her counsel.

He saw her into a cab at the side door, and she drove away, the air already strident with the yellings of the newsboys: "Mauleverer Trial," "Sensational Ending," "*Alibi* of the Prisoner," "The Duchess Vivienne," "Duchess in the Dock." She wondered what it all meant. She hardly realized it all related to herself. She simply seemed to see nothing except the fat white hand of the judge, stretched out and groping along to grasp the black cap. Try as she would she did not—she could not—realize what the meaning of the day's events was to her. Herbert Mauleverer, her cousin, had been murdered. Well, she was sorry—he was a pleasant enough companion, but that was all. She couldn't break her heart over him—but what did it matter—what did anything matter? All she remembered, and like a wave it came tumbling back into her memory, was that afternoon but a few short weeks ago when she had plighted her faith and troth and trust to Jack Mauleverer—yes, he was really the only man she had ever loved. Poor Jack! and he was dead, too, and she was alive and had stood her trial for her life that day and yet it all seemed unreal, and she picked at the sable ribbons of her dress of deep mourning in a vain attempt to bring her thoughts back to actuality. Poor Jack! How she had enjoyed that afternoon! But at last everything came crowding back in her brain. She was the Duchess of Merioneth, and she was Vivienne Vane, and what would everybody say? Instinctively she turned cold all over, and she cowered as if she expected a physical storm to burst upon her there and then. Suppose Jack had lived to know? Suppose Jack did know, now? And at last the tense nerves snapped and the superhuman fortitude broke down. Had the game been worth it all? Oh, had it been worth it? and the scalding tears trickled slowly down her face as, with blind unseeing eyes, she gazed from the cab window on the old familiar streets. At last she sat up straight and the grip of the face came back, as she murmured to herself—

"I've played the game, I've played it twice over, I've had a right royal time, and now I've got to pay. Why should I squeal?"

In a few minutes the cab drew up at her door, and with all her old *insouciance* and fearless carriage, and with the sweeping trail of her skirt, by which society reporters often identified her, she walked up the steps to her door, and passed in as *debonaire*, as careless, and as young as when she had left it weeks before.

In the course of the next few days the Crown issued a formal pardon to the Duchess of Merioneth, under the name of Vivienne Vane, as was only to have been expected, in consequence of the evidence produced in court after her conviction. But the evident innocence of the Duchess in both her capacities of the murder of Herbert Mauleverer simply left the mystery doubly intensified. True, Webb remained under arrest for the murder of the Scotland Yard detective and the attempted murder of Anthony Mauleverer, but it was evident he could have had nothing to do with the other murders, and there were four to be accounted for. The proof of *alibi* by the Duchess seemed to have swept away at once every clue upon which the police and the detectives had worked. It was not merely a slip in the final step by a wrong identification, it was the crumbling of the whole edifice. As Yardley put it to himself: "It's a clean sweep, building and foundations together, and we've just got to start again from the very beginning. But——" and then his visit to the Bond Street milliner flashed across his mind, and he talked to Scotland Yard, and two days later the whole of Europe was scandalized and horrified by the rearrest of the Duchess of Merioneth—charged with the murder of Jack Mauleverer and his two brothers.

There were not wanting those who considered that, having been once tried for the murder of Herbert Mauleverer, it was an unnecessary refinement of cruelty to again put the Duchess at the peril of her life. It says much for the impartiality of English justice that such action was taken.

CHAPTER XII

THE public interest in the case, which had scarcely subsided, was again strung up to fever pitch, and so greatly was popular sympathy with the Duchess, that Colonel Mauleverer found it necessary for his own personal safety to issue a statement to the effect that the responsibility for the rearrest and prosecution rested entirely with the Crown. Portraits of the Duchess figured prominently in every illustrated paper which was published, and the *Daily Tale* netted no little advertisement and notoriety by making and publishing a collection of every known photograph which had been taken of her either as Duchess of Merioneth or as Vivienne Vane. It was at once noticed that every portrait in the latter character was in exact profile and in evening dress; every portrait as Duchess was full face, and taken in a hat, and, as was eventually disclosed in a very interesting Chancery suit, the copyright in the whole of the latter belonged to the Duchess herself. Public excitement over the case was intense. The whole of the kingdom divided itself into duchessites and anti-duchessites, though the latter were generally popularly bracketed with the Little-England anti-everything body.

The usual formalities of a State trial took place in their due and allotted course, and the Lord Chancellor, as Lord High Steward, and the other members of the House of Lords passed in procession to Westminster Hall on the morning of the day allotted to the trial. With damning eloquence and with a merciless logic, unholy in its scathing denunciation, the Solicitor-General, in his raucous voice and familiar nasal brogue, surely, step by step, and with seemingly infallible accuracy, built up the charge against the Duchess. Even Tempest—who was again, by the express wish of the Duchess, alone for the defence—shivered as he realized the impregnable indictment which had been created against his client. Dealing with the evidence he intended to produce, the Solicitor-General started with the first of the long series of murders—that of Captain Mauleverer in his quarters at Knightsbridge. He showed, on the evidence of the unfinished cheque, how Captain Mauleverer had been visited by a lady disguised as a Sister of Charity; evidently disguised, because the pose was proved to be false by the cheque given the Sister by Major de Crespigny being still uncashed. That had been asked for and obtained merely to give the pretending Sister an opportunity of diverting suspicion from herself by the announcement of intention not to call on Captain Mauleverer. Then, alluding to the handkerchief which had been found in Captain Mauleverer's chambers, counsel pointed out how the curious perfume clinging to it when it had been found had been identified as one which, in this country, was exclusively used by the Duchess of Merioneth. He told how he intended to produce evidence to show that the Duchess had purchased from a well-known firm of theatrical costumiers the dress of a Sister of Mercy, and had posed in that costume in a hospital scene for the benefit of a South African charity in some tableaux illustrative of Life in Mafeking during the Siege, which had been one of the great functions of the previous season. The sentries on duty would give evidence as to the arrival and departure of the Sister of Charity. Turning to the murder of Mr. Herbert Mauleverer, for which the prisoner had stood her trial and been convicted, the Solicitor-General, in spite of the vehement protests of Mr. Tempest, pointed out that she had been pardoned on evidence that had never stood the fire of cross-examination, and said he proposed to produce medical evidence that would go to prove it to be quite possible that the murder had been committed at an hour which made the appearance of the Duchess at her house in Park Lane no *alibi* at all. Then, piece by piece and strand by strand, he rewove around the prisoner the whole of the evidence upon which, as Vivienne Vane, she had been already convicted of the murder of Herbert Mauleverer. Unless the *alibi,* on the strength of which she had been pardoned, could be infinitely strengthened, the evidence which had been so damningly fatal at the previous trial was doubly intensified in its effect upon the present issue. Pointing to what all the world knew of—the subsequent engagement of the Duchess of Merioneth and Jack Mauleverer—he stated that this at once explained the allusion in the letter which had been found, at once made clear the reason of the murder of Herbert Mauleverer, the only obstacle standing in the way of the engagement; and the expressed opposition of Herbert Mauleverer was of course explained by the notorious fact that Mr. Jack Mauleverer had been for some time the devoted slave of the Duchess, and had, as was well known, constantly and repeatedly urged his cousin to marry him, and that her opposition was, of course, a consequence of the simple fact that Herbert Mauleverer had discovered the identity of Vivienne Vane and her Grace of Merioneth. In the light of these explanations, every fact that had been urged against Vivienne Vane in the former trial simply gained added force when pleaded against the Duchess as corroborative testimony in relation to the other murders.

Turning to the murder of Jack Mauleverer, counsel showed how the Duchess had dispatched a note summoning him to her the same evening, and that he was on his way to her in accordance with her summons, at what was certainly an unusual hour for a gentleman to call upon a lady, when he met his death.

"I cannot," said counsel, "prove the direct agency of the prisoner in the perpetration of this murder. I am inclined to infer the presence in this case of the hand of an agent or accomplice, but I do unhesitatingly allege the direct complicity of the Duchess in the murder of her betrothed. The fact that around the neck of the body was found the knotted cord, which is the one common point of all the murders, was proof positive of premeditation, of preparation, and of foreknowledge that murder was to be committed. Knotted cords do not make themselves, nor do dead men hang them around their own necks. The note was sent to Mr. Jack Mauleverer at the New Club in Grafton Street, and Lansdowne Passage was the most direct route therefrom to Park Lane. Now, who except only the Duchess could possibly know that he would be passing through Lansdowne Passage on that evening and at that hour, unless in collusion with the Duchess?"

Then, turning to the death of the younger brother at Oxford, counsel described how Henry Mauleverer, in response to a written invitation, had gone over to Merioneth House, one of the seats of the Duchess in the immediate vicinity of Oxford, on the afternoon of his death, dressed in his flannels; and how the two had played tennis in the afternoon; how, after tea, the Duchess had told the butler to cut some sandwiches for Mr. Mauleverer, and had pressed him against his inclination to take a flask of whisky with him, and had herself run up to her bedroom and fetched her own flask and held it whilst the butler filled it with whisky and water, and how the two had left the house together, walking in the direction of the river; how the post-mortem examination had proved that the death. was due to poison—strychnine—and not to drowning; and how the Duchess had not been present in the house for dinner, but had returned between nine and nine-thirty, and had explained her absence by saying she had fallen asleep in one of the rustic shelters of which there were several in the park.

Turning next to the attempts on the life of Anthony Mauleverer, counsel stated that the Duchess was, for an amateur, an expert and clever bicycle rider; he said he should prove that when in the country she always discarded the use of petticoats, wearing knickerbockers under her skirt, and a grey tweed cap, but that neither could now be found. The waist measurement of both knickerbockers and belt which had been found on the railway line, approximated closely to the ordinary measurements of the Duchess. Counsel pointed out that the attempts on the life of Anthony, as they had been carried out, were an absolute impossibility, except to someone intimately acquainted with the premises and the neighbourhood of Tibberton Mauleverer.

"That," said counsel, in low tones, but with telling emphasis, "was the original home of the Duchess, who, her parents being deceased, was, in her early life, before being sent to her convent school, brought up at Tibberton with the Mauleverer family. I admit I cannot account for her absence from the train when it was searched, if the theories put forward at the trial of Webb are correct. Her maid, who was on the train, has stated (and the Duchess has admitted the statement to be correct) that she had received express instructions to travel on that particular train, and to meet her Grace at Newark, where the latter intended to join the train at the conclusion of a visit she had been paying, unaccompanied by her maid, to a Mrs. Ellis. No doubt the intention was that after the attempt on the life of Anthony, the Duchess would change her clothes and present herself in *propria persona* to her maid on Newark platform. In the bustle and confusion of the arrival of a mail train, such an arrangement was very feasible. But the train did not stop at Newark, so the maid travelled to London alone"; and counsel could only suggest that the Duchess had managed to leave the train, on one or other of the two occasions in the journey when the train had been slowed down to a crawling speed because of adverse signals.

This was the evidence of fact which would be stated by various witnesses, and counsel addressed himself to the evidence of motive—which, as he remarked, was of all motives probably the strangest combination that could be conceived of several entirely separate motives, all converging upon and pointing to one common line of action, and therefore constituting one motive, and that of a degree and intensity amply sufficient to account not only for one murder, but for twenty.

"One was told in one's childhood," said counsel, "how one lie created the necessity of another, just as a pebble thrown into a pool created an ever-widening series of ripples till the limits of the pool were reached. So in this case—whether she intended it or not—whether indeed she contemplated the whole gamut of the crimes with which she is charged when she forged her first link in the chain, I cannot tell; I hesitate to think she did, but having taken that one first step, I believe she has been simply whirled along in a very maelstrom of events which, finally, she was utterly powerless to either check or control. The motive in the first murder was not apparent without a little investigation, and only came into the hands of the prosecution by accident. Captain Mauleverer happened to be one of the trustees of the marriage settlement of his cousin the Duchess. I don't pretend the Captain knew or cared or troubled one atom about business matters; as a matter of fact, the contrary was notorious. Goodness only knows why he was ever made a trustee: he couldn't add a column of figures correctly, he never knew or troubled enough about his legal affairs to 'come in out of the rain.' But he was wise enough to recognize his own incapacity, and to employ a remarkably clever firm of solicitors, Messrs. Downton and English, of Bedford Square. Unlike so many other firms of equal standing accustomed exclusively, like themselves, to dealing with the affairs of the upper classes," counsel remarked, "that firm deliberately eschews the fatal policy of *laisser faire*, and when a client places himself in their hands his interests are treated as if they were the personal affairs of the partners in the firm. When Captain Mauleverer put his affairs in their hands they acquainted themselves with his responsibilities, and not liking the manner in which his trusteeship had been conducted—as he said, 'I just signed what her lawyers asked me to'—commenced to make very thorough inquiries as to the whereabouts of the assets of the trust. If we succeed in putting him in the witness-box, one of the partners in the firm will presently have to explain in his evidence, which we have had vast difficulty to procure, that they had stumbled across and asked for an explanation of a certain matter, which explanation most certainly would at once have disclosed the double life of the Duchess, and a great deal more. Two days later Captain Mauleverer died, his trusteeship ceased, and that firm of solicitors have necessarily had no further interest in the affair.

"The murder of Herbert Mauleverer was necessary to close his mouth as to the identity of Vivienne Vane and the Duchess of Merioneth, and the hand of the Duchess was forced by Herbert Mauleverer's threat to disclose his discovery to his eldest brother. Whether or not Herbert Mauleverer had any suspicion of his cousin's connection with the murder of Captain Mauleverer must remain a matter of surmise, but it was by no means unlikely; in fact, the mere question of the disclosure of identity, if that were the only threat Herbert Mauleverer held over the head of his cousin, hardly seemed sufficient motive. A disclosure would have put an end to the marriage of his brother and the Duchess certainly, but the good name and good repute of his own family would have prevented a complete revelation which would disgrace his own relative so completely. But the death of Jack Mauleverer and Henry Mauleverer belong to another chapter in the mystery.

"The Duchess of Merioneth was reputed to be wealthy for even her ducal position. She enjoyed a jointure of £30,000 per annum from the Merioneth estates for life, and an additional £30,000 during widowhood, with the use and enjoyment of the several residential seats. As the only child of her deceased father, Lord Wendover, she had succeeded to property which produced an income of about £40,000. The Duchess has no family to provide for, the Merioneth seats and estates are kept up from other sources, the income she inherited from her father is invested in coal mines and railway shares. So that after her widowhood and after attaining her majority, events which occurred within the same twelve months, she had at her personal disposal some £100,000 per annum, absolutely uncharged and unencumbered. We have discovered amongst the papers of the Duchess a very methodically kept account-book, which discloses on her part no little business ability. Commencing within a few months of her widowhood, the accounts are entered up practically to the present date. These accounts have been placed in the hands of a firm of accountants, who have made the amazing discovery that of the £100,000 per annum placed to the credit of the Duchess, in the first year an aggregate of £50,000, in the next year £60,000, and so on, increasing each year up to last year, when it was £95,000, was paid by cheques for various amounts to one or other of ten names. The whole of the ten were recipients in the first year, the same ten are recipients in the last year. The fact, however, is plainly apparent that, during the last twelve months, of the £100,000 she nominally received, a sum of only £5000 remained for the personal use of her Grace.

"The Duchess of Merioneth is the best dressed woman in London, every newspaper says so; her establishments are not run on £5000 per annum, or anything like it; and Miss Vivienne Vane has been the most wildly extravagant young person of whom London has knowledge. It has been her exuberant extravagance which has so largely attracted attention to her in that personality. I need only remind your Lordships that she paid one thousand guineas for rent alone for a furnished house for a week simply that she might play a practical joke upon the Lord Bishop of Leominster. The rest of her extravagance has been on the same model. The real truth is, and was, that the Duchess of Merioneth is, vulgarly speaking, 'hard up,' and at her wit's end for money. For the last two years the remnant of her income cannot have kept up even her town establishment, and there can be no doubt she has been gradually getting deeper and deeper into debt."

Counsel paused, and a ringing laugh startled the House. Even in her peril the Duchess was amused.

"I am afraid the Duchess," said counsel, "must have forgotten her own figures. The curious point about this huge drain upon her income is, that it is difficult to account for, and we are absolutely at a loss to trace the money. There are certain possibilities. It may represent interest on mortgages. The objections to such a supposition are that none are registered, and mortgages on estates settled as are those at the enjoyment of the Duchess could only have been created by fraud, and could be so easily upset that the security for them is worthless. It also seems difficult to believe that mortgages to this extent should have been created whilst all the time property remained in the Duchess's hands in the form of railway stock at her absolute disposal, and the sale of which would have caused no comment. None of the shares have been realized. The payments may possibly be blackmail, and there are many events in the past life of the Duchess as to which she may well have been willing to purchase silence. But this drain commenced four to five years ago, and the aggregate paid away is enormous. A gang of criminals profiting by blackmail to this extent must infallibly have attracted the attention of the police. And yet the increasing sums and the rapid increase in the amounts of late seem astonishingly like blackmail. The curious point is, that we can get not the slightest clue as to the people who are receiving the money. There are ten accounts in as many banks in London into which these payments find their way. In no single case of those ten have the bank officials ever set eyes on their client. It turns out that each account has been opened through the post by a well-known firm of solicitors, writing from an address in Lincoln's Inn Fields, in favour of one or other of the ten names, and the copies of signatures to be honoured have been supplied by the solicitors. That firm, it now appears, have never had an address in Lincoln's Inn Fields. The banks appear to have been carefully chosen, for each one happens to be a bank which makes a practice of returning the cancelled cheques to its clients when the pass-books are made up. Now each account had been made up before we commenced our inquiries, and there is no single cheque in the hands of any one of the ten banks that we can subject to examination or use for comparison. The ten model signatures bear no resemblance. Since the first arrest of the Duchess and Vivienne Vane, no payment has been made into any one of the ten accounts. No cheque has been drawn against the accounts. We have, therefore, only the bank ledgers available. In each case the accounts seem to have been used in the ordinary way. There are payments of various amounts to various well-known firms, but there is one curious point about each, that at varying intervals a commissionaire or a District Messenger boy (or at any rate, persons in these uniforms) would arrive in a four-wheeler with a cheque for a considerable sum payable to bearer, which sum would be taken away in gold. Now sovereigns cannot be traced. The only payment of a sum to excite remark is a cheque drawn on one of the accounts to the order of 'Armstrong' for £25,000. That particular account had been accumulating. I suggest that that is a payment to Armstrong, Mitchell and Co., Limited, of Newcastle-on-Tyne. Naturally they decline to confirm our suspicions. Under the circumstances they could hardly do other. In each of the other nine accounts there is still a very large credit balance.

But we can gain no other clue from them to account for this drain upon the Duchess. The only certain fact is, that from her was extorted, or otherwise obtained, the greater part of her income, and that she must have been for the last two years heavily in debt. Now, where was she to obtain money from? Now it is necessary for me to digress. Colonel Mauleverer, as is well known, has recently inherited a large fortune. It was this inheritance which caused him to retire from the active pursuit of his profession and career in the army. Rumour places that income at £150,000 per annum, but Colonel Mauleverer informs me it is really between six hundred and seven hundred thousand pounds per annum. In this income he has only a life interest under the terms of the deed of settlement, it passing after his death to his sons in the usual form of remainder. The Tibberton Mauleverer estate had been resettled by the father of Colonel Mauleverer, in anticipation of Colonel Mauleverer's marriage, on Colonel Mauleverer and his issue, and then on the Colonel's brothers, both of whom were killed in action and were unmarried. That original deed of settlement had the usual final remainders to the heirs of the body of the grandfather of Colonel Mauleverer. Failing male issue, the next heir— in fact, the only other known descendant of the Mauleverer family until a much more remote period—is the granddaughter of Colonel Mauleverer's Aunt Elizabeth, who married Earl Town-

send—in other words, the heir is the Duchess of
Merioneth. The fortune to which Colonel Mauleverer has just succeeded it was known must eventually devolve upon his line, and consequently was
provided for, and was included in the deed of settlement. It is chiefly house property in London, let
on lease, and, until the last few years, producing a
comparatively small income. The motive now becomes clear," said counsel, "because only the lives
of Colonel Mauleverer and of Anthony Mauleverer
now stand between the Duchess of Merioneth and
an income of nearly £700,000 per annum. The
Duchess needed money. She first contemplated
obtaining that income by marrying the heir, Mr.
Jack Mauleverer, hence the length she was prepared to go to that her marriage should not
be prevented. Hence my positive assertion that
she murdered, or caused to be murdered, her cousin,
Herbert Mauleverer. It was the necessity of obtaining this income, and not affection, that placed
the Duchess in the wildly unnatural position of,
after having been first the mistress of Herbert
Mauleverer, having sought to become the wife of
his brother, Jack Mauleverer.

"That opens up the question of how her own income had become sequestrated to the disposal of
the ten people who apparently appropriated the
whole of it, for what purpose it was applied, and
why the Duchess wished to obtain the immediate
reversion of the Mauleverer fortune, instead of

waiting for it to pass to her use as the wife of Jack Mauleverer."

The Solicitor-General then repeated the evidence as already given at the previous trial, explaining how the wife of Colonel Mauleverer was the daughter of Admiral Hay, and the granddaughter of Sonia, professedly the elder daughter of Sir William Codrington, but really undoubtedly the daughter of Prince Ivan Soyonoff, ruling Prince of Moritania, the sons of Colonel Mauleverer being successively the right heirs of that sovereignty.

"Olga, the younger sister of Sonia, married Earl Townsend, by whom she had a large family. Of all her children only one son left issue. He eventually married Miss Elizabeth Mauleverer, the aunt of Colonel Mauleverer, and had an only child, Lady Abigail Townsend, who married Lord Wendover. Her only daughter is the Duchess of Merioneth. So we get this curious position, that the five Mauleverer brothers were the only descendants of Sonia, the elder sister, and the Duchess of Merioneth was the only descendant of Olga, the younger sister, so that if the five brothers could be removed, then the Duchess becomes the only descendant of Prince Ivan, and, as such, the true heir to the sovereignty of Moritania. Four of those brothers had already been removed. The life of the fifth had been attempted. Although the death of the fifth would not put the Duchess of Merioneth in possession of the Mauleverer property during the lifetime of Colonel Mauleverer, the death of Anthony would prevent the breaking of the entail and a resettlement, and as next in remainder, the Duchess could at once raise a large sum on the security of her reversion, an event which would synchronize with her becoming heiress, the very moment at which, as the then heir and claimant to the throne of Moritania, she would need a large sum of money for the revolutionary purpose she plainly had in view.

"There is yet another mystery to be found in the antecedents of the Duchess of Merioneth. I am sorry to have to rake up these scandals. Lady Abigail Townsend was born abroad, and spent the greater part of her life in Paris. Her English relatives saw little, if anything, of her. She was of age before either of her parents died, and after that time she continued to live in Paris. In the year 1867—that date is rather important—she returned to England, and during the next five or six years she appears to have occupied her time in this country. We find her renting various hunting and shooting boxes for brief periods, but she made no permanent home here. About 1873 she met Lord Wendover, and in the following year married him. A brief three years of most unhappy life followed, and then as every one knows, on at least two occasions Lord and Lady Wendover separated for short periods before the final separation. It was known that when she finally left him

Lady Wendover was expecting to have a child. From that moment her Mauleverer relatives lost sight of Lady Wendover. Three years later, as a result of negotiations conducted by Lord Wendover's solicitors, the expected child passed into his Lordship's custody, and all trace of Lady Wendover was lost. Colonel Mauleverer informs me that Lady Wendover is understood to have wandered about Algeria, Tunis, and Egypt, and in the year 1882 Lord Wendover sent to Colonel Mauleverer a brief note to the effect that his wife was dead. There is no doubt Lord Wendover knew the history of his wife's life during those years. Beyond a bare statement on one occasion to Colonel Mauleverer that his wife's life was entirely reputable, however, Lord Wendover kept that history to himself, and we have been unable to trace it with certainty.

"When his daughter, now the Duchess of Merioneth, was ten years of age, Lord Wendover died, his daughter became a ward in Chancery, and Colonel Mauleverer's father was appointed her guardian. As was only natural, she was removed to Tibberton Mauleverer, where the next few years of her life were spent. At the age of fourteen she was sent to a French convent school, where she remained for between two and three years. Meanwhile Colonel Mauleverer's father had died. Colonel Mauleverer was in India, and Tibberton Mauleverer was shut up. By her own suggestion

Miss Wendover, as she was then, remained in France, living with a French family. Colonel Mauleverer made inquiries about this family, and, to the best of the opportunities he had, satisfied himself that Miss Wendover was in good hands. In the summer of 1896 Miss Wendover, then nineteen years of age, wrote to Colonel Mauleverer, saying she wished to have other arrangements made for her home, as she was not comfortable. The Colonel, being just about to return home on furlough, cabled to Miss Wendover to procure a suitable companion and meet him at Port Said. She did so, afterwards proceeding to England, and again living for a brief space as a member of the Mauleverer family at Tibberton Mauleverer. She there met the Duke of Merioneth, who became infatuated with her beauty, and, in spite of being considerably her senior, married her, after a very short engagement, in the year 1897. The following year found the Duchess of age and a widow. That, my lords, in brief is the ostensible account of the life of the Duchess of Merioneth, to vouch for which there are scores of witnesses, chief amongst them being Colonel Mauleverer. Now, the Duchess of Merioneth has identified herself with Miss Vivienne Vane The Russian police have identified, and they believe accurately, Miss Vivienne Vane with Mademoiselle Sarcelle. Now, it seems almost incredible that one person should successfully personate three individualities, but I cannot do other than draw attention to certain facts which seem to fit that hypothesis. They may be only a curious series of coincidences after all, but they seem to dovetail into everything else too well to be lightly dismissed as coincidences and nothing more. In the year 1864 his late Majesty the Czar is believed to have contracted a morganatic marriage with a Mademoiselle Sarcelle. The lady, afterwards celebrated on the Parisian stage, was not then an actress. Who she was and where she came from, not even the Russian police ever discovered. All that was known was that she was a devout Roman Catholic, living a very retired life both before and after her marriage. Of the actual fact of the marriage no proof has come to hand, though the fact is generally accepted. In 1867 the connection between the two came to an end; there had been no issue thereof. The Czar was married to the present Dowager Empress. Here is the first coincidence. In the year 1867 Lady Abigail Townsend, a devout Catholic, came back to England. Mademoiselle Sarcelle is not heard of again until the spring of 1877, when she reappeared in Paris in company with the Czar. A month or two later she appeared on the stage, and in December of that year her daughter Vera was born. A little later on Vera Sarcelle was at that time stated to have been sent into the country to be nursed. She was then about two or three years old. It is difficult to obtain the exact dates, for neither the mother nor the child were then under the observation of the Russian police. Here is the second coincidence, for the Duchess of Merioneth went to live with her father, Lord Wendover, in 1880. Both Mademoiselle Sarcelle and Lady Wendover are reputed to have died in 1882. Miss Vera Sarcelle comes into notice and prominence as a Russian revolutionary in 1895, and was closely watched during that year and the following year. From 1894 to 1896 Miss Wendover was living as an inmate of a French family, according to Colonel Mauleverer's belief; but the Colonel now admits that Miss Wendover herself made the arrangements, merely appealing to him for sanction for her proposals. Colonel Mauleverer was in India, and instructed his solicitors to make inquiries about the family. He learnt that they were a family of the highest respectability. All his subsequent letters to Miss Wendover were addressed to her at some number in the same street as that in which that family was certainly living, but it was now quite impossible to ascertain whether this family lived at the particular number to which Colonel Mauleverer wrote. Colonel Mauleverer's solicitors have turned up their letter-books, and find they simply inquired as to the respectability or otherwise of a M. Huret, of the Rue de Passy, Paris, no number being specified, and the Colonel cannot now remember the number to which he was accustomed to write. Both M. and Madame Huret are now deceased, whilst their only daughter married some years ago and went to Brazil, and the Duchess professes entire ignorance of either her present name or address. M. Huret and his family appear from the Colonel's recollection to have travelled a good deal, and though Colonel Mauleverer always addressed his letters to the Rue de Passy, Miss Wendover's letters were seldom written from that address. In 1897 the Russian police lost sight of Vera Sarcelle, and though they believe her to be in England and know her revolutionary propaganda is being pushed with untiring energy, they cannot locate the lady, unless she is identical with Vivienne Vane, a lady nobody had heard of before 1897. The Duchess was married in 1897. In 1902 a battery of quick-firing guns, made by Armstrong, Mitchell & Co., was smuggled into Moritania by a firm of piano dealers, and I would remind you of the cheque for £25,000 paid in 1902 to Armstrong, to which I have already alluded. I submit, therefore, that there can be no doubt whatever that Pauline, Duchess of Merioneth, Vivienne Vane, and Vera Sarcelle are one and the same person. Now we have arrived at a point at which we come into contact with the underground history of revolution in Russia. Apparently the first idea of the Duchess must have been marriage with the true heir of Prince Ivan, and no more ideal figure-heads for a revolution could have existed—they might have been made to order—than Mr. Jack Mauleverer, a universal favourite in Russian society, a man of fascinating manners and appearance, the true heir to the Moritanian throne, with his wife, who was at one and the same time a descendant of Prince Ivan and a daughter of the Czar, and, as such, one who to many Moritanians would seem the true heir of the Czar. The ancient law of Moritania, like the law of Hungary and other countries, has no knowledge of his morganatic marriage.

"There can be little doubt, these things being known, that this was the end both the Duchess and her revolutionary committee in Moritania had in view. The principal member of that committee was Prince Kentchikoff. But man proposes, the devil disposes, and the consummation of that revolution needed money to be poured out like water. Two things happened. The Russian Government obtained knowledge of the dimensions and actuality of that movement, and sequestrated the estates and revenues of Prince Kentchikoff some twelve months ago. Almost at the same time the Moritanian committee joined hands with the Balkan revolutionaries, and the moment for action seemed to have come if the funds could be procured.

"Whether the Duchess disclosed her plans to Mr. Jack Mauleverer, and he refused, or whether it was thought the simpler plan to place the Mauleverer fortune at the disposal of the Duchess, so that she could raise funds upon the reversion, I am unaware. I think it quite possible Moritania, or perhaps her Balkan allies, may have thought that a woman would suit their purposes better than a man. The ways of Englishmen are rather straight for the Balkan politician. Anyhow, I assert that Jack Mauleverer was killed, not by the Duchess, but with her knowledge, and in her interests, Henry Mauleverer was murdered, and the life of Anthony Mauleverer has been thrice attempted.

But the crime has not been ordinary crime; it is not the crime for which precedent can be found in the criminal records of this kingdom. It is a high political game, involving issues of a magnitude to which we are unaccustomed. The way to thrones is through the shambles of either battle or assassination, sometimes of both. Her Grace of Merioneth was playing for a throne, throwing the dice with fate in a wild gamble for the Crown of Moritania and the ultimate reversion of the Empire of all the Russias. Only Russia and the Duchess know the point to which the balance tottered, or how near she was to gaining her end. The end justifies the means, and in success the shambles would have been overlooked. England as yet has made no extradition treaty with the Realm of Moritania. There would simply have been one other coronation at which no representative of this country would have been present."

At the close of the Solicitor-General's speech the House immediately adjourned. As the Duchess left her seat in the courteous custody of "Black

Rod," the change was plainly noticeable. Her impassiveness had vanished, to give place to poignant anxiety and an utter bewilderment. Tempest himself was no less surprised. With the identification of Vivienne Vane as the Duchess, he had concluded that any question of identity with Vera Sarcelle was absolutely at an end. He was previously entirely ignorant that the Duchess was next in remainder to the Mauleverer estates, and had not the slightest knowledge that the Duchess was a descendant of Prince Ivan. She herself denied being aware that she was doubly related to the Mauleverers, or that she was likely to inherit under the Mauleverer entail, or that she was a descendant of Prince Ivan. · Nor had she known anything of her mother's life. She was utterly bewildered, and Tempest was staggered by the case he had to meet.

The trial lasted more than a week, and every barrister who followed the case, either as it occurred in the House or as it was reported in the Press, marvelled at the ability with which Tempest fought each point and contested every inch. Finally, in sheer desperation, he put the Duchess in the witness-box, and told her to tell the whole history of her life, in her own way, as a prelude to his examination. In a low musical voice, and without a trace of hesitation, she did so. She described her early life at Wendover Manor with her father; she had no recollection whatever of her earlier life in Paris with her mother. Then she described the death of her father, her life at Tibberton Park with the Mauleverers, and then her school-life at the convent in France. Then she described how Amalie Huret had been her school companion and great friend, and how, as she knew Tibberton Park was then shut up, she had written to Colonel Mauleverer to suggest she should stay as a paying guest with the Huret family. She described her life in Paris, and travelling all over Europe with the Hurets, and emphatically and indignantly denied having during that time been aware that such a person as Vera Sarcelle existed. Then M. Huret died, and Madame became an invalid, and Amalie got engaged to the Brazilian she shortly afterwards married, and she had written to Colonel Mauleverer, and subsequently met him at Port Said, as the other side had said, and then returned with Colonel Mauleverer and three of his sons, Anthony, Henry and Herbert, to Tibberton Park.

She had there met the Duke of Merioneth, and flattered by his attentions and the prospect of becoming a Duchess, she had married him, only to bitterly repent it within a week of her wedding-day. Speaking slowly and impassionately, she said: "He was usually drunk; he was personally repulsive in all his habits; he was immoral and loathsome, and the £60,000 a year for which I had sold myself was dearly bought by the awful twelve months I passed as his wife. Soon after

I was married, in sheer devilment, in the hope of some little amusement and pleasure, I went to a fancy dress ball at Covent Garden. Beyond my costume, the only disguise I wore was a large wig of bronze-coloured hair, and I was perfectly astounded when, meeting my cousin, Herbert Mauleverer, he failed to recognize me. Doubtless with him, as with everybody else, the utter improbability of the Duchess of Merioneth and Vivienne Vane being the same person was in itself sufficient disguise. We had supper together, and I then realized what a charming companion my cousin was. He pressed me to meet him again, which I did, and I was, oh! so glad to get away from the loathsome creature I was married to. I don't profess that I was in love with Herbert, but I was glad to be with him as a relief from my husband. My husband brought not one but half a dozen mistresses to my house, and I felt no compunction on that score in letting things take their inevitable course in my relations with my cousin Herbert. Had I known I should be a widow so soon, I should probably have acted differently, but the Duke was only fifty-five, and I looked forward to twenty years of torture, which seemed to me a prospect of an eternity of pain, and I was tempted to seek distraction. No doubt it was the ease with which I managed to deceive Herbert as to who I really was, that led me to adopt the double life. I liked Herbert, but what chiefly appealed to me was the wild excitement I could obtain as Vivienne Vane which was wholly denied to me as Duchess of Merioneth. Consequently, I carefully laid my plans to avoid detection and to facilitate my double existence. So safe did I think myself that I took absolutely no precautions to safe-guard the reputation of Vivienne Vane; in fact, it seemed to me that the more notorious her reputation became the less chance there was of any identification. I hardly expect to be believed, but, except my cousin Herbert, no man can truthfully say I was ever more to him than a friend and a companion in escapades. I have known many men; they have been friends, intimate friends of mine, and companions in the fooling which has made Vivienne Vane so notorious, but that is all. That name has been joined with the names of many men. I have seen half a dozen in this house during my trial with whose names that of Vivienne Vane has been linked. They know as well as I do that what I say is correct. But I was always 'game' for any devilment that could be suggested. To make my movements easy, I took a small house at Ryhope, in Staffordshire, in the name of Mrs. Ellis, and I took a flat in Russell Square in the name of Vivienne Vane. But I always told my maid that Mrs. Ellis, who was an old friend of mine, only had a small house, and that I could take no servants. So it was easy to drive to Euston, have my luggage put in the train for Stafford, and start. Sometimes I really did go to Ryhope; at other times I merely changed at Willesden, came back to Euston, and drove to Russell Square as Vivienne Vane. Great stress has been laid upon the ten banking accounts. I ran them to prevent the possibility of being identified. I was the only person who drew on them. If you will hand me a piece of paper, a J-pen, a stylograph, and a quill pen, I will write you the ten signatures." This the Duchess did "I made a point of always writing with a quill pen as the Duchess of Merioneth, and with a stylograph as Vivienne Vane. The cheque to Armstrong's was for my share in a well-known racing yacht, which raced under the name of its ostensible owner. I had planned everything carefully, and things went on without a hitch for several years, till my cousin, Jack Mauleverer, began to pay attention to me as Duchess of Merioneth. I have no wish to hide the fact that I did fall passionately in love with him. Jack is the only person I have ever really loved. He asked me several times to marry him, but, knowing the life I had been leading with his brother, I refused him. But he was always badgering me, and," with a pathetic little smile the Duchess added, "it's a temptation to marry the man you love. One day I gave him an answer which, whilst not an acceptance, was not a refusal. I said I would think about it. Jack pressed me till I admitted I did love him. He was very delighted, and appeared to' think it was all settled, for I knew he told his father and his brothers. It was a strange fatality that a few days later my wig got caught and fell off, and Herbert Mauleverer at once recognized me. He was more upset than I expected. He wrote me saying that if I would give up Jack and leave England he would say nothing. I was then at Ryhope, and I determined to see Herbert and have it out with him. I wrote him the letter of which part has been produced. In that letter I told him I should come to Jermyn Street to see him. I travelled from Ryhope to Euston, and called at my flat for one of my wigs. I found Herbert there, and drove with him to Jermyn Street. There we had a long and bitter discussion. Jones is perfectly correct in his description of the interview as far as he knew. Herbert finally agreed he would not interfere. I left Jermyn Street without my wig (Herbert put it at the back of his bookshelves) at five-thirty, and drove to my own house. The evidence of my butler is absolutely correct. I never saw Herbert Mauleverer again. I know nothing about his murder. I know nothing about the murder of my cousin, Captain Mauleverer. I was never in his quarters, and I have not the ghost of an idea how my handkerchief was found there. I don't think it is one of mine. I had told Herbert I should not confess to Jack unless he asked me to marry him again. When he did again ask me to, Herbert was dead. He was the only one who knew, and at first, I am ashamed to say, I succumbed to the temptation and did not tell him. Afterwards I thought better of it, and one evening I sent a note to Jack asking him to come and see me. You have the note, and you will see I wrote: 'I have something serious to tell you, so come at once.' I gave the note to my maid to send off. That was the ending. He never came, and I know nothing of his murder. I know nothing of the attempts on the life of my cousin Anthony.

"My cousin Henry was very much upset by the death of his brother, Captain Mauleverer, and, knowing this, I did what I could to try to cheer him up. I sent him a note one day, and asked him to come over and have an afternoon's tennis at Merioneth House, which is about five miles above Oxford. The poor boy came, sculling up from Oxford, and we stayed on playing for a bit, and having tea and talking. Until it was too late, I quite expected I should persuade him to stay to dinner, but—I think it was about seven o'clock—he insisted on going. He told me he had an appointment which he could only just manage to keep. I asked him how he would arrange about dinner, and as he seemed to think it quite needless to trouble about a meal, I had some sandwiches cut and lent him my own travelling flask. Then I walked with him to the river to where his boat was tied up, and I saw him start, and I never saw him again alive. With regard to the evidence of my maid as to the arrangement I had made to meet her at Newark,

I had been visiting in Yorkshire, and as I was changing my housekeeper at Ryhope, I went there. My maid has relatives in Yorkshire, and I told her she could visit them for a few days, and meet me at Newark on the mail train on the night of the 30th, and return with me to London. She did so. Unfortunately I had left Ryhope early in the day, intending to break my journey so that I could try some horses I was buying from one of my tenants near Stafford, but I found the trains wouldn't fit, so I waited in Stafford instead, and then travelled to London by L. and N.W. route; but I changed my mind, and went to my flat in Russell Square, posting at Stafford a telegram to be sent from Ryhope that I was not returning for two or three days. No doubt this may have excited my maid's suspicions. I did not know until I heard it in court on the opening day that I stood a chance of inheriting the Mauleverer money, though I dare say it is quite correct, as I know I am now their nearest relative; but really I have plenty of money of my own. My income is not charged in any way, and I find I have nearly £150,000 to the credit of one or more of my banking accounts. As to my descent from Prince Ivan, I really could not have told you with any certainty what my great-grandmother's name was, but I have heard of Olga, Countess Townsend, if she is the lady who has been referred to. I have always supposed that I was the daughter of Lord Wendover.

I have lived with him as his daughter. I may be
really the daughter of the late Czar; how am I
to know? I have no recollection of my mother,
and really know nothing about her; but this I do
know, that I am not Vera Sarcelle, and I certainly
have never been mixed up in any way with any
Russian revolutionary affairs. I know nothing of
Russian politics except from novels. I have visited
Moritania certainly, but merely as a guest of Countess Sassulevitch, who is a lady I was at school with
in Paris. I have one or two other Russian friends,
and as Vivienne Vane I had several Russian ad-
mirers. His Excellency did me that honour, I
remember," she added, with a dry but wan little
smile towards the Russian Ambassador, who was
present in the House. "My Mauleverer cousins
were the only relatives I had in the world, and it
is almost the cruellest part of all my troubles that
Colonel Mauleverer or Anthony should think it
possible I had anything to do with the murder of
the others. One's chickens come home to roost
with a vengeance. I have always so carefully
planned my arrangements to avoid identification
that I admit there is no single point in the account
the Solicitor-General has recited that I can put my
finger on and say, 'I can prove I was not there.'
All I can say, my lords, on my honour as a peeress
and as the promised wife of my cousin, Jack Mauleverer, whom I loved passionately, is, that neither
in thought nor in deed have I done or wished any

one of them ill. We were all brought up together, and I was very fond of them all, as I think they all were of me."

A scathing cross-examination followed by an adept at the art, who had been specially briefed for that purpose. So brutal were some of the questions which were asked that some of the peers made angry remonstrance. Young Lord Wendover vigorously denounced what he termed the "brutally abominable" method which was being pursued. "We are gentlemen in this House, and are not accustomed to the beastlinesses of the police courts." The Lord High Steward called him to order. Flaming with indignation, he reminded the Lord Steward that the House only could call him to order, and he promptly challenged a division on his motion that the cross-examination should cease. The motion was lost by a single vote. Noticing that the Bishop of Leominster had recorded his vote, Lord Wendover again rose. A well-known member of the "Union," he was a polished speaker and a brilliant debater, and for the next ten minutes, with cutting sarcasm and pointed invective, he voiced a very general consensus of opinion as to the propriety of the Bishop in the House. Identified with no political party—in fact, unknown to the majority of the House—the young peer was unhampered by considerations which must have deterred many more prominent men, and the Bishop suffered in consequence. "Her Grace, the Duchess of Merioneth," Lord Wendover concluded, "has said she has no relatives. The blood relationship between us is so remote that, when she has denied it, I am not justified in claiming connection; but I bear a name which formerly was hers, and I will not sit calmly and hear her 'baited' by a man who has no claim to admittance amongst the rank in which she was born, and to which she still belongs."

Though the motion had been lost, the hint was taken and the cross-examination ceased; but through it all the Duchess never flinched, and no point had been thereby gained against her. Steadily denying any knowledge, answering every question without hesitation, her manner carried a conviction of innocence to many. But at length the long-drawn-out trial came to an end. There could be but one result, and sentence of the extreme penalty of the law was passed in a solemn hush, made vividly and doubly impressive by all the quaint formality and ceremonial with which it was surrounded. "Oh, thank God it's over! I could not have stood much more," had been the only comment of the Duchess. There had been many peeresses present, and most were in tears. The short winter afternoon had closed in, and the gaslights flickered in the draughts, as the building slowly emptied. The Lord High Steward broke his wand across his knee and left, followed by most of the officials, but still the Duchess sat gazing straight before her. Her face was by now haggard and weary, yet still beautiful in every line. Without a sign of movement she sat until the Sergeant-at-Arms gently touched her, and asked her to follow him. As she passed Ashley Tempest she stopped, and taking both his hands in hers she pressed them.

"Don't be disappointed," she said; "you've done all that was possible. I've had my fun, and now I've got to pay."

Tempest could not speak. Raising her hands to his lips he let them fall, and she passed on with the wonderful carriage he knew so well.

CHAPTER XIII

PASSING through the lobby he met Lord Wendover.

"I suppose you are going to petition, Mr. Tempest?"

The man's lips were trembling, and a lump was in his throat, as in a voice quite out of his own control he answered—

"Certainly a petition will be sent in. I'm just going to see her solicitors, but petitions matter so little, and the time will be so short, and I've got to prove her innocence. She had nothing to do with it whatever, from beginning to end. And there must be something wrong with our law when she can be convicted twice over as she has been."

"I know, I know," agreed Lord Wendover. "I want to help: what can I do?" said the young peer. "I suppose you don't want money in this case, do you?"

"No; we haven't been hampered that way."

The strain had told fearfully on Tempest. For the second time an innocent client whom he had defended had been convicted, and the man's pride in his profession and his confidence had collapsed. He was forty-four years old, though as a rule he looked a full decade younger, but his hair had turned grey in the last few weeks, and as he spoke he might well have passed for sixty-five. As the two men walked side by side out of the building and turned up Whitehall, Tempest broke down and clutched at Lord Wendover for support. Without a word the latter whistled for a hansom, drove straight to Harris's, the chemists in the Haymarket, and quickly explaining matters, dosed Tempest with a strong pick-me-up, which pulled him together. Going straight from there to White's Club, he refused to discuss matters, but stood over him and literally forced him to eat. It was the first meal Tempest had had for nearly forty-eight hours. Passing cigars across the table, Lord Wendover suggested that they should go into the open air and talk things over. A hansom quickly dropped them at the entrance of Hyde Park, and Lord Wendover unfolded his plans.

"We've got to find out the truth, but that will take time, and to get time we must have a reprieve. A big petition ought to get that, and I suggest you leave that part to me. As to the other part, what do you suggest?"

"Well," replied Tempest, "I've been thinking. I'm going to try myself, but I want somebody used to detective work as well. I think I'm going to try Dennis Yardley."

"But he's on the other side."

"Quite so; but he's done his work, and got his

conviction. If he can now find out the true solution it will be the biggest thing he has ever done. Money is a big inducement to him, and he knows already every in and out of the whole business. He is abreast of it. It would take a new man some time to get level with all the facts, and time is all-important. Yardley knows them."

"You're right," said Lord Wendover.

The two men parted, Lord Wendover driving to the *Daily Tale* office in Melcarite Street. Asking to see Sir Frederic Badsworth, he was lucky enough to ascertain that the Baronet happened to be on the premises, and eventually was shown into his room. Prefacing the conversation by asking if he could have the front page of the *Daily Tale* on the following day, and learning this could be arranged at a price, Lord Wendover sat down deliberately to talk Sir Frederic Badsworth round to his view of the case. He met with less difficulty than he had anticipated. The romantic aspect appealed to the journalistic sense of the clever newspaper proprietor—his personal sympathies were with the Duchess—and in a short time the two men were planning out one of the biggest newspaper campaigns that has ever been launched. Calling Mr. Barlowe and Mr. Hildred into their counsel, a list of the daily papers was made and divided into two classes—those that could be bought and those that could not. Then the telephoning began from every instrument in the office. The former class of papers were each given a full page advertisement, on condition they adopted editorially the standpoint of the absolute innocence of the Duchess, and undertook to retain that attitude in constant editorial and other articles so long as the subject remained of popular interest. To the latter class—some half-dozen in all—Sir Alfred telephoned personally, getting into communication with the responsible editor in each case, and asking how they proposed to treat the trial. Four were for the Duchess, and the advertisement was given them "for sweetening purposes," as Barlowe remarked. The other two were huffy, and were left alone. Though it may be worthy of comment that the chief advertisement canvasser in each case called on Lord Wendover the next morning. The advertisement that was given to each paper was simply a copy of the petition for a reprieve, with blank spaces for signature, to be filled up and sent to Lord Wendover, who that night spent a year's income, and would have been fleeced of three, but for the knowledge and assistance of Sir Frederic Badsworth. Once committed to a particular line, the consummate genius of Sir Frederic carried the public excitement to a wild fever-heat, and the signatures to the petition for the beautiful Duchess, whose portrait occupied the whole of the magazine page, in a couple of days had far outnumbered the record petition of the old days of the Chartists. Entering into the spirit of the thing, the lust of journalism and

sensationalism carried Sir Frederic to the fullest
tether that the enormous advantage of the chief
proprietorship of more than thirty journals gave
him.   He, as an old hand at journalism, knew that
"effect" is cumulative.   Taking the control out
of the hands of Lord Wendover, he cleverly engineered it; and as each post brought in the signatures, these—five thousand at a time—were
despatched alternately to the Home Secretary at
his private address and to Lord Knollys.   Day by
day the figures were telephoned round to the press,
and the excitement increased rather than dimin-
ished.   The journalist was "in" the game, and,
declining to take any further payment, the form of
the petition and the spaces for signature appeared
day by day in the *Daily Tale* and other journals
under his control.   Applying his personal influence,
Sir Frederic induced many of the other daily and
evening papers to follow his example.   The result
was that nearly 3,000,000 people signed the petition, and the Home Secretary's butler made nearly £50 by the sale of waste paper.   It was not the
first time that the *Daily Tale* had interfered in the
course of so-called justice.

Telephoning to Yardley, Tempest had met him
an hour after leaving Lord Wendover.   Yardley
at once agreed to join forces with Tempest.   His
professional services were on the market.   If the
Duchess were the real criminal, then his engagement with Colonel Mauleverer had automatically

ceased. If she were not, then all the more reason, in Colonel Mauleverer's interests, that he should pursue the matter further, and to the right end. He would be earning payment from both sources.

"You are sure the Colonel won't object?"

"Lord love a duck! he'd only be too glad, for he doesn't half like the conviction of the Duchess; for, in spite of the evidence, he doesn't believe the Duchess herself is guilty."

The two men were sitting in Tempest's Chambers in New Square, Lincoln's Inn, a week later, and far into the night they sat and talked.

"Has it ever struck you, Yardley, that if the Duchess is not guilty, Anthony Mauleverer is in as big a risk as ever?"

"Yes; but all that's provided against, as far as my wits can suggest—and they go a long way."

"Well, as I've said before, if those murders were done in order to obtain a *future* object, there would have been no mark to identify them as the work of a gang, or to give the slightest clue. But there still remains Anthony to be killed, and unless the murders *are in themselves the object to be obtained,* there would have been no knotted cord. The murders *are* the object and the end of some episode. In all the theories which have been built up round the Duchess, the murders are never the end, but always a preliminary to something else. That is where they are wrong. I tell you I am as certain as I am sitting here that the murders mark the *end* of some episode, and that the cord in each case is as it were a notch cut in a stick—so much of the end accomplished. It is an advertisement of that end, and a challenge to somebody of a fact accomplished; and there is nobody but Colonel Mauleverer that it can be a notice to. The boys had no other relatives than the Colonel and the Duchess."

"I've asked the Colonel that very question, and he denies all possibility."

At that moment a District Messenger boy brought a note addressed to Tempest. He read it twice, and passed it to Yardley. The note was curious, and without address or signature.

"If Mr. Tempest wishes to benefit the Duchess of Merioneth he will accompany the bearer of this note. The writer relies on Mr. Tempest to act on his honour as a man, but makes no other stipulation, although vast interests are jeopardized by this present action."

"I'm going," Tempest said; "you'd better come as well."

Hastily putting on an overcoat and hat, Tempest went out, and Yardley followed. At the side gate in Chancery Lane they found a hansom waiting. The messenger boy who accompanied them emphatically declined to answer questions, adding that he had been instructed to say that Mr. Tempest could come or stay away, as he pleased, but if he came he must do as he was requested, and ask no questions. The cab turned into the Tottenham Court Road, and stopped at a well-known night club in Percy Street. Leaving Tempest and Yardley in the cab, the messenger entered the club, and soon emerged, accompanied by a powerful man well over six feet in height—broad in proportion, and plainly a pugilist by profession. He spoke with a foreign accent, and at once demurred to Yardley accompanying them.

"I was," he said, "to accept Mr. Tempest's mere word, but that doesn't include a —— detective."

Tempest solved the difficulty. "I don't suppose I am wanted here. I expect you are to take me somewhere else. Suppose you introduce us here, and put some friend of yours to watch us whilst you take a note for me, and then come back."

The suggestion evidently appealed to the foreigner, who agreed to do as Tempest asked.

Hastily writing a note, explaining that Yardley had no connection with the police, but was heavily paid to work in the interests of the Duchess, Tempest undertook on his personal honour that Yardley would act in no way except under his directions.

In the course of an hour and a half the messenger returned, accompanied by a companion of even brawnier proportions than himself, but apparently quite unable to speak a word of English. The carriage in which he returned was a well-appointed pair-horse brougham, and Yardley's quick eyes noticed a coronet on the panels. The four men took their places in it, and were quickly driven to one of the largest houses in Cromwell Road. At that hour of the night the streets were quite deserted, but when the carriage stopped it was evident their arrival was awaited, for the whole house was brilliantly lighted. The doors were flung open by liveried servants with powdered hair, and Tempest and Yardley were ushered into a room on the ground floor. They waited some little time, until at last a footman entered and said that "Madame la Comtesse" desired their presence upstairs. Bewilderment plainly written on their faces, they followed the servant to the next floor, and through the drawing-room to a small boudoir beyond. As they entered the room, a girl half rose from a couch to welcome them and motion them to be seated. Tempest gasped for breath, and his heart thumped with sickening thuds as he fought to master his astonishment. To all appearance it was Vivienne Vane, or, save for the flaming red hair, the Duchess of Merioneth herself, in whose presence they were. The Countess, who understood, smiled at the man's surprise and embarrassment.

"So you recognize the likeness, Mr. Tempest. Who do you think I am?" The man hesitated, and she continued: "I'm the Comtesse Varigny, but I don't suppose that helps you much. I suppose you will only have heard of me as Vera Sarcelle. I know you English always doubt a foreign title, but I'm not masquerading. I am really Vera Sarcelle, and I am really Comtesse Varigny. Perhaps I had better explain that, in order to help me to avoid the espionage of the Russian Secret Police, who are very far from being really under the control of the Emperor, my father had a dated patent drawn out for me, in which the names were all left blank. These he filled up with his own hand, and gave the patent to me. The blank patent is registered in Russia, so that I or my descendants can claim recognition when it suits me, but when I disappeared from Paris I dropped the name of Vera Sarcelle, and I reappeared under my title in England, and I have so far managed to evade recognition. I tell you this because I must impress upon you that the Russian Secret Police do *not* know my identity, and there are many reasons why they should not. I am putting myself in your hands by telling you. It will surprise you, I have no doubt, but my father hated the way all power in Russia has passed into the hands of the police. He made many attempts to alter it, but whatever he did he was always checkmated, and it was plainly shown to him that he was only allowed to rule on sufferance. His life was always in danger. But I expect you know Russian Court history. My father knew and sympathized with all I was doing, and he was very jealous of the different life and the freedom the English Royal Family enjoyed. But his hands were tied. All my so-called revolutionary actions were really done with his full knowledge and approval, with the intention of making for him the opportunity for a *coup d'état,* by which he could upset the present régime. Force has to be met by force, and I was trying to forge a power and create a force that he could use, to initiate a constitutional government equal to the power which sustains the arrangements he hated. That was why I managed to do so much in his lifetime; but our plans got known, and as anybody in Russia can tell you, my father was slowly poisoned. Now I am playing for my own hand and for Russia, and there is a big reckoning to be made. My brother is a fool, or I would have worked for him."

"Then you are really Vera Sarcelle?"

"I am. You"—turning to Yardley—"find it necessary to know things, I suppose. You know there is such a person as the Comtesse Varigny living at this address?"

Taking a key from her bracelet, the Countess opened a bureau and showed them the Letters Patent creating "my dearly loved daughter, known at present by the name of Vera Sarcelle, and presently residing in Paris, to be Countess Varigny in the Empire of Russia."

Again seating herself after locking up the patent, she asked Tempest—

"Will you, as a barrister, and as the counsel for the Duchess, tell me plainly, please, how far the verdict against her was due to her identification as Vera Sarcelle?"

"It is difficult to say exactly," he answered, after a pause. "It's almost impossible to estimate, but there is no doubt that it went a long way, because it clinched up so many divergent possibilities which otherwise were in opposition, and by which divergence she ought to have benefited; and it seemed to prove motive. Besides, an English jury will believe any crime to be possible when you hint anything about a Russian Nihilist."

The Countess laughed merrily. "The English public needs educating badly about Russian politics. They think there are only two forces at work in Russia, the Czar and the Nihilists. I wonder when they will recognize that the Nihilists are a small body of utter outcasts, every man's hand against them, their hands against every one. Suppose you in England were to class everybody who didn't belong to the Primrose League as a Nihilist. But we are not here to discuss Russian politics. As for me, I don't believe the Duchess is guilty. Now, will it help her if I come forward as Vera Sarcelle? Will it get her liberated?"

Tempest thought for some moments. "Candidly, I don't think it would obtain her liberty right away, but if you are prepared to do that, it throws doubt on the evidence on which she was convicted, because nobody could say how far the verdict was a consequence of the identification. They can't put her on her trial again. They would be bound to reprieve her, particularly if we left it to the last moment, and there is an invariable rule that a prisoner once reprieved shall never suffer the extreme penalty. That gives us, if necessary, her natural lifetime, during which we may hope to establish her innocence."

"Then you may make arrangements to that end. All I ask is that my identity is not divulged except to the Home Secretary personally. And, Mr. Tempest, please remember that my future comfort is at your mercy. If you can do without me I shall be the better pleased."

Tempest at once applied for an interview with the Home Secretary. No doubt the reason for which it was desired was anticipated, for he received the usual stereotyped regret that the Home Secretary was unable to grant his request. Tempest merely said "Damn" as he threw down the letter, but the Home Secretary, when he returned that evening to Mount Street from the House of Commons soon after midnight, was greeted by a figure which was seated on his doorstep with the remark—

"Look here, old man, why the plague don't you keep decent hours?"

The two had been at University College together and had been fast friends, but it had needed a very extraordinary inducement before Tempest

had presumed upon the acquaintance for professional reasons.

"Good God!" was the Home Secretary's reply.
"What on earth are you here for?"

"I've come to beg a whisky-and-soda."

"Why don't you go to your club—it's near
enough—or any other beastly pub? Look here,
Tempest, if you've come to talk about the Duchess's trial, it's no good. Friendship's one thing,
shop's another, and I'm not going to have them
mixed up."

"All right, old man; but I want that whisky-and-
soda."

"Oh, come in, then," said the other, ungraciously.

Tempest coolly divested himself of hat and coat
and passed into the library with the Home Secretary. The two men sat in easy chairs on either side
of the fire, and talked in a desultory manner about
any subject in the world but the one Tempest had
come about. At last Tempest came to the point.

"You've got to reprieve that woman."

"I told you I would not discuss that subject on
a private footing."

"I can't help it. You didn't suppose I sat on
your blessed doorstep for two hours for fun, did
you? You must listen to what I've got to say for
the simple reason I daren't tell you officially."

"Then I can't act on it."

"Yes you can. Just listen to me," and without
waiting for further comment or consent, Tempest

told the Home Secretary the history of his visit to the Countess Varigny.

As the story progressed the Minister dropped his cigarette, and slowly sat erect, his hands tightly gripping the arms of his chair, his eyes wide open with amazement.

Tempest concluded, "You see, I couldn't tell you officially and have the thing minuted backwards and forwards and initialled and countersigned till every clerk and messenger in the Home Office knew all about it."

"We don't work that way."

"H'm. Well, I wasn't going to take the risk."

For several minutes neither spoke, then the Home Secretary broke silence.

"I expect you wondered why I wouldn't see you. But, Tempest, you know as well as I do there have been all sorts of undercurrents in that curious trial. I'm not talking for publication, but *you* may as well know—it's not to go any further at present. The Duchess is going to be reprieved. Knollys wrote to me to-day that the King, at the earnest request of the Russian Ambassador—that means the Czar, of course—had consented to a reprieve if he could be advised it would be in the interests of justice. I told the Duchess myself to-night. She's still in custody in the Clock Tower. But the amazing thing is she is going to be reprieved because she is Vera Sarcelle, and now you come and want her reprieved for the one single reason that she isn't that person, and I and a good many others have been none too certain there ever was such a lady. Oh, yes, she'll be reprieved sure enough; but what puzzles me is what reason we are to publish. We can't give Russian intervention as the reason. Good Lord! just think of the *Daily News* on that for a text! And just as certainly we can't give your reason; think of Swift McNeill in the House. If you can imagine any decent and plausble lie that will do for the papers you'd better let me know it. The best I can think of so far is to put the reprieve down to the tenderheartedness of the Queen, and say she interceded. That would be a popular kind of cry. But, Tempest, if you love me, do for Goodness' sake choke off that Badsworth man and his petitions. Tell him I'll postpone his peerage till the next time we're in Office—and I'm sure I don't know when that will be—if he doesn't drop them."

The two men parted, and Tempest went whistling down the street. He felt as if a mountain of nightmare had slipped away. His chief point was gained; for, given time, he was confident that sooner or later he could prove that the Duchess had had neither part nor lot in any of the murders. For the first time for weeks he slept soundly through the night. It was late when he woke; and, when he left his bedroom, he found Yardley waiting, busily occupied in keeping his breakfast warm for him. Without giving any details, Tempest told him in confidence that it was settled that the Duchess was to be reprieved, the sentence being commuted to penal servitude for life.

"She'll go into hospital at first, and they suggest she should be trained as one of the nurses. Things will be made as easy for her as they can manage, and they can do a good deal. Russia wants her extradited; but, of course, that's impossible—luckily for her."

Tempest, whatever the Home Secretary might have said, was by no means ungrateful for the assistance they had received from the *Daily Tale,* and when the time came for public notification, he carefully engineered matters so that the information was "exclusive" to that paper twenty-four hours before the official announcement was circulated through the usual channel.

"Tempest," said the Home Secretary, when they met a week later, "of course it was your doing that that halfpenny rag got out with it a day before any other paper. Why did you do it? It's putting a premium on newspaper interference with the course of justice. The public will believe the *Daily Tale* pulled the wires and were responsible for the reprieve, and it's bad for that sort of idea to get about. It's a bad precedent, and it lowers the prestige of the King's prerogative."

"Quite so; but it's only reciprocity, your pet word in the Cabinet. Beyond what we have paid for, there is a huge advertisement bill we owe in

Carmelite Street, which has not been sent in to us, and which I dare say never will be. I'm not Cecil Rhodes or Cruden's Concordance, but there's a text somewhere in the Bible about doing unto others as they do unto you, or something of that kind. Don't you be too precious keen on what the public think. That's the worst of the present Government. They are getting almost as sensitive as the Radicals to popular ebullitions of feeling."

Chapter XIV

TEMPEST and Yardley drew opposing conclusions from much of the evidence; but the production of Vera Sarcelle, they both agreed, put an end once and for all to any Russian connection between the Duchess and the crime. Tempest insisted that it wiped out every Russian trace; Yardley, remembering Jack Mauleverer's attaché-ship, was by no means equally positive. But they were on common ground in agreeing that they must go back to the actual material facts composing the evidence and eschew "high falutin" theory, as Tempest stigmatized it.

Tempest resumed: "There are certain facts which are beyond dispute. In each case there is the knotted cord; then we get the half-written cheque, the scented handkerchief, the clothes from the train, the certainty that whoever attempted Anthony's life was on the second train from York for the whole or a part of the journey. The clothes may possibly be a blind; they have been that, for they have practically been traced to the Duchess, though I doubt if that was intended. *A priori,* she was too "unlikely" for any one, after premeditation, to trouble to throw suspicion in her direction. If she had ever worn those clothes as Vivienne Vane, there might be a different conclusion possible. Then there's another fact—we've got to find some one who is an expert revolver shot, an expert bicyclist, and a more than average athlete. The Duchess is a good bicyclist, but she's not an athlete, and she tells me she has never fired a revolver in her life. Those dogs needed some shooting at Tibberton. If the clothes are not a blind, then we are fairly certain that a woman was taking part. So we want a woman who is an athlete, a bicyclist, an expert revolver shot, and a woman with a grievance against Colonel Mauleverer."

The next step forward was a letter from the rolling stock Superintendent at King's Cross. Would Mr. Yardley or Mr. Tempest call on him?

Yardley, when shown into the office, was briefly made acquainted with the fact that one of the cleaners had noticed that a cushion from a first-class carriage had several hard lumps, and a minute examination had shown that one of the seams of the cushion had been undone for about twelve inches, and subsequently resewn. Whilst the seam had originally been machine-sewn, a space of about twelve inches was noticed, when examined, to be oversewn from the outside. The cushion had then been opened and a pair of shoes found inside it. A reference to the records of the making-up of trains had shown that that particular coach had formed a part of the second train from York, after the attempt on the life of Anthony. Yardley carefully examined the shoes. They were of canvas, with india rubber soles, much worn and covered with mud. There could be no question, from the style, size, and shape, that they were a lady's pair of shoes. That clinched the fact that the person they were looking for was a woman. The shoes bore the name of the makers—the North British Rubber Co., Ltd., of Leeds. But inquiry in that quarter proved the pattern to be a stock one, of which, even in that particular size, some ten to fifteen thousand pairs were sold each season. There were no other marks by which the retail tradesman could be traced. In the cushion and together with the shoes was found a knotted cord, clearly a ready-made noose. There remained no doubt, therefore, that that pair of shoes had been worn on the eventful night at Tibberton; but here, once again, they had run up against a blank wall.

"Did you ever think of trying to trace the bicycle, Yardley?" asked Tempest, the next time the two met. "You had it in court."

"Oh, yes, that is a regular stock police line of investigation; it was one of the first things they tried. But they couldn't get any forrarder."

"Why not? I thought all bicycles were numbered."

"So most of them are—all the good makes; but there's rather a fad amongst some people to have their own bicycles 'made up.' Don't dressmakers advertise, 'Customers' own materials made up'? Well, there are a lot of bicycles made that way. A man will buy a set of B.S.A. fittings; then he thinks he can only ride with some fancy-shaped handles, and he has his own particular weakness in tyres and lamps and gears, and he either buys the parts himself and sends them to one of these local bicycle shops to be made up, or else he draws out a specification and has a machine built by one of these small men in accordance with that. Well, that kind of bicycle never gets numbered; and besides, even if it were, what's the good of a number unless you can apply to the maker to trace it?"

"True. Is there room for these specifications to vary much?"

"Why, it's like trying to identify thumb-marks that have never been classified. It's a game of permutations and combinations."

"Yardley, we'll advertise that specification, and offer a big reward for the maker."

It was a simple matter to get hold of an expert bicycle agent to draw up a detailed and exact specification of the machine which had been produced in court. As the two men watched him carefully measuring each part, gauging sizes, and noting patterns, they wondered at the intricacies involved.

Tempest asked if the machine were an old one.

"No; you see that," he said, pointing to a certain

part of the mechanism; "that particular pattern was only brought out in 1901, in the spring. Well, it would want two or three months to get known and talked about, even amongst those who watch the changes in the cycle world closely. Unless that part has been added since in repairs, this machine has been made since the summer of 1901."

"Well, it seems to have had a lot of wear."

"Oh, I don't know;" and glancing at the cyclometer, which registered exactly 1794 miles, he added: "I should guess the cyclometer is about the same age as the bicycle, and has been running on from then without alteration. But the tyres are new. They haven't gone fifty miles."

Within the next three or four days a prominent advertisement appeared throughout the press offering a reward of £100 for the maker of a bicycle built in 1901, or since that date, to the specification which was annexed.

A few days brought amongst many purposeless letters two others which seemed to be what Tempest and Yardley needed. One was from a small bicycle-repairing establishment in Leeds to say that they had in December, 1901, made a bicycle to the order of a Mr. Frederick Walker, a clerk in the employment of Messrs. Kitson and Sons, Ltd., engineers, of Leeds. A second reply came a post or two later from the Agincourt Cycle Works in Park Street, Camden Town, to state that they had made a bicycle to the advertised specification which had been delivered in June, 1902, to a Mr. Sidney Barnes, of 175, King's Road, Camden Town.

"I expect the first is our man," said Yardley; "it's in the neighbourhood. I don't want him just slipping through our fingers, so I'm going to Leeds at once."

But only disappointment awaited him. When he got there Walker at once admitted he had had such a bicycle made, but after it was delivered he had found it much heavier than he expected, and he sold it second-hand to Messrs. Griggs, of Harrogate, who let out bicycles for hire. Sick of heart, Yardley went on to Harrogate, and called on Messrs. Griggs. Yes. They admitted they had had such a bicycle, but it had been hired from them on October 28, and had never been returned. They promptly laid claim to the one in the charge of the police, but they had no recollection of the person who had hired it. Yardley returned to town. Things were going very crookedly. As he said, "It's almost a dead certainty, it's that machine. Harrogate is only eight miles from Tibberton Maul-everer. It's all in that neighbourhood; we've simply chucked away £100."

"I'm afraid we have; still there's always the bare outside chance it might have been the other machine. You'd better inquire about that."

Yardley had considerable difficulty in doing so. He found Mr. Barnes had moved, and it took some time to trace him to his new address. At last he was run to ground. He admitted having had such a bicycle, but he stated that when on a bicycle tour in Yorkshire, during his holidays, he had lost it. He had entered a hotel at Thirsk for refreshment, leaving his machine outside. He said that he had stayed in the hotel a short time, and on going out he had found his own bicycle had disappeared, and in its place was another with one of the tyres badly burst, and with the chain jammed and broken. He added that the bicycles of his two friends which were with his own had plainly been purposely damaged, no doubt to prevent pursuit, and that the broken bicycle which had been left was a Racing Model Humber of much better quality than his own, and that consequently he had made no fuss, but simply had the Humber machine repaired, and used that one since. It was still in his possession. Yes, he knew the number—37859.

"Do you use a cyclometer, Mr. Barnes?"

"I had one on my own machine; but, of course, it was stolen with the bicycle."

"I suppose you don't remember what it registered when it was stolen?"

"No, but I can tell you pretty nearly. You see, there were three of us on a bicycling tour, and we started that day, it was Thursday, from Thirsk. I wanted to know how far I rode during my holidays, so I remember setting the cyclometer before I started. It was then standing at over 1700 miles, seventeen forty something, I think. I made up my mind I would put it at a figure I could remember. I was then living at No. 175 at my mother's. So I thought I would put it at 1750 miles. To make it that figure I went for a short spin the evening before, and rode about till I got it exactly 1750 miles. Well, we trained to Northallerton, where we stayed the night. We started the next morning. I don't know how far it is from Northallerton to Thirsk, but if you add the distance to 1750, then that's what my cyclometer must have registered when it was stolen.

"Could you remember the way you went from Northallerton to Thirsk?"

"I think so."

"Well, will you come down to Northallerton with me on Saturday and show me?"

This was arranged, and the following Sunday morning the two men started from Northallerton to bicycle to Thirsk. Each had a cyclometer carefully set before starting. When they reached Thirsk, Yardley took the lead in a straight line to Tibberton Mauleverer. Leaving the high road by the turning to Boroughgolds, he made a complete circuit of Tibberton Park, and went on to the point at which the bicycle had been left outside the park wall on the night on which the attempt to murder Anthony had been made. Turning, he led the way to York by the route that Anthony had spoken of. Dismounting at the station, they found that since

leaving Northallerton each cyclometer had registered forty-four miles.

"Seventeen hundred and fifty and forty-four
make 1794 miles. Mr. Barnes, the attempted murder was done with the help of your bicycle, so now
I must hunt up the owner of Racing Humber
37859."

A little investigation and a few inquiries proved
that the bicycle had been sold from the Holborn
Viaduct Show Rooms of the Humber Company in
1899. The order had been received by telegram;
in fact, the whole of the negotiations had been conducted in a series of telegrams, and the machine
been sent in accordance with instructions to Oxford
Station to await the order of "T. Symonds."

The firm had been advised that another bicycle
of their make was being returned to them, and they
were asked to make an allowance for that machine
on the price of the new one. The whole of the correspondence with T. Symonds had been addressed
to the post office at Oxford, "to be called for." The
balance on the new machine had subsequently been
paid by telegraph money orders. The machine sent
back to them was one of their make, but of a
very old pattern, and was electroplated all over.
They, unfortunately, could not trace for whom they
had made it.

"But isn't it rather unusual to electroplate a
machine all over like that?" asked Tempest.

"Well, it is rather; but we have made some number for exhibition riders and trick riders in the music halls."

"Yardley," asked Tempest afterwards, "has it struck you why the bicycle was sent to Oxford Station 'to await orders'?"

"I can't say it has."

"Then I think I can tell you. The person we are looking for is a woman; this is a man's bicycle. It would have excited comment if a lady had claimed it, or if it had been sent to the home address of the rider. Therefore it is sent to the station to be called for. The telegrams tell us several things. Several days elapsed between the first telegram and the last ones wiring the money. So it was not a question of urgency. The lady could have gone to London, taken the one bicycle and brought back the other in an afternoon if time had been an object. Then you may have noticed the first telegram wired for price, but there was an interval of six days before the second telegram wiring for amount which would be allowed on old bicycle which was being forwarded. There was no necessity to wire, as a letter would have brought the reply quite as soon, because nobody in their senses could expect a reply till the firm had seen the bicycle. There is no doubt the telegrams were primarily adopted for the purpose of concealing a revelation of sex by the handwriting, because I doubt strongly that the *method* of the crime was premeditated so long beforehand that the possibility of identification through the

channel of the handwriting could have been anticipated and provided for. I expect it was nothing
more than the sex which was to be hidden. That
was why it was paid for by telegraph. Then it is
evident that whoever was concerned was not mistress of her own address—or why have all the com-
munications been addressed to the post-office?—and
not mistress of her own time. Hence the delay.
Then there's another point. It's the etiquette of
'the' profession never to write a letter when a telegram will do, so a professional naturally thinks
about telegraphing first. Hence the arrangement
by telegram instead of by means of letters in an
assumed handwriting; therefore, bearing in mind
the electroplating, we are now looking for a 'professional' But advertisement to 'the' profession
is the breath of their nostrils, and if it had been
any one on the boards now you would have had
everything done with much bold advertisement of
the full name. Then again, professionals have
always their mornings free, so why the delay of six
days between two of the inquiries? And then, how
do you account for the disposal of a bicycle which *is*
a 'professional property' for one which certainly
would be of very little use on the stage?"

"Oh, I give it up."

"Excuse me, Yardley, that's what the other
donkey did. Yet it's simple enough. You know
now that you are dealing with a person who *was* a
professional, but had finally left the stage when

those telegrams were sent. And, as I have said, for a lady who rides a man's bicycle and wishes to conceal her sex—one who is evidently within reach of Oxford, and one neither mistress of her address nor of her own time. It's a pretty wide problem still, but we are slowly narrowing it down. She may be a visitor, a younger member of the household, or an employee. Now, you get two telegrams on two successive days, so she can't be far from Oxford—she can't be at such a distance that she must 'get permission' to go by train every time she needs to come into the city. Yet the other unnecessary interval of six days proves she was not sufficiently near to be popping into the office every day. I should guess she lived between a radius of three and a radius of seven miles from the town. Now, a professional to have been on and come off the stage on which she was some success (or she wouldn't have ever been in a position to possess an electroplated bicycle, even as a stage property) must be of such an age that she would not be under control at home to any appreciable extent. It is possible, of course, but not very probable. That leaves us the alternatives of visitor and employee. Yardley, you had better come down to Oxford with me."

The two men went to Oxford, and Yardley, claiming the help of the local police, methodically made a list of every person within a radius of seven or eight miles who was accustomed, or even likely, to undertake bicycle repairs.

At last they were successful. It was, of course, by the nature of things, the last address at which they made their inquiries, for they happened to have paid several fruitless calls to the address previously, in a vain endeavour to catch the proprietor of the business in question. A few desultory inquiries prefaced the remark:

"Do you know much about racing-machines— road-racers, I mean? I am trying to trace a Humber, 1899 pattern, that has been about this neighbourhood."

"Well, I expect I can tell you something about that sort of machine, because not only have I often repaired one, but I actually had one left in my charge, worse luck."

"Why worse luck?"

" 'Cos he rode off about four or five months ago and I've never set eyes on him since, and he owed me twenty-five shillings for a quarter's rent and taking charge of it, to say nothing of a small bill of five or six shillings for oil and one or two little repairs."

"You haven't got the machine here now, then?"

"'Oh dear no! else I shouldn't feel anxious, for it was a good machine. Must have cost a lot of money! He'd only had it a year or two! Before that he had another all electroplated—used to be admired a lot in my place here. I rather liked having that about for folks to see, though it was old-fashioned. But he didn't ride that machine much

—more like as if he valued it, and was just paying me to keep it in good order. Then, as I say, he sent that away and got this racing Humber, and then he was for ever going out. He had his money's worth out of me in the cleaning of his machine alone—very particular and finnicking about it he was, too. I used sometimes to think I'd ask him to take himself and his machine somewhere else, only there were times when he'd never be near the place for weeks together."

"What was his name?"

"Well, what might it be worth to you gentlemen to know it?"

A five-pound note changed hands and they were at once told the name, T. Symonds.

"What was he like?"

"Oh, he wasn't much of a chap—about middle height, but very slim, and small feet and hands; and his face looked as if he'd never had a hair on it in his life."

"Where did he live?"

"That I never knew. You see, I didn't trouble so long as I had the bicycle as security. It never struck me—not till afterwards, of course—that it wasn't much of a security when he could ride away on it and never come back. Leastways he didn't actually ride away the last time."

"How was he generally dressed?"

"He was always dressed the same—white canvas tennis-shoes, black stockings—a well-shaped pair of legs he had, by the way,—grey knickerbockers and coat, and grey cloth cap, and a white jersey thing. But he always carried a black bag with him. Sometimes he took it with him, strapped on the machine; but he generally left it here whilst he was out riding, taking it away with him again when he came back. It was always locked, I know. But there was one curious thing about him: he was always dropping hairpins about the place. I told him I'd make him pay if I got any tyres punctured through it; but he said he always carried some loose in his pocket to clean his pipe with. He wasn't a bad-looking chap in a womanish sort of way."

"When did you see him last?"

The man scratched his head and turned up the small ledger which answered all his purposes of account—semi-daybook, semi-ledger, debits and credits, all mixed in a confusion he alone could interpret.

"Let's see now; he paid me up to March 25 last year, then there's one quarter's rent due to June 30. It was after that. Oh, and then he had some oil on July 15. If I remember right, it would be about a week or perhaps a fortnight after that he came in one day, said he was going for a bicycle tour for his summer holidays, and would I pack the bicycle and send it to him to the cloak-room at King's Cross Station. I sent it off, and that's the very last I've seen of him or the bicycle. As Yardley and Tempest returned to town in a first-class compartment they had to themselves, Tempest said:

"That's the right person, there's no doubt."

"Yes, I should say the hairpins settled it, if the clothes and the machine by themselves weren't enough."

"Well, we are a step or two further on. His story disposes of the casual visitor theory. The woman was evidently an employee, probably a companion, and to rich people with two or three places, which would account for her not using the machine at times for two or three months together. The date he went off with the machine finally would fit. Yes, and it tells a good deal. July 15, and a week or a fortnight after that, means the end of the London season, and King's Cross means grouse and Scotland, or possibly the Yorkshire moors. We are getting warmer, as the children say.

"I suppose it never struck you, old man," said Yardley, "that Merioneth House is near Oxford, and we may simply be tracking the Duchess à la Vivienne all the time."

"Oh, rats to that for a tale! I hadn't overlooked the proximity, and if the Duchess had had a companion, I'd go straight now and arrest her; but the Duchess never had one, and as I don't, as you know, believe the Duchess had anything at all to do with it, the proximity of Merioneth House is a mere coincidence. Besides, the Duchess wouldn't bother with all this subterfuge merely to get an occasional bicycle ride.   She always rode as much as she wanted to.   I remember talking 'bike' one night for hours with Vivienne Vane, and she told me she had tried knickerbockers and skirts, and preferred skirts.   But what struck me as curious then, and it proves what I say now, was that she told me that whether riding in a skirt or knickerbockers, she much preferred riding on a lady's machine.   The remark was quite uncalled for, but that being her opinion, I doubt her bothering to keep a man's machine like this.   Besides, the Duchess has got much too good a figure for any one to call her slight if dressed in a man's clothes."

"What are you going to do next?"

"Make a list of everybody in the county of Oxford who is in a position to keep or has kept a lady companion.   Then your man, Yardley, I've no doubt, will be interested in taking each one separately, and sorting out those who are (1) companions in families owning two or more houses, and who (2) can ride bicycles, and who (3) were here on May 30 when 'Henry was murdered, and on July 15, and were in Yorkshire on August 30 when Anthony was fired at.   Then we shall have something to go upon, and we will hunt up their antecedents, till we find one who has been on the music-hall stage as a trick rider.   That will sort the thing out."

Yardley and his assistants did the thing thoroughly, and in the course of a fortnight the list Tempest had suggested was made out, and rather elated by the expedition with which his assistants had worked, and the thoroughness with which they had made their inquiries, Yardley started out to Lincoln's Inn. In each case they had managed to secure the approximate age and a description of appearance. Yardley wisely had not even hinted to his assistants the very narrow limits within which the final selection would be made, fearing that if the elimination lay in their hands, they might eliminate a little too thoroughly. As the requirements were to a certain extent guess-work, Tempest needed the list to work upon if other qualifications proved more correct than those he had outlined to Yardley.

The two men, after Yardley had undone the bundle of records which had been collected, sat down to go through them together, both considering each case separately. Finally, they had found four who fulfilled the requirements laid down. They were (1) Miss Janet Spurrell, aged about 50, companion to Lady D'Abernon; (2) Miss Edytha Jones, aged 27, companion to Mrs. Hoggenheimer, a wealthy woman, devoid of aspirates, the void, as her other deficiencies, and they were many, being suitably filled with gold-stopping; (3) Mrs. Clancy-Clancy, aged 35, a penniless widow, for whom a home was provided in return for her services by Lady Jenkins, the widow of a Jubilee knight; (4) the Hon. Thomasina Simmons, aged 23, daughter of Lord Cinderton, a recently created peer of untold wealth.

She, it appeared, usually spent eight or nine months of every year ostensibly as a visitor, but really as the unpaid drudge of her exacting old aunt, the Countess of Stewartsdale.

As Yardley picked up the last form from the heap he said:

"My man was very dubious about calling this superior person a 'companion,' but I thought we'd better not omit her."

Tempest looked at it. "Why, that's the celebrated 'Tommy' Simmons. Lord! fancy you not knowing 'Tommy' Simmons. She's one of the leading lights at the Bath Club, and a simply magnificent athlete for a girl."

All the four, it had been ascertained, possessed and presumably were accustomed to ride bicycles; all were usually resident within a radius of seven miles from the town; all were near Oxford on July 15; all were in various parts of Yorkshire about the end of August.

"I saw Miss Spurrell," said Yardley; "she is very stout, wears bloomers, has a red face and an aggressive manner."

"She won't do, then."

"That I knew when I saw her, and a deuce of a bother I had to see her; but, honour bright, it was worth all the trouble simply to see her back view on her machine. Miss Edytha Jones," he continued, "didn't seem very likely either. It takes up so much of her time trying to convince people that, in spite of her name, and also in spite of her present association with Mrs. Hoggenheimer, she really does know what an 'h' sounds like, and has been taught how to eat peas with a fork, etc., and consequently she certainly is not likely to waste time undoing her efforts by wild unconventional careering about in male bifurcations. Mrs. Clancy-Clancy, down there, is known as a bit of a hot lot. Old Lady Jenkins lives at a place called Kidlington Grange, and the village seem to have no other topic of conversation than the manners and customs of Mrs. C-C. She always seems to be up to some piece of unconventionality, and has been known once to turn out in knickerbockers. But she spends all her time running after a tame curate."

"Ah, then she's no good for us."

"Miss Simmons I never saw, though I tried hard. She's gone 'off duty' now for two or three months."

"Oh, I know Tommy well enough. As I said, she's a splendid athlete, she's bound to be a revolver shot, and she's got a bit of a reputation as a lady cyclist."

"Well, do you think she's the one we want?"

"I don't know, I'm sure; the name is certainly a strange coincidence, and she's got the face and figure that might pass for a man, and it's rather a habit of hers to be always dropping hairpins. They say at the Bath Club that one of the attendants gave notice; said she'd been engaged to clean out the dressing-rooms, etc., and not to collect hairpins.

Said she didn't mind finding one occasionally, but she drew the line at it as a regular job. Some of the other members certainly did send a round robin to Tommy, asking her to change her pattern. 'Scientific' hairpins have business ends that are unpleasant to bare feet."

"Has she ever been on the stage?"

"Not that I know of. May have acted as an amateur, but that's all. Certainly not as a trick rider. But, then, our chief basis for that is the electro-plated bicycle. Now, if it was a ten-year-old pattern, as the Humber people said, it was bought when Tommy was, say, fourteen. Now, at that age she wouldn't buy her own bicycle. The old man would make her a present of it, and that's just about the sort of thing he'd buy. He's got some taste, of course, but only just about as much as one of his own wheelbarrows."

"Steady on; if her father bought it, he'd have bought a lady's machine."

"Right! but Tommy has a brother much about her own age, and she certainly is the only one of all the four from these reports who would have had the money either to buy such a bicycle as the Humber one, or to spend all that money in telegrams over it."

"You are making it very black against her."

"Well, I'll tell you something else. She knew all the Mauleverer boys, and I've heard of her staying at Tibberton. But I can't think she would be concerned in this murder business, because I don't think I ever met a sunnier-tempered girl. She never offended a soul and wouldn't kill a fly, and as to this secrecy with the bicycle, all I can say is that if she wished to wear knickerbockers she'd rather take a delight in shocking her old aunt. She isn't the sort of girl at all to do things 'on the quiet.' "

"But, then, we come to another point. The two attempts on Anthony's life were on September 30 and August 30. Henry Mauleverer was murdered on May 30, Jack Mauleverer on July 30, Herbert Mauleverer on June 30, and Captain Mauleverer on April 30. Whoever committed these murders must have been in London on April 30 and June 30 and July 30; in Oxford, May 30; in Yorkshire, on August 30; and in London, September 30. They were all in Yorkshire on August 30, and in Oxford July 15-30, but Miss Spurrell, Miss Jones and Mrs. Clancy-Clancy were all, as far as you have been able to ascertain, in the Oxford neighbourhood the whole of the time from April to the end of July. Now I know 'Tommy' was in London till pretty late on in the season, because she won that big open Swimming Tournament the last week in July. So she is the only one possible out of the four."

"Well, are you going to do anything?" asked Yardley.

"I'm not going to have her arrested, if that's what you mean. A Duchess twice convicted is quite enough crime in high life for the present. It will take the halfpenny rags a long time to forget that."

"What's the next step, then?"

"Yardley," said Tempest, rising to his feet and stretching himself, "they always say there's a perfect fortune in front of any man who can invent a new and a really good game. I've invented a magnificent one, and I'll have all the country talking about it before long."

CHAPTER XV

TEMPEST knew his time to get hold of Sir Frederic Badsworth, and when shown into the latter's office, explained that he had come to enlist Sir Frederic's assistance again.

"My dear chap, the Duchess is dead as mutton—of course I mean for the purposes of copy—unless you can revive her in some extraordinarily thrilling manner. Now, that's one thing I pride myself on having taught the British Press, that news must be fresh, alive, up to date, brought down to five minutes ago. The *Daily Tale* never publishes mutton; nice tender, juicy lamb is what I'm buying. Now, if you can release the Duchess, or really prove she is innocent after all, or if you've caught anybody else instead, then there may be something in it, and I don't mind saying that Barlowe would take a column from you, to oblige you, at our usual rates, you know; he might even stretch a point and make it two columns. We are short of a sensation for to-morrow, I hear; half the staff are at the telephones now trying to rake one up. So now's your chance."

"That isn't what I mean. How much do you want to lease *Replies* to me for next week's issue?"

Badsworth roared. "My dear chap, to-day's Wednesday; next Saturday's *Replies* is printed already. They are already working on Saturday week's now. You're a day behind the fair, sonny."

Tempest looked depressed; his knowledge of journalism was limited, being chiefly confined to the *Saturday Review,* an office where they start to "make up" on a Thursday afternoon.

"You seem to have wanted it badly; can I offer you *Home Talk* or *The Pansy?* Let me see, is *Home Talk* mine or Mearson's? 'Pon my soul, I sometimes forget which are my papers and which are his. But fooling aside, Tempest, if you really want me to help you, tell me what you want done, and I'll see if I can suggest anything."

"You know we are trying to prove the Duchess did not commit the murders, and consequently I'm trying to find out who did, and we've been working on the evidence we collected from the attempts on the life of Anthony Mauleverer. They've got a chap in custody now for that—Webb, you know."

Badsworth nodded. "Jury disagreed, didn't they?"

"Yes; he's coming up for trial before another jury in a month or so. He's a most complete and accomplished scoundrel, but he didn't commit this particular crime. If he is convicted and sentenced I can get him off with the evidence I have, but at present he suits me better where he is. Prison is no novelty to him, and a few weeks more or less for him in the hands of the police simply means so much the less crime of the blackmailing variety. There are many people whose lives would be easier if his came to an end. But I've found out who did commit the crime."

The instincts of the journalist were aflame in a moment.

"We'll have that two columns."

"No, you won't, because I can't put a name to the lady yet, and that's where I want you to help me."

"It was a woman, then?"

"Yes; there's no doubt about that." Briefly sketching out what he had done, he said: "You see, I can describe her pretty exactly in a good many particulars, but I haven't the ghost of a notion who the woman is, what her name is, or where to look for her. Now, anybody who has ever come across that particular woman would recognize her in two seconds from the details I can give of her life. But if I advertise that that particular woman is wanted, and offer a reward for her conviction in the usual way—well, I should be simply defeating my own ends. Her friends would never give her away, she wouldn't answer herself, and I should not get a step further forward. The usual Scotland Yard dodge is to advertise a legacy, or a 'will hear of something to their advantage,' but I can't, because I don't know the woman's name. So I thought I would hire your paper, and start an entirely new kind of competition. You're great on competitions, so nobody would smell a rat. I intended to put up a prize of £1000, or £10,000, if you think that better. I'll be guided by you, and I should announce that the particulars of the identity of a certain person were in a sealed envelope lodged at your bank, and the prize would be given to the first person who was able from the published particulars to give the correct name and address, and then I meant to publish all the particulars I had collected.

"That's a very smart idea of yours, Tempest. How much did you intend to offer for the paper?"

"Oh, I'm in your hands."

"And you're open to put up £10,000 as a prize?"

"Yes."

"I'm curious to know what you expected to pay."

"Well, I thought if I let you take sales and advertisements as usual, you'd let me run the thing for £500 or £1000."

"Tempest, you're perfectly infantile over journalism. Are you spending your own money or the Duchess's?"

"Oh, a big sum like this I shall get back from the Duchess. I don't bother her estate for small sums, but this would be different. So long as she is in prison she can't spend her income, and it would be worth £10,000 to her to get released. I'll make it more if you like. You see, we shouldn't have to pay if we didn't find the woman we want."

"If nobody got the £10,000 there would be ructions."

"Oh, you could say the award would be made in three months' time, and then you could publish a full, true account of the whole, reasons and everything. I don't think anybody would kick up a fuss, because, unless you do get the right person, nobody *could* have won. It isn't like a thing which there are two ways of working out."

"That's so," admitted Badsworth. "But what I was going to say was that no paper has ever given a £10,000 prize for a competition, and it would be such a huge advertisement for *Replies* that, instead of charging you, I don't mind myself finding a couple of thousand. We can do nothing this coming week; but for Saturday week I can put in an extra four pages, outside those already printed and inside the cover. The first two I'll use for advertisements, because you can't page them; the last two we can page, and you shall have one for your competition."

Picking up the telephone from the table, Sir Frederic at once gave the necessary instructions to *Replies,* and told one of his assistants to inform every other publication under their control of the £10,000 prize, which he required to be boomed for all it was worth.

"It wouldn't be half a bad idea to take that for the *Daily Tale* to-morrow as our usual sensation. I'll talk to Barlowe about it; he may object, but I'll see what I can do.   Will you pay half, Tempest, if we get out posters all over the place ?"

"Certainly."

Consequently, on the appointed day *Replies* announced that they proposed a competition on a gigantic scale such as had never previously been attempted in any publication.   Readers of *Replies* had no doubt already seen all over England huge posters announcing that "*Replies* will give £10,-000."   *Replies* intended to be as good as its word, and would pay £10,000 to the first person who sent in the correct answer to the competition.   A certain person in the United Kingdom had been selected, and an account of the method of selection and a full narrative of every detail in connection had been lodged in the hands of the manager of Lloyds Bank, Laws Courts Branch, in a sealed envelope, together with the sum of £10,000.   On that day three months the said bank manager would make the award, and would publish the letter in his charge in such manner as he thought fit.   To aid readers in the identification of the selected person, clues would be found stated at length.

The advertised clues were:

(1) The person to be found was a female over age; (2) medium height; (3) slight build; (4) was an expert bicyclist and athlete; (5) was a good revolver-shot; (6) waist measurement was twenty-three and a half inches; (7) wore shoes size four; (8) had a regular occupation; (9) had been a

music-hall performer as a trick bicyclist, but was not now on the stage; (10) had lived some time in the neighbourhood of Oxford, but was sometimes in Yorkshire; (11) has a habit of dropping hairpins; (12) answers to the name of ——, and a space was left for the insertion of the name.

The excitement produced by this announcement was beyond anticipation. Not even the pound a week for life, not even the missing word competitions, had produced one tithe of the excitement. A few retaining fees judiciously distributed, and in every topical music-hall song, in every moment of "patter," could be found some allusion to this monster competition. The overwhelming shoals of replies produced a result and a complication which had never entered Tempest's head when he had planned the competition. He had doubted whether a claim would be made. More than twenty thousand names were sent in. After consideration, it was decided to send a reply-paid postcard to every person who had competed asking for the professional name under which the person whose name was submitted had appeared in public as a trick bicycle rider. Less than a thousand of the postcards came back, but of these more than five hundred named a certain Jenny Delano, who had been a member of the famous Delano cycle troupe, and a popular favourite some twenty-one or twenty-two years ago. Inquiries concerning her elicited the fact that her chief "act" consisted of breaking glass balls with a revolver whilst riding head downwards on a bicycle saddle. This exhibition, though at the time it had excited enormous enthusiasm, had been of brief duration. A lamentable accident to a member of the audience, and the obvious danger to the public, had led the authorities to intervene.

A further reply-postcard, sent to all who had named Miss Jenny Delano, asking for her present address, very plainly showed that most of those who had entered the competition had simply done so "on the chance," having nothing beyond the recollection of the combined bicycle and revolver performance. One person, however, wrote to say that he had seen Miss Delano about twelve months previously in Oxford, and had pointed her out to a friend, recalling to him her famous performance.

Yardley at once went down to Oxford and interviewed the writer of the letter. He was positive he had seen Miss Delano. He did not speak to her—had attempted to do so—an act she plainly resented. He had known her well as Miss Delano, and was certain he was right. He took Yardley to see his friend, who confirmed his story of the meeting and identification. Asked to describe her present appearance, he said she looked thirty-five to forty, but might possibly have been a year or two more; was very quietly dressed, very handsome, and dark, had a very slight figure and an aquiline nose. No, she was not bicycling when he met her. She was dressed in black, but not mourning.

"Doesn't that read like the typical companion?" said Tempest, when Yardley called to tell him the result.

In the course of the next few days Yardley unearthed a quondam member of the Delano troupe, and learnt further details of Miss Jenny Delano. Her real name, if he remembered correctly, was Brown. She had joined the troupe when quite a child thirteen or fourteen years old, but had not taken any very prominent part in their performances till she was seventeen or eighteen, when the revolver act was introduced. She had always been fond of revolver-shooting, and it had been her own idea. The accident, when one of the audience was shot, took place in Dublin. Soon after that there had been trouble in the troupe with Miss Jenny, who, without any notice, went off to spend a week in a trip with one of the officers then stationed at the Curragh. There had been high words amongst them all on her return, and she had got huffy and cleared out, and he had not seen or heard anything of her for seven or eight years. Then they had wanted a new lady member for the troupe—the troupe was always changing—and they had advertised, and she had come back and performed with them for nearly ten years longer—in fact, until the troupe finally broke up. She had saved a bit of money; she was always—well, he wouldn't say mean, but very careful with her money, and she was always having jewellery sent her, which she promptly sold, and when the troupe came to an end she had about £40 a year coming in from her savings. He had no idea at all what became of her afterwards. She always kept herself to herself, and he had never met her in any of the old haunts. Tempest thus found himself checkmated again. In his own mind he had not a shadow of doubt that the woman he was looking for was Jenny Delano; but how was he to put his hands on her? He advertised in the *Era* for the present address of Miss Jenny Delano, but got no reply. It was evident that she had absolutely dropped all connection whatever with the profession, and to the present generation she was scarcely even a name.

"Still," as he said to Yardley, when they talked things over, "we are a step or two further on."

It was with a deep sense of depression that Tempest waited the pleasure of the prison authorities when he presented himself for his next interview with the Duchess. His hopes had been high; he had felt so certain of his ability promptly to demonstrate her entire innocence to the world; he had even succeeded in imbuing the Duchess with some of his own sanguine aspirations. On the previous occasion her spirits had manifestly improved during their conversation. He had practically promised her that on the next occasion he came to see her it would be to triumphantly announce her innocence and freedom. On the previous day he had had a long interview with the Home Secretary, and had laid before him the results of his discoveries, and had vainly urged that they were sufficient for him to release the Duchess on a ticket of leave, even if they did not warrant the issue of a free pardon.

"My dear Tempest," was the reply, "I quite agree with you that you have proved that the Duchess was not the person who attempted the life of Anthony Mauleverer; in fact, it seems to me you've proved Webb's innocence as well, though as it hasn't come before me officially, he had better stand his trial when it comes on. If the Duchess had been convicted for the attempted murder of Anthony, I would let her out; but, as you know, she was actually convicted on the indictment for the murder of Captain Mauleverer, and the other indictments were not proceeded with. Now, you haven't produced to me one particle of evidence relating to Captain Mauleverer's murder. I can't do it yet, Tempest. If she weren't the Duchess of Merioneth—well, we might. No, even in that case I don't think we could; but as she is a Duchess it's impossible. Of course, you can deposit your papers if you like, and I'll send them on to the Lord Chancellor for his opinion, or you can have the police put on to the Delano track; but it seems to me you've so far done better without them than with them, and I have very little doubt you are getting to the truth. My advice to you is, go on in your own way. Come to me again if you get any fresh evidence of any weight. Tempest, I knew the Duchess well, and I liked her. From my personal knowledge I don't myself believe she would be guilty of such crimes, but you can't get over the evidence as it stands at present. Bring me anything I can act on honestly, and I promise you I will act, and act promptly."

And with that Tempest had been forced to be content, but it was a sorry report for it to be the best that he could take to the Duchess.

It seemed an eternity to the waiting man before a warder presented himself to conduct Tempest to the interview.

The Duchess showed her eager anticipation when their eyes met. She read his failure in a moment, but for his sake she kept up a brave show. Utterly downcast, he related his simple, straightforward tale of what had been done.

"Oh, it's awfully good of you all, Ashley," she had said, as he began; but as he proceeded with his bare facts one after the other, piling fact on fact, proof on proof, telling in a few brief words the gleanings of his many weeks of labour, the smile died from the Duchess's face, and in its stead came a growing look of horror and wild amazement. The woman seemed to absolutely flinch and recoil as the story was unfolded, her eyes dilated, and over her beautiful face came such wild, sheer terror and alarm that for one moment Tempest himself lost his faith. Was he simply telling her of her own

guilt? Was he just shutting for her one by one
the avenues through which she might have escaped?
Had he been fooled all along? What was the
meaning of that horror with which, dumbstricken
and amazed, her eyes darting from their sockets,
she gazed petrified as he came to the end of his
story? In a hoarse, guttural whisper, ere he had
quite finished, and with the words tumbling over
each other from her lips, she gasped:

"Then you've proved it was Jenny Delano?"

"I think there can be no doubt left."

"And you don't know who she is?" and her
voice rose in a piteous, wailing moan. "My God,
if only I had guessed! my God!" and then in a
broken shriek came her statement: "She was my
maid."

CHAPTER XVI

THE watery sun of an April afternoon was flickering through the trickling raindrops on the window-pane of the consulting-room of Dr. Forsyth, in Harley Street, as a trim, white-capped maid ushered in a lady plainly dressed in black.

The physician bowed, and motioning her to a chair, settled his glasses, and read the name upon the card again, as the lady informed him she had once before consulted him some fifteen months previously. Rapidly turning over the leaves of his case-book, he found the entry he was looking for, and read his notes.

"Ah, yes; I hope you are now relieved of your anxiety. I trust the cure will prove permanent. It's always a pleasure to hear that one's treatment and advice have produced the desired result. It's a pleasure we doctors seldom have. Our patients, I'm sorry to say, don't come back and pay us consulting fees simply to let us know they are keeping well."

"I'm afraid I'm not an exception."

"But aren't you better? Wasn't the operation a success?"

"I never had the operation."

The firm, kind mouth of the doctor closed tightly on the thin lips.

"Madam, that's difficult to believe. You came to me, and I told you that the simplest operation, a very slight operation, would have removed all trace of the disease and put an end to any danger, and I told you the operation would scarcely cause you any pain at all, the progress of the disease was then so slight. You told me you had no friends you could consult, so I asked you what fee you could afford for the operation, and I gave you a letter of introduction to a surgeon who, I knew, would perform it satisfactorily for that fee. And you tell me now you never had it done. How could you be so short-sighted? What *can* I do for you now?" The kind-hearted old man was plainly upset. "I hope you haven't been misled by your own medical man," he added in a kind of after-thought.

"Doctor, don't worry, please; I never consulted any one else. I never meant to have it performed. One comes to have a consultation to find out things, not always to be cured; sometimes one doesn't par-ticularly want to be cured. You doctors are always trying to prolong life. Some of us aren't any too fond of things as they are, and don't want them lengthened out; life isn't so precious to everybody. I've been quite satisfied with the length of mine. When one lays down a certain life's action, and one gets quite close up to a completion of that action, well, to put it plainly, one has had enough of this world's worry and woe. I've had enough. I came to you before to know for certain what was the matter. I've simply come now to know how much longer I've got to live, that's all. Will you, doctor, as a gentleman, please tell me the exact and definite truth, and the Truth in capital letters, please, doctor?"

The physician, world-wide in his celebrity, rang for the presence of his nurse, and made the necessary examinations. The nurse deftly assisted the patient to rearrange her clothing, and then retired. The doctor then said:

"Madam, it is grievous, very grievous to me indeed, but you've literally thrown your life away— thrown it away with both hands. Then you could have been cured; now it is quite impossible."

"I know, I know; but how long, doctor?"

In very gentle tones, his firm white hand lightly resting on her shoulder, he said:

"If there's anything you want to do, you had better do it at once. Your time is very short indeed, I'm afraid; a week or ten days, I should think; a fortnight at the outside. But one can't really tell. If you're making arrangements better think of ten days. Oh! why didn't you do as I advised you? But I'm afraid you must be in very great pain. Perhaps I can lessen that for you."

"Pain—why it's been the tortures of the damned;

they say one gets used to pain. I haven't got used to this. I dare say some people would consider that all my life I'd been booking a saloon ticket through to hell, but I guess this pain must have about worked off most of my sins."

There and then administering a strong dose of morphia, the physician wrote out instructions and prescriptions which would, as far as his knowledge went, minimize the pain she was bound to endure before the end came, and afterwards the woman left. It was not until his patient had been gone some ten minutes that he noticed she had placed the usual two guineas on his table. He was sorry she had done so.

The woman, who seemed relieved after her interview was over, walked down Harley Street in the direction of Oxford Street, and passed into the Park, where she sat drowsily and lazily whilst the drug deadened her pain. It was the first relief from pain for longer than she cared to remember. She sat in the Park for some time, and then slowly made her way to Berkeley Square.

CHAPTER XVII

COLONEL MAULEVERER had come
in from his club and was in the library
pretending to scan the paper. But he
had read it much earlier in the day,
and he was in reality half dozing until
the dressing-bell should announce that the afternoon
was over. The Colonel in the last few months
had lost his interest in many things, and the murders of his sons had told upon him heavily. He
looked a broken man, and as the hardness of his
face relaxed whilst he dozed in his chair the changes
seemed more marked. The enormous strength of
will, which of old had been the dominating characteristic, seemed to have gone, and in its place had
returned a certain sensuality which the twenty years
on the Indian Frontier with its responsibilities had
largely effaced. The original man showed out
brutal, cruel, sensual, and now to these qualities
there was added fear, and it was not a pretty pic-
ture. Anthony was seated at the writing-table;
and in an easy-chair, keen and alert, sat one of
Yardley's assistants.

The butler came in. "Please, sir, Mr. Tempest
has telephoned to know if he can see you if he drives
here at once. He says it is most important."

"Very well, tell him I'm here."

Ten minutes later one of the men-servants from the hall came in to tell the Colonel that a Mrs. Brown wished to see him for a few minutes on business.

"Ask her to send a message in," said the Colonel, drowsily.

In a few minutes the man-servant came back.

"Please, sir, she says the business is private, and she would rather not send a message."

"Does she look respectable?"

"Yes, sir, I think so."

"Do I know her? Has she been here before?"

"I don't remember her having been here before, sir, but her face seems rather familiar to me, sir. I'm not sure, but I think I must have seen her at the Park, sir, that time I went down there with you, sir."

The Colonel, who was constantly backwards and forwards, was in the habit of maintaining a complete staff of servants at each house, and it was exceptional for the servants of one house to be at the other.

"Oh, well, send her in. What do you say her name is?"

"Mrs. Brown, sir."

"Oh! When Mr. Tempest comes bring him straight in." It might shorten her visit, the Colonel thought.

In a few moments the door opened again to

admit a dark, strikingly handsome woman. She was apparently about forty years of age. Bowing slightly, she stood and waited for the Colonel to speak.

Making a movement to rise from his chair, a movement he quickly arrested, he waved his visitor to a seat, as he asked:

"Well, madam, what can I do for you?"

"Don't you recognize me, Colonel Mauleverer?" she asked, in a low husky voice.

"I'm afraid I don't call the privilege of your acquaintance to mind, madam."

"I used to be on the stage."

"Oh," and the Colonel looked her over with growing interest, whilst a little smile formed itself on his mouth, "I'm not surprised to hear it."

The woman's lip curled in scorn, and her eyes met his steadily, and she deliberately looked him down.

"You've not altered. You always were a beast, Mauleverer. Well, I'm Jenny Delano."

"I'm afraid I don't recollect the name."

"Good God! and it was you—you, for whom I threw up my living and ruined my character, and you don't even remember my name. Well, you've got to remember me. Have you forgotten the bicycle troupe that performed in Dublin when you were stationed at the Curragh? Have you forgotten the night I shot a man by accident?"

Recollection was coming back to the Colonel.

"Why—why, you're little Jenny!"

"Ah, you remember now. Do you remember bringing me over here to London? I never expected you to marry me, but I did draw the line at living with you as you suggested whilst your wife was still alive, *and* supporting myself all the time into the bargain. You were a cur."

"Anthony," said his father, "you'd better leave the room."

The boy rose; but with ineffable scorn the woman said:

"No; he'd better stay. You'll want some witnesses presently."

"Mr. Tempest, sir," said the butler, as he ushered him into the room.

"The more the better," was the woman's only comment.

She had remained standing by the door. Tempest crossed to the other end of the room, and took a seat by the Colonel in ill-concealed impatience.

The woman stood for a moment or two and the strain became intense. The silence was irritating, and as she made no attempt to break it, the Colonel interjected:

"I don't know what your object may be in coming here after all these years; but if it's money, I'm in a better position now than I was then, and I have no doubt something can be arranged."

"When I want money I'll ask for it."

"Well, then, I fail to see the object of prolonging

this interview. I have many other matters to attend to."

Again she hesitated, and it was evident she was at a loss not for what to say, but how to say it, and she spoke slowly and with difficulty. At last she asked:

"Do you know what the date is, Mauleverer?"

"It's April 30," put in Tempest.

"Quite so. And what's it the anniversary of?"

The Colonel stared, and Tempest and the detective started.

"Oh, I'm not referring to your son's death last year. Where were you the year before?"

"In camp on the frontier."

"Yes, I know. And what happened on April 30?"

"How the devil do you suppose I know? Do you think I keep a diary, madam?"

"Ah, then I must tell you. There was a court-martial, and you hung two of your soldiers. What for?"

"For selling their rifles to the enemy on active service."

"You liar!"

"The men were properly tried by court-martial and were found guilty. They were two twin brothers named Brown. Were they any relation of yours?"

"They were my sons, and I say they were not properly tried. You know the court sentenced them to be imprisoned, and you overrode that sentence and had them hung. And the whole camp knew, any one of your soldiers could have told you, that the rifles were stolen from them and not sold."

"They were caught red-handed in conversation with some of the enemy."

"They were caught with some native women, and you know it. They were simply boys, not twenty-one, and just like their father in that. He was always after women."

"They were properly tried and found guilty."

"But the Court did not sentence them to death —you did, you damned murderer! You were a bully to women and a bully to your troops."

The woman's voice, hoarse with passion, rang though the room.

The Colonel, affecting bravado, said, with a sneer:

"Well, then, I suppose you've come here now to pay it back upon me."

"Pay it back on you? You! Did you murder me? No; you only ruined me. You broke my heart and broke my name, and spoiled my living; but you didn't murder me. You murdered my sons. You took me from the stage, and then only a week afterwards threw me away. I knew I had run a certain risk and I had lost, but I didn't squeal. You needn't trouble any more about that in this world. You'll be called to account for it afterwards, perhaps. Not that you have troubled **very** much up to now. Why, you'd even forgotten who Jenny Delano was."

Tempest jumped to his feet.

"Colonel, the Duchess told me——"

"Hold your tongue, you——. I've found out all about your dirty spying. Sit down," she screamed, and then fell back to the hoarse tones in which she was speaking to the Colonel. "You murdered my boys, not me, and you hung them, you beast! and I——" and the woman leaned forward and looked him in the face—"and I had to bear the pain. 's worse than being murdered yourself. I had to find that out, and now you've found it out. I've seen to that. I went to Captain Mauleverer's quarters at Knightsbridge and I shot him."

Tempest strode towards the woman, for now everything was plain to him.

"Sit down, I tell you. I'm not going to run away."

The dominating will-power of the woman had its unconscious effect, and Tempest paused. Locking the door, she threw the key on the table between them, and the heavy portière fell back into its place. Tempest sat down, but the detective, who had been sitting near the window, was slowly and quietly edging his way round the room in her direction. Like a flash she turned on him and pointed a revolver.

"Hands up! Hands up! I say," and she

stamped her foot as he attempted to rush forward. A bullet grazed his cheek. "Hands up!" and he obeyed. "Go and stand behind Colonel Mauleverer," and he went. "I simply took one of the Duchess's fancy costumes—I suppose she has told you I was her maid, and that my father used to be one of the keepers on the Tibberton estate," she said to Tempest—"and I dressed up as a Sister and went and asked your son for a contribution, and the silly boy sat down to write a cheque, and I shot him whilst his back was turned, and then walked out. It wasn't the Duchess's ha lkerchief; it was one of my own, and I used he. scent. Henry I made love to, and he had promised to take me on the river, and I poisoned him from my own flask when it was getting dusk, and sculled the boat ashore under the willows and tipped his body out and walked back to Merioneth House. And then a month afterwards I was going through Jermyn Street, and I saw Herbert looking out through his open window. He'd seen me before somewhere else—he was like his father, always after women— and he asked me to go up and have a drink, and I did, and I told him he would have to write me a cheque, so he sat down at his writing-table to do it, and as he hunted for his cheque-book I wandered into his bedroom and looked round, and I saw his razor and picked it up and went back and cut his throat as he was writing. You could do anything with Herbert if you were a woman. I was wearing the watch they made such a fuss about; and Jack Mauleverer I shot when he was on his way to my mistress. She gave me the note to send off, and I read it, and I guessed he would go through Lansdowne Passage, so I waited for him there, and then I shot him. If he hadn't come that way I could have waited. I'd have killed him some other time. And," she paused, dropping her words out one by one, "and—I've—taught—you—what—it—means—to—have—your—sons —murdered. And do *you* like it?"

The Colonel had sunk all in a heap in his chair, his jaw had dropped, and he gazed paralyzed at the woman as she stood there jeering at him. It was like a cat playing with a mouse.

"Did you like it, you cur? Damn you! Have you learnt what it means? Damn you! You hung my boys, but they were your own boys. They were your own sons, do you understand?—your own blood sons by me, and you hung them. And I've murdered four more of yours, and you've hired this dirty scum to protect your last. Do you think he can? Oh, damn you both! Oh, may every devil in hell and God Himself forever damn your soul!"

There was a flash and a report, and without another sound the body of Anthony gently toppled in his chair, and the smoke cleared away, and screaming, "You blasted murderer!" she flung the empty revolver straight in the face of the Colonel.

Tempest and the detective sprang at her together.

CHAPTER XVIII

ANTHONY'S body, without a cry or groan, simply crumpled up into a limp heap on the chair and slowly toppled forward to the ground, whilst the blood trickled down the Colonel's face from the wound the revolver had made. Tempest could never tell what was the force which had held him motionless. Honestly, he knew it had not been fear, but rather the dominating power of the fascination of the woman's mood and will. She had compelled both awe and admiration as, standing like an avenging fury, the torrent of curses had burst forth from her lips, and now she stood leaning against the door, her bosom panting as her breath came in quick gasps. Reaching her hand to a decanter on a side-table close by, she poured herself half a tumblerful of brandy and drank it undiluted. The commonplace action quickly brought Tempest to his senses. Picking up the key, he unlocked the door, and told the butler to telephone for doctors and the police, and then told him to get hold of a magistrate at once.

The woman's excitement was cooling and soon the reaction set in. Sorrow she had none—none was pretended, but after a succession of sobs she quietly began to cry, and the tears streamed down her face. A few moments brought the police. Tempest, who gave her into custody, insisted that she should remain until the arrival of the magistrate, before whom her confession was taken down and signed. As handcuffs were locked upon her wrists, she broke into a peal of hysterical laughter. "You fools," she said, "how soon can you try me? Why, I shall be dead before then. Go and talk to Dr. Forsyth. He told me this afternoon I should not live a fortnight"; and again she burst into laughter.

Doctors had arrived, and Tempest left Colonel Mauleverer and the body of his son in their keeping. As he passed into the entrance hall Dennis Yardley bounded up the steps and, scarcely speaking to Tempest, he confronted his assistant. "You unutterable coward," and he felled him to the ground with a blow from his fist. The man stumbled to his feet without speaking and stood shamefacedly before his employer, who struck him again with a savage passion that seemed absolutely without control. He fell unconscious. Yardley turned on his heel and left him lying where he had fallen.

Tempest, with the signed and witnessed confession in his pocket, drove rapidly to the House of Commons, and passed through the corridors to the Home Secretary's room. Briefly recapitulating his interview with the Duchess that afternoon when she had identified the person he was in search of as her maid, Tempest also told how he had arrived at Colonel Mauleverer's during the interview between the maid and the Colonel, and he related the tragic ending. The Home Secretary carefully perused the confession, and verified the signature of the attesting magistrate.

"You can't call it coincidence, Tempest; it isn't coincidence; much of it was too carefully planned, and the evidence was all true. I can't see where judge or jury went astray in dealing with that evidence, but there's something radically wrong in our system when an innocent woman can be twice convicted of crimes she had nothing to do with."

"Man alive, do you think I don't feel that? I've been at the Bar for more than twenty years, and you know my reputation in the Courts. I've twice defended that woman, knowing each time that she was absolutely innocent, and yet each time I've failed. I feel as if I never dare again take the responsibility of defending a person from such a charge. How soon can you act on it?"

"Well, if one does it in full form, I suppose I should, in the ordinary case, act to-morrow, and release her then, but," and he smiled grimly, "I don't mind taking the responsibility—you can have the Duchess out to-night if you like. Here, I think your efforts deserve it. You shall take a letter from me to the Governor of the gaol authorizing her immediate release, and I'll tell him the official papers are following to-morrow. I'll see to the formal pardon as soon as I can get at the King for his signature. It will only be two or three days. Anyhow, whatever is necessary shall be done without delay. If you'll sit down a few minutes I'll write that letter for you." Tempest sat for a few minutes thinking.

"May I use your telephone?" he said.

"Oh, certainly."

He rang up the Countess Varigny, and on getting the answer that she was at the instrument, said:

"We've got to the bottom of the mystery. The murders were committed by the Duchess's maid. She has signed a confession. I am going down now to get the Duchess out of prison. Will you do her a good turn?"

"Certainly, if I can. What is it?"

"Well, I don't know where to take her to. She can't go home and face all those grinning servants of hers by herself; and I don't know of any friend of hers in London who will stand by her now. You know her story. Will you?"

"Yes, of course. She shall come and stay with me here. Can't I come with you?"

"You're an angel! Be at Baker Street in half an hour. I'm just telephoning for a special. And get your maid to put up some clothes for her. She will have none—none she can come away in," he hastily amended.

He then rang up the *Daily Tale* and read the

confession verbatim through the telephone. It was the only paper to receive it. Tempest rang off and called up the Great Central Railway, and ordered a special train to be in waiting.

"Hullo!" said the Home Secretary, as he looked up from sealing the letter. "Special trains, eh?" —and a smile came to his lips. "I fancy there's a balance left at my bank which will run to a special train," answered Tempest.

In a few hours the three were travelling back to Town, Vera's arm tightly encircling the waist of the Duchess. The latter was crying quietly. Leaning across to Tempest, she took his hand and pressed it between her own.

"Ashley, can I ever thank you enough for all you've done?"

A week later Tempest dismissed his hansom in Cromwell Road, at the house of the Countess Varigny. Ever since the day when he and the Countess had together brought the Duchess away from her imprisonment he had written, begging her to see him; but with one excuse or another she had refused to do so, till to-day he had received a wire asking him to come to her. He wondered as he followed the man upstairs what she would say; he knew what he should say to her.

She was alone, and waiting for him. Tempest scanned her face anxiously as he took her hand.

"Why wouldn't you see me, Pauline? Have you been ill?"

"No; not ill. I *couldn't* see you or any one. I have simply tried to think of nothing—to eat, drink and sleep. To meet the eyes of any one is torture to me. My soul is naked and ashamed. Oh! you don't know what I've been through." Her eyes looked hunted, and Tempest saw how utterly the long suspense and publicity had broken her down. It was what he had feared.

"I know; but it's over, don't forget that. It can never come again. Come and sit down, and let me tell you some plans I've been making."

She let him put her on the sofa and pile cushions round her.

"I asked you to come and see me to-day," she said, "because I've never thanked you properly for all you did. I owe you my liberty, and perhaps my life, I know."

"Yes," Tempest assented gravely. "Do you know, Pauline, if I hadn't won your life for you I should have blown my own brains out. I *couldn't* have stood the knowledge that I was too big a fool to get off even the woman I love."

The Duchess flushed uneasily. "You mustn't say that," she said. "But I didn't quite know till the Countess told me how hard you've worked for me, and how bad the evidence looked against me. Surely even you must almost have doubted. I didn't understand how black it was. You see, all along I knew I was innocent."

"So did I! Don't let's talk about it any more." He leant towards her. "I want you to give me every moment that remains, to let me make you forget it, to blot it all out. I want to see your dear eyes smile again as they used to. My dearest, will you marry me now?"

"You ask *me* to marry you again!" Her voice was hard and incredulous. "Have you forgotten what I am?—that now no woman of my acquaintance will know me any more?—that henceforth I am a pariah, an outcast? Every one knows my face! I daren't go out! They would point at me! They would say, 'There's the Duchess who was on the streets!' Oh, my God, the shame of it —the shame of it!"

She sprang up and paced the long room, her hands clenched in uncontrollable excitement. Tempest rose and went quietly to her, taking the hands in his.

"You're talking nonsense. Listen to me a moment. We will be married by special licence at once, and I will take you abroad. No one will know you there, you will drop your title and be just Mrs. Tempest, and I cannot flatter myself that my name is of world-wide, or even European celebrity. We have neither of us ties in England, we have nothing to bring us back here. We will go where you like, my darling; all lands are alike to me if I have you with me. Surely we shall never regret leaving this dreary England."

She was calm now, and she looked at him in silence for a moment.

"And do you mean to say," she exclaimed, "that you are seriously asking me again to marry you, knowing all that I am? Your profession—what of that?"

Just for an instant Tempest hesitated, then he threw back his head, and looked straight into her eyes.

"Lord knows I've loved my profession," he said. "But I love you more, Pauline, and it can go. It doesn't matter much monetarily, you know; I've enough without it."

The Duchess turned away, and buried her face in her arms on the tall mantel-shelf. Tempest put his arm round her waist.

"Don't, Pauline. Only trust things to me. You know I'll see they come out all right."

She turned round, her eyes wet with tears. "Oh, I know you would, I know you would. And I'm tempted, oh, Ashley, *how* tempted, to just do as you say and leave things to you. But I'm not selfish enough for that yet. I can't spoil your life, your brilliant career. I know that now, after your defence of me, you're the finest barrister in the king-dom. I won't marry you, Ashley; I'm going away; that's partly why I sent for you to-day, to say good-bye. But I thank you, oh, a thousand times, for

offering me your name, in place of my own notorious one."

Tempest gripped her arm till it hurt. "You are
going away! Where?"

"I'm going to Moritania."

"The Countess has——"

"I'm going with the Countess—going in with
her in everything. It's the only thing left for me
—the only niche I can fit myself into. Why, they've
all said I was a revolutionary. When they told it
all in court I almost believed it myself, it sounded
so real. Well, I will make them right. What
they said I was I will be. Vera has done much;
she and I together can do more. And my money,
that will help."

"Pauline!" the man's voice was a cry, "you can't
do it—you daren't do it! What will be the end—
what always is the end? Think of it! Arrest!
Siberia! or death! My God, you tell me this, and
I love you, Pauline! I'd give my soul to save you
an instant's pain! You shall not—you shall not!"
He flung his arms round her. "Say you will
not!"

The Duchess did not struggle, all her old strong
nerve and will were broken, and she seemed only to
drift with the strongest current.

"I've promised," she moaned—"I promised
Vera."

"You had no right to promise—you couldn't.
Haven't I done more for you than she has? Your

life's mine. Mine—I saved it for you. You *shan't* fling it away."

He held her close in his arms, and looked up as the door opened. Countess Varigny entered.

"Mr. Tempest, is Pauline ill? I hope nothing is the matter."

She ran to them and drew Pauline's half fainting figure from his arms into her own.

"Ah, I see that she has told you."

"Yes, she has told me," Tempest answered, shortly and sternly. "Countess, you've done a wicked thing. But it seems that you have done it pretty thoroughly. I came here this afternoon to ask Pauline to marry me. She knows and you know, too, that I have long loved her. If she will marry me I will give up my profession, and we will leave England at once, never to return to it. For her all notoriety would be over; as my wife she could make for herself, and I would try to make for her, a new life in which the old could be forgotten. Pauline!" he took a step towards her, "think again!"

There was silence in the room. The Countess Varigny gently drew back, a look of pitying comprehension on her face, and left the Duchess standing by herself between them. Tempest held out his arms, his face broken up with intolerable longing, and the Duchess slowly looked from one to the other. Her lips parted, but no sound came. Tempest broke the silence in one mad cry:

"Choose me, Pauline! Oh, for God's sake, choose me!"

But she turned and clung passionately to the Countess.

"Vera," she cried, "tell him I must go with you."

The Countess gently put her arm around her, and faced Tempest.

"Mr. Tempest," she said, "there is one thing I can honestly say to you. I wish she had chosen you! But, if it is any comfort to you, as far as I can, I will take care of her."

Tempest stood motionless. Something seemed to have snapped in his brain, and he watched calmly the two women before him, so alike, both so beautiful. One of them he loved more than his life; for months past she had been in every thought, and after to-day he would probably never see her again.

"Thank you," he said dully. "It is a comfort to me. I believe you will. Good-bye, Countess."

He held out his hand to her, and she gently pushed Pauline, who still clung to her, into a chair, and, turning, took it into both of hers.

"Good-bye, Mr. Tempest. Try not to hate me because I take her away. It is the only medicine I can give her—now. Oh! you can't understand, but *I* understand, and this is the only way. She *could* not love you now; some day—who knows—"
Her voice dropped to a hurried whisper. "Let me doctor her; believe me I can and will. She will run risks with me. I can't save her that danger;

but she will get back her old self-confidence. She will remake her own life. Surely that is something! Don't despair, don't despair!"

Tempest looked down earnestly into her eyes.

"Then you think——" he began.

"I think nothing," whispered the Countess, with a smile. "But I like you, Mr. Tempest, and—don't give up! Wait! It is the only thing I can say to you. Yes, there is one thing more. I hope with all my heart that Pauline will some day marry you. I can wish her no better fate! Now you must go; again, good-bye."

Tempest bent, and kissed the hand he held. "Thank you," he said.

The Countess walked to the windows. Tempest knelt down by the side of Pauline's chair.

"It's all right, darling," he whispered "I'm going away, and I shan't bother you again. But you'll know; you'll always know that I haven't forgotten you. I shall be just waiting for you to want me. Look at me and say good-bye."

She looked at him, and Tempest saw the hesitation in her eyes, and was man enough to resist it. For the Countess was right!

"Oh, Ashley," she said, "I'm sorry!"

"Then don't be sorry any more; not for me! Once more, my darling, my darling, good-bye. And do, for God's sake and mine, take care of yourself."

He looked back from the doorway.

The Countess had run from the window; her

arm was round Pauline, she was speaking softly to
her. Tempest walked quickly downstairs and out
of the house. A hansom was passing, and he hailed
it and gave the address of his chambers.

"Wait, indeed!" he growled to his reflection in
the little looking-glass. "Wait! good Lord, she
forgets I'm forty-four!"

AFTERMATH

DRIVING sleet, a wet promenade, and out towards the sea a heavy, clinging mist, through which came the sullen plash of the waves. The wind whistled along the Front at Brighton, empty and desolate on a dismal, dull November afternoon. Slowly and with halting steps a decrepit wastrel of humanity gingerly drew a bath-chair along the pavement. Seated therein was a white-haired, jibbering figure, which dribbled at the mouth, and with muffled hands pointed here and there.

A smart, well-built girl, in a trim tailor-made costume, swung briskly along, and as she passed, turned her face to look at the occupant of the bath-chair. A leer—animal and beastly in its depravity—overspread the face of the man who was being drawn along.

"Jenny," he said, grabbing at the girl as she went by, "I'm damned tired of waiting, but I knew you'd come. Now, let's give 'em all the slip, and go to London. You know, Jenny," he added admiringly, as the girl whisked her skirt from his clutch, "I've always said you had the finest pair of legs upon the stage."

The human beast of burden chuckled, and as he turned the bath-chair to go back again, said:

"You're wrong again, Colonel, as usual. That ain't no Jenny of yours. Why carn't yer be'ave yerself?" and he pottered back along the Front.

THE END

Lightning Source UK Ltd.
Milton Keynes UK
UKOW06f0853290915

259471UK00016B/541/P